Refuge *on* Crescent Hill

Refuge on Crescent Hill

A Novel

Melanie Dobson

Refuge on Crescent Hill: A Novel

Published by Kregel Publications, a division of Kregel, Inc., P.O. Box 2607, Grand Rapids, MI 49501.

Library of Congress Cataloging-in-Publication Data
Dobson, Melanie B.
Refuge on Crescent Hill : a novel / Melanie Dobson.
p. cm.
1. Women photographers—Fiction. 2. Ohio—Fiction.
3. Family secrets—Fiction. I. Title.
PS3604.O25R43 2010 813'.6—dc22 2010002120

ISBN 978-0-8254-2590-5

Printed in the United States of America

10 11 12 13 14 / 5 4 3 2 1

For

Esther Cottrell Wacker
My beloved grandmother
August 1918–January 2007

and

Aunt Ruth Cottrell
I'm grateful for your love and generosity
and for always encouraging me
to pursue my dreams.

The North Star beckons in the dark
Luring forth to freedom stay.
Hunters race on bloody heel
To capture massa's runaway.

Ghost train moves in black of night.
Hold your breath, child. Be still.
Cross the river. Don't stop running
Til you reach the Crescent Hill.

Circa 1853

CHAPTER ONE

The glass door was locked, but that didn't stop Camden Bristow from yanking on the handle. The imposing desk on the other side of the glass was vacant, and the receptionist who usually greeted her had disappeared. Behind the desk, the *Fount Magazine* logo mocked her, whispering that the money she so desperately needed had disappeared as well.

She pounded on the glass one last time, but no one came to the door.

Turning, she moved to a row of windows on the far side of the elevator. Sixteen stories below, swarms of people bustled toward their next appointment. Someplace they needed to be.

Not long ago, she'd been rushing too, up and down Park Avenue to attend meetings at ad agencies and various magazines . . . including the suite of offices behind her.

Whenever the photo editor at *Fount* needed the most poignant pictures for his magazine, he called her, and nothing stopped her from capturing what he needed for the next edition. Human rights. Natural disasters. Labor disputes. She'd dedicated the past five years to responding to Grant Haussen's calls, but after she came back from Indonesia two months ago, he stopped contacting her.

She'd e-mailed him the pictures of the earthquake's aftermath along with her regular invoice of fees and expenses. He'd used the pictures in the next issue, but apparently discarded the invoice. She never received a check, and he didn't return even one of her many calls.

A few years ago, she wouldn't have worried as much about the money—those days her phone rang at all hours with freelance photography assignments—but her clients slashed their budgets last fall and were using stock photos or buying photographs from locals. The results weren't as compelling as a professional's work, but keeping the lights on—the rent paid—trumped paying for the best photography.

Her clients may be making rent, but she hadn't been able to pay hers for two months. Her savings account was depleted, and the income from her Indonesia shoot was supposed to appease her landlord. Even though she hadn't heard from Grant Haussen, she held out hope that she might at least recoup the expenses for her trip so she could pay off the whopping flight and hotel charges on her credit card.

All hope shattered when she read the morning's headline.

FOUNT MAGAZINE DECLARES BANKRUPTCY

Others may have skimmed past this article, but the news stunned her. Three hours ago, she had left her studio apartment and started walking to the Reinhold Building in Midtown. A few staff members might remain at the *Fount* office, packing things up, or if there were some sort of bankruptcy proceedings . . . maybe she could collect a few thousand dollars. Just enough to pay a portion of her bills while she tried to find more work.

It appeared that no one had stuck around for the aftermath.

The elevator dinged behind her, and she turned away from the windows and watched a skinny man in overalls push a mop and bucket into the hallway. He was at least two inches shorter than her five foot six.

She forced herself to smile, but he didn't smile back. She pointed at the office door. "I need to find someone from the magazine."

He grunted as he dipped his mop into the gray water and wrung it out. Shoving her fists into the pockets of her long jacket, she stepped toward him. "They owe me money."

"You and half this dadgum town."

"Yes, but—"

"They ran outta here so fast last night that the rubber on their shoes was smokin'." He flopped the mop onto the tile floor and water spread toward his boots. "I'd bet good money that they ain't comin' back."

Camden slumped against the window. Even if she were able to track down Grant, it wasn't like he would personally write her a check for money the magazine owed. He was probably out hunting for a job already, or maybe he was stretched out on his couch watching *Seinfeld* reruns, enjoying the luxury of not having to report for duty. He could collect unemployment while he scrolled Internet sites for a new gig.

Unfortunately, freelancers earned no unemployment.

The janitor pushed the mop across the tile in straight strokes like he was painting instead of cleaning it, taking pride in his work.

She understood. At one time she had been proud of her work too. There was nothing more exhilarating than flying off to a country rocked by tragedy and immersing herself into an event that most people only read about. She was on-site to see the trauma, feel the aftershocks, though she never allowed herself to get personally involved. It was her job to record the crisis so others could help with the recovery.

Because of her travels, she hadn't accumulated much stuff over the years. All she needed to do her job was her camera equipment and laptop. Her landlord furnished her flat before she moved in, and for the almost five years she'd lived there, the apartment and everything in it felt like hers. It was the longest she'd lived in one place her entire life.

But tonight, her landlord was changing the locks. Someone else had rented her home.

The man pushed his mop by her. She couldn't blame him for his indifference. This city was full of people who needed a job—he was probably doing everything he could to keep his.

She would mop floors if she had to. Or scrub toilets. It wouldn't pay enough for her to make rent, but maybe it would keep her from having to contact her mom and beg for cash.

She hopped over the wet trail left by the mop and stepped into the elevator.

Her landlord said she had until five o'clock to pack her stuff and vacate the building. The little credit she had left on her card wouldn't pay for a week in a Manhattan hotel. And the few friends she'd made when she wasn't traveling were struggling as much as she was. One of them might let her sleep on a couch, but she'd be expected to help with rent.

The elevator doors shut, and she punched the button for the lobby.

Where was she supposed to go from here?

The town hall basement smelled like burned coffee and tobacco. The navy carpet had faded to a dull gray, and the dais at the front of the room was scuffed with shoe marks. Five men and two women sat behind a table on the platform—the bimonthly summit of Etherton's City Council.

As the town mayor, Louise Danner presided over the city council from the middle chair. Her hoop earrings jangled below the signature Bic pen she propped behind her left ear. Copper-colored bangs veiled her smudged, penciled eyebrows.

Three steps below Louise's chair, Alex Yates drummed his fingers on a stack of proposals and tried to listen as Evan Harper begged the councilors to let him tear down the barn on his property and replace it with a guesthouse.

In the eight months since he'd moved to Etherton, Alex learned that Louise Danner was almost as permanent a fixture in Etherton as the town hall. Within days of him taking this job, she told him exactly how she became mayor over the eleven thousand people in their town.

She had been born in a small house off Main Street and reigned as valedictorian over Etherton High's class of '67. Armed with a degree from Marietta, she returned home after graduation and worked in several businesses until she secured the job of hospital administrator. Louise served on almost every town committee for the next thirty years, from historical preservation to the garden club, but when she landed the mayorship almost eight years ago, she dropped anchor.

She'd spent a boatload of money to retain her position during the last election—some said she bought her seat. With the state of the town's economy, she would have to fight to keep her job when voters went to the polls in five months.

Alex rechecked the time on his phone. It was almost lunchtime, and Evan Harper was still pleading his case. Alex saw the dilapidated barn every morning on the short drive to his office. Guesthouse or no guesthouse, he agreed with Evan—someone needed to put the structure out of its misery. A hearty gust of wind would end its life if the council wouldn't approve demolition.

Alex stifled a yawn as Evan named all the people who could stay in the guesthouse including his wife's elderly parents and his daughter's college friends. Apparently, no one had told the man he couldn't get his way by filibustering city council. If the mayor didn't curtail Evan's speech, he'd probably pull out the local phone book and read until the councilors adjourned for lunch. But once they walked out of the room, they wouldn't reconvene for two more weeks.

Alex couldn't wait that long for approval. He needed an answer today.

For the past month, he'd quietly courted the owner of the ten-acre property at the edge of town—part of the old Truman farm. If the council concurred, the owner was ready to sell the land and farmhouse for a pittance. The town could buy it and use the property to help with their plans to revitalize the local economy.

Alex caught the mayor's eye and tapped his wrist.

"Thank you." Louise interrupted Evan before he finished listing off every construction supply he'd purchased for the guesthouse. "I think that is all the information we need to make a decision."

Evan plucked another piece of paper from his stack. "But I haven't read the neighborhood petition."

"We appreciate all the time and thought you've put into this, Evan." Louise propped her chin up with her knuckles. "Have a seat and we'll let you know if we have any other questions."

Evan sat on the wooden folding chair at the end of the row, and Alex leaned back as the council began discussing the hot issue of preservation versus progress.

Most of the councilors were successful business leaders and attorneys, passionate in either their pro-growth or anti-development stance. Today Alex needed to convince them that voting yes on his proposal would commemorate the town's history and lay the foundation for their legacy while generating new revenue and development.

Alex glanced at his phone. If it took the councilors forty minutes to decide the fate of a rickety barn, how long would it take them to make a decision on his proposal?

When he parted ways with corporate mania last year, he thought he'd left behind the constricting strands of red tape that kept him from doing his job, but he'd learned that Etherton's residents, along with the city council, rode the high of debate until they were forced to vote. Sometimes the debate lasted weeks, or even months.

Edward Paxton led the charge against development. He didn't want *his* town to change—nor did he want Alex involved with any of the town's business. Rumor had it that he wanted his grandson, Jake, to take the economic development position that Louise had created last spring to solicit new business. The only problem was that no one else on the council wanted Jake Paxton to work for the town, and now Edward held a personal vendetta against him for stealing his grandson's job.

At least the mayor was on his team. She'd gambled when she hired him, but he assured her and the council that he'd deliver. On their terms.

After almost an hour of discussion, Louise called for a vote, and Evan smacked his knees when they approved his guesthouse with a 4–3 vote. He saluted the row of councilors as he rushed out, probably on his way to rent an excavator. Alex guessed the barn would be in a heap when he drove home tonight.

He sighed. *If only getting the council to approve a project was always this easy . . .*

Etherton needed the tax revenue from new businesses to fix its brick streets, increase the police force, and build a high school. The city's officials expected Alex to find a way to merge their small town charm with big city business.

Blending these two ideals was no small feat. Not long after he moved to Etherton, he worked a deal to build a WalMart Supercenter on a piece of farm property at the edge of town. Some towns didn't want a WalMart, but since Etherton's local economy had tanked, he thought most of the locals would welcome the store. After all, most of them drove forty-five minutes each week to visit the WalMart in Mansfield, and this would bring discount clothes, groceries, car care, and—most importantly—jobs to their back door.

He was wrong.

When the council voted last December, residents of Etherton packed town hall, a chorus of dissension over why their town couldn't bear the weight of a conglomerate. The icy room turned hot as tempers flared. Small business owners threatened to overthrow the seats of every council member who supported the proposal.

In the end, the council rejected his plan. The town desperately needed the revenue and the jobs, but apparently not enough to put out the welcome mat for a mega-store. A local farmer bought the field to plant corn, and Etherton missed out on the much-needed sales tax that would flood into Fredericktown when Wal-Mart opened its doors there this fall.

The council told him they wanted new business, but they wanted something quaint that would fit the town's celebration of all things old. It was a hard task—but he'd found the perfect solution. If the residents were willing to risk a little, he was ready to deliver both quaint and classy . . . wrapped up in a pretty package and tied together with a sound financial bow.

Louise slid the pen out from behind her ear and tapped it on the table. She dismissed the few people in the audience, explaining that the rest of the meeting was a closed session, and then she pointed at him. "You're up, Alex."

He straightened his tie and stood to face the councilors. It was about to get hot again.

CHAPTER TWO

Six o'clock was the wrong hour to cross the George Washington Bridge into New Jersey. Horns honked on every side of Camden's car, as if the noise could prod the traffic forward, and she massaged her temples to rub away the stress that came whenever she drove her old Miata out of the parking garage and attempted to escape Manhattan. Usually she had an idea where she was heading—upstate New York or Long Island—but tonight she was driving until she found a cheap hotel. Very cheap.

Four hundred and fifty-six dollars would max her MasterCard, and when her credit ran out . . . she didn't want to think about what would happen then.

If her father were still alive, he'd reprimand her for flushing her finances down the toilet. Timothy Bristow had been a successful businessman in Columbus, Ohio, and as far as she knew, never had trouble with money. When he died, he'd left behind a couple million for his second wife. Camden was eleven when he passed away. She didn't know much about wills at the time. She just missed her dad.

Camden's mother never forgave her ex-husband for leaving both her and her daughter out of the will, but Camden understood. Her mother spent money faster than her father saved it. Any money left behind for Camden would be long gone by now.

When requests for work were pouring in, Camden tucked ten percent of every check she received into savings. Like her father would had done. And, after a few years, she'd built up a healthy rainy-day fund.

Problem was, she'd anticipated a rainy day . . . not a torrential storm. New York City was brutal on contingency funds.

Her savings account emptied in six months. She could still sell what was left of her camera equipment, but without it, she had no hope of getting back on her feet . . . and she wouldn't receive even close to what she paid for it. The Miata could sell for three or four thousand dollars—she probably should have sold it months ago—but it was her only ticket out of town. And when she reached the limit on her MasterCard, it might be her only place to sleep.

She could call her mother to ask for money, but if she called, her mother would pass the phone to her latest boyfriend—a retired egomaniac living outside Madrid. Camden would rather sleep in a shelter than grovel to him. The boyfriend might pay her way to Spain, but then what? She'd spent most of her life tagging along behind her mother from boyfriend to boyfriend, country to country.

If she followed her mother back to Europe, she had no doubt she would get trapped in the drama and instability again. Her mother loved her, but she'd never been able to take care of herself or her daughter without help. Even though they might throw some cash her way, Camden refused to ask her mother's boyfriends to help her as well.

Her car crept forward a few feet, and she glanced between the steel braces on the tower beside her. The sun glistened off the Hudson River, sparkling against the backdrop of industrial buildings and smokestacks.

No matter where she traveled, there always seemed to be a glimmer of beauty in even the most dire of situations. She'd spent her life searching for beauty and hope in other people's lives. Now she just needed to find it for herself.

She squeezed the steering wheel, staring at the taillights in front of her.

Desperation was a feeling she despised. From age eighteen, she had been independent. Self-sufficient. After high school, she said goodbye to her mother and her mother's latest boyfriend in London and flew to New York.

Photography had been her passion since her father had sent her a Kodak Fun Saver for her eighth birthday. In New York, she'd found work as a photographer's assistant, and she'd taken pictures of families—hundreds of them. Her boss preferred shooting the pictures inside the family's house instead of the studio, because the home reflected the character of the family. The colors. The art on the walls. The style of furniture. Camden could feel the warmth of a happy family or the stale coolness of a family who didn't get along. They didn't tell these families, of course, but they always recommended the unhappy ones have their pictures taken in the studio. Her family would have been among those whom her boss would have kindly suggested to appear at the studio.

After five years as an assistant, she began selling her own photos to a few magazines and agencies until she had enough of a client base to make it on her own. And for almost four years, her business thrived.

The freelance business was lucrative, but it was a death sentence on relationships. Most of her friendships lasted the duration of an assignment—guides and translators and other photojournalists who joined her on her journey.

On that last fateful trip to Indonesia, though, the guide she trusted stole her duffel bag. Later she was told that the woman probably sold her clothes but tossed the pricey equipment that Camden wasn't carrying on her that day. The stuffed dog that Grandma Rosalie had given her was gone too; her faithful companion, Ash, had traveled the world with her.

There was no justice. Thousands of people were displaced and wounded; the few police working the scene would have laughed at her request to recover her bag. She never would have asked them to stop their work anyway. Stolen luggage was a very small problem compared to what the locals were facing.

It wasn't about the luggage anyway, not really. It was about being violated by a woman she'd trusted to escort and translate for her. A woman she'd befriended.

She cracked her window for some fresh air, but the surge of exhaust fumes changed her mind. Rolling the window back up, she turned on the AC. Even though she had left her apartment over an hour ago, she was still hovering on the line between New York and New Jersey.

As she edged toward the other side of the bridge, she saw a billboard for *Les Miserables*, and she began humming the lyrics to "In My Life."

You will learn truth is given by God

to us all in our time, in our turn.

Her grandmother used to sing that part of the song from the Broadway musical over and over when they worked together in the garden or took a walk in the trees below the hill, by the river and the cemetery. A very long time ago.

Camden blinked.

The summer of 1992, she was supposed to spend with her father but, once again, he'd been too busy working and traveling to care for her. Eloise, her stepmother, was too occupied shuttling her nine-year-old—Camden's half-sister, Liza—to ballet, French, and piano lessons. She didn't have time to babysit Camden as well. So instead of keeping her in Columbus, her father took her to the same place he did every summer since she was five years old—to his mother and the home where he'd spent his childhood. A place called Crescent Hill.

Crescent Hill had been the one constant in her young life.

During those summers with Grandma Rosalie, she'd felt like she had a home. For two months of the year, she didn't worry about her mother breaking up with her current boyfriend one night and yanking her out of school the next morning to move someplace new. Instead she roamed the hill behind the enormous old house and spent hours watching her grandma paint and blow glass in her studio. Together they planted flowers and picked flowers and then arranged them until the house filled with the scents of rose, hibiscus, and scarlet carnations.

That was the same summer her grandma gave her the stuffed dog, and she named him Ashter after the river she'd grown to love. Grandma Rosalie called him "Ash" for short, after the Bible verse in Isaiah that talked about trading beauty for ashes.

The name Ash stuck, and she treasured that puppy for eighteen years.

Camden checked the dashboard clock. Ohio wasn't that far from New York. A day's drive at the most . . . or an overnight trip.

She hadn't seen her grandma since that summer when she was ten. Her father died in a motorcycle accident the next year, and even though she'd begged to go back to Etherton, her mother thought it frivolous to pay for plane tickets to send her to the States. After all, Rosalie Bristow was her ex-husband's mother, and she had no affinity for anyone related to him.

At first, Rosalie mailed Camden wonderful notes, written on hand-painted cards, but over the next few years, she and her mother moved again and again. Camden sent letters and postcards to her grandmother, with their latest address, and her grandmother mailed her back—until Camden and her mother moved again, usually without leaving a forwarding address. Gradually, the cards stopped arriving in their mailbox.

With every move, her mother had wanted to forget the past. It was Camden who wanted to remember.

As she got older, she immersed herself in photography instead of relationships. Pictures, at least, were permanent.

Her car inched off the George Washington Bridge and crept into the Garden State.

Her grandmother had cared for her, and in every letter she had written, she invited Camden back to Crescent Hill.

Maybe she would let her stay again for a few weeks, until she got back on her feet and found work. Surely, her grandmother wouldn't turn her away. Not like her father.

The clock on her dash clicked past six, and she hit the accelerator as traffic picked up speed.

She didn't need to spend money on a hotel. If she drove all night, she could be in Ohio by morning.

The Bristow family mansion watched over Crescent Hill like a battered Union soldier. Rain had pounded the brick walls for almost two hundred years, and a hailstorm had crumbled one of the four chimneys a decade ago. In spite of the weather that threatened to topple her, the house held strong, braving Ohio's volatile weather like she'd braved the War. And like a good Yank, she harbored secrets deep inside her walls.

Jake Paxton wasn't interested in the architecture or the history of the old house, but he was very interested in its secrets . . . or at least Edward was.

Now that Rosalie had kicked the bucket—and the crowds of visitors were gone—he promised his grandfather that he would search the mansion, top to bottom, in a day or two. He needed to be sure none of the visitors were still hanging around town.

Edward made him swear he wouldn't get caught this time, like it was his fault that the detective caught him selling Mrs. Rolling's silver on Craig's List. How was he supposed to know her ugly platter was worth ten thousand bucks? Or that it was stolen? Or that Mrs. Rolling would try to buy another platter, only to discover that the replacement platter she purchased was in fact her family's heirloom?

Buck Houston had given him the stupid platter to pay off a gambling debt, and Jake had done what anyone else would do—sold it. If he'd known it was worth something, he would've asked a whole lot more than two hundred dollars. Mrs. Rolling never would have dumped ten thousand to buy the platter off Craig's List. A collector would've bought it instead, and he'd be scot-free.

Instead Edward bought his freedom. Jake still didn't know how he did it, but his grandfather paid the right people a truckload of cash—or at least, that's how much Edward said he paid—to get him out of the county jail. Edward considered it an investment, and he refused to let Jake forget that at any moment, he could put Jake in the slammer.

Edward would make Jake pay for the rest of his life. His only hope was that Edward's lifetime might not last too many more years.

Jake tromped through rusty iron gates that once guarded the gravel driveway. The expansive yard leading up to the mansion was mostly dead grass and weeds. The meadow on the east side of the hill sloped down to a forest that wrapped around the property and hid the Ashter River below. A pond lay beyond the trees along with acres and acres of fields, newly planted with corn.

On the west side of the house, across the street, was another slope. This one dotted with homes that weren't as lofty as the Bristow mansion, or as run-down.

When a tornado ripped across a field outside town a few years ago, its winds tore scads of shingles off the old mansion and delivered a branch through one of the cupola's windows. The tornado damaged many homes in town—ripping apart clapboard siding, shutters, and shingles—but unlike the Bristow mansion, their owners repaired the homes to their former Victorian glory.

There was no one left to repair this house—or at least no one who wanted the hassle of trying to patch it back together.

Maybe if they knew what was inside its walls, someone would try to keep it standing a little longer. But according to Edward, no one knew the most valuable secret of this old place except him . . . and now Jake.

He would search every inch of the house and prove he wasn't the idiot his grandfather thought he was. It didn't matter if the legend was a hoax. Edward was convinced the treasure was still there, and until someone proved him wrong, Jake would try to find it.

He bounded up six cement steps to the lofty doors of the Bristow mansion and rang the bell. No one answered the door so he strained his neck to look into the darkened window of the sitting room on his right. He could see the edge of the couch and an end table through the smudged glass, but nothing else. Eyes might be watching him from the other side of the room, and he wouldn't know.

The thought made him shiver.

He wasn't the least bit frightened of any *person*—except maybe his grandfather—but the supernatural terrified him. He didn't care what anyone else said, ghosts were real and dangerous.

He rapped the knocker one last time, but no one came to the door.

Most of the town had eaten Sunday brunch or dinner at least once in this house, but Rosalie Bristow had never invited the Paxton family over for a meal. At least, not his side of the family. Edward's cousin Dotty Sherman had been a regular over at the house, but she never invited him along, even when Rosalie hosted the annual Christmas party for what seemed like half the children in town.

But now, after thirty-one years of living in this rat hole of a town, he would explore the house on his own terms. There was no one to stop him.

He put his ear to the door and listened.

Silence.

He'd give it another day, to make sure all the visitors had really gone home. Then he'd find out if Edward's story was true.

CHAPTER THREE

Petunias spilled over the hanging planters around Etherton's town square in splashes of red, white, and purple. Anchored atop cast-iron lampposts, the spring flowers sprinkled color and much-needed life into the worn downtown.

Below the flowers was a small, grassy park with a towering statue of a Yankee soldier that faced south. Steady hands clutched the soldier's musket, resolution and strength etched in his face. He wasn't threatening his enemies or cowering from them. Instead he seemed to know that trouble was coming to Ohio, and if called, he was ready to fight.

From his booth at the Underground Cafe, Alex watched the cars race down the brick street in front of the soldier. Gray clouds hovered over the town square, but it hadn't rained yet this morning.

Some days it seemed like he was in a battle. The stakes for him weren't nearly as high as for the Yankee soldier, but it felt like the future of the town that bred so many of these soldiers was in his hands. No large business was interested in relocating to a dying town—Wal-Mart had been their last hope for a major shot to the economy. Still there were other things they could do to create new work and revenue. If only the council would rally around him and fight for it.

He took a bite of his turkey sandwich and then washed it down with Coke.

When he proposed the plan yesterday for the town to acquire the Truman farm, he had spelled it all out—how they could hire locals to build a first-class community center along with a park and space for a restaurant and a few small shops at the edge of town. The town could rent out the community center and then when tourist traffic—and income—picked up again, they would be ready.

The council shot down his proposal, 6–1. Louise was the only one who voted for it. A courtesy vote. They all wanted a bigger property, a bigger business—just not a mega-store or a shopping mall. Like his phone was ringing off the hook with businesses begging to relocate or build in Etherton.

The council wanted new business, of course, to respect the quaint, Americana feel they wanted to maintain. They just didn't want to bother with courting and wooing, or with the give-and-take. He couldn't think of a single business that would give in to all their demands.

Alex broke off a piece of bread from his sandwich and dipped it into his corn chowder.

Members of the city council thought he didn't appreciate the past—that he was trying to desecrate their town's noble history—but that wasn't true. He could spend all day appreciating the exhibits in a Civil War museum, but if he got too caught up immortalizing the past, he wouldn't be able to help Etherton's citizens today. That's why they had hired him—for a fresh perspective . . . and because neither he nor his family were tied personally to a single building downtown.

History, he'd tried to explain, wouldn't put more policemen on the streets or increase their capacity to provide water or build a much-needed hospital. Without new business and its tax revenue, Etherton would fade away like so many other small towns along the Ashter River. When residents of Erinville and Mannings migrated to better jobs in Columbus and Cleveland, their towns disappeared.

He'd resigned from his position with a lucrative marketing firm to take this job in Etherton, and he was glad to move on. He hadn't just left South Carolina. He'd run away from it and never planned to go back.

When he moved to Etherton, he'd done it because he was searching for a new life, and he'd found it. In the months he'd been here, he'd discovered a relationship with God that he never imagined he could have, and he'd made friendships that he was certain would last for a lifetime. He could see himself staying here for the rest of his life. But except for giving a face-lift to some of the old buildings in town, he hadn't done much since he arrived. The council had vetoed every one of his ideas to invite new business and put unemployed residents to work.

Alex set his spoon on his plate and looked back out the window at the soldier.

His wasn't a battle of life or death like the many soldiers who'd come from Etherton, but even so, he would do his job and fight for this town.

Whoever decorated the Underground Cafe had a passion for color, and—fortunately—an eye for it. Plum cushions on flax-colored couches, midnight blue walls splotched with taupe paisleys. Carpet with bold circles dyed ruby red, orange, and a plum that matched the curtains.

Camden eyed the board of specialty coffee drinks above the café's front counter and saw her favorite—a chai latte—but instead of splurging on a latte, she ordered a regular coffee and mixed hazelnut creamer into the drink.

Collapsing into a pumpkin-colored chair, she forced her eyes to stay open as she sipped her coffee. She'd stopped a few hours at a rest area outside DuBois last night, finishing her drive this morning. Once she'd decided to come back to Etherton, she didn't want to waste time sleeping. She wanted to see her grandmother.

She should have returned for a visit years ago, and as she crossed the miles in Pennsylvania, she tried to remember the reasons why she hadn't. When she first moved to New York, she didn't have the money, but when work and money began to flood in, she was too busy traveling out of the country to go back to Ohio.

Once, when she was shooting photos of mill workers in Cleveland, she almost rented a car and drove down to see her grandma, but then she'd gotten an urgent call from Grant who needed her in the Philippines the next day. She packed her bags and caught the next flight out. It never occurred to her to turn down the job and come to Etherton instead.

When she first moved back to the States, she attempted to call her grandma several times. When Rosalie finally answered the phone, her grandma mumbled that she couldn't hear whoever was on the other end of the line. Camden stood there shocked, phone in hand. Grandma Rosalie hung up on her.

After the telephone episode, she wrote her grandma a letter, and her grandma responded right away, saying she would love for Camden to come visit. Camden wanted to rush to Ohio, but part of her was scared.

It probably didn't make sense to anyone else, but she was afraid of ruining the treasured memories she experienced with Grandma Rosalie. Her grandma might reject her as an adult and that would end the one constant relationship she'd enjoyed since she was a child.

So she settled for writing about her travels and sent Rosalie some of her pictures. Her grandma replied, her writing barely legible though her words were filled with love and grace. She encouraged Camden in her work and always asked how her relationship was with the Savior.

How long had it been since she received a letter from her grandma? Six months, possibly a year. Way too long. In her last letter, her grandma almost begged Camden to visit, but she hadn't done it. In the busyness of her work and then the aftermath of trying to find work, she hadn't traveled to Ohio. Nor had she written again.

Would her grandma be angry that she hadn't come before now? She deserved it if Rosalie was furious. She should have visited years ago.

She took another long sip of coffee, forcing her eyes to stay open.

Even if Rosalie was angry, surely she would forgive her for taking so long to get to Ohio . . . and for waiting to visit until she was desperate for help.

She would go this morning, knock on Rosalie's door.

The only problem was—the last time she was here, she'd been a kid. She needed directions to Crescent Hill.

Scanning the café, she saw two women gossiping over lunch, a man eating ice cream with a couple kids, and a guy in his early thirties looking out the windows. The man sitting by himself had dark brown hair and was dressed in a business suit designed more for a workday on Wall Street than lunch in Etherton. His face was angled toward the window, but she liked the confident set of his jaw. Or was it stubbornness?

She sighed as she swirled her coffee. He was probably married, like all the good-looking ones seemed to be these days. Even her last boyfriend tied the knot over a year ago, seven weeks after he'd broken up with her. He said that she was the one with commitment issues, which made her laugh until a mutual friend showed her his wedding invitation.

She didn't have a problem with commitment. She just hadn't met the right guy.

Retrieving her handbag from the floor, she strolled toward the business suit in the booth. Maybe this guy wasn't from Etherton, but if he was, she guessed he could give her directions to her grandmother's home.

When she cleared her throat, he swung his head toward her, and his eyes were a clear green, the color of a lagoon she'd visited near Bali.

She flashed him a quick smile. "I'm wondering if you can give me directions."

He pushed back his empty bowl. "I'd be glad to try."

Relieved, her worn smile grew bigger. It was good to be in a place again where people were nice to strangers. "I'm trying to find Crescent Hill."

The man's lips parted slightly, and then he shut them. When he searched her face, she wondered what he was trying to find. Maybe he didn't trust the shadows under her eyes, darkened from lack of sleep.

She stepped back and tucked a stray blond hair behind her ear. "If you don't know . . ."

He shook his head. "It's not that."

When he paused again, she buttoned up her jacket. She'd go find a gas station, maybe the attendant wouldn't make her beg for directions.

"It's not far from here," the man finally replied with a nod out the window. She followed his gaze toward the glass as if she could see her grandmother's house from the town square. "Take a right on Elm and follow that until it dead-ends on Crescent Hill."

She flung the strap of her handbag over her shoulder. "Thanks."

He leaned toward her. "What are you looking for up there?"

She hesitated before she spoke again. "My grandmother."

CHAPTER FOUR

Camden slammed the car door and basked in the sight of her grandma's home. Clematis overran the north wall, its vanilla scent sweetening the breeze that gusted over Crescent Hill. Sap from the pine trees blackened the brick walls of the mansion, and beech tree limbs dusted the ornate eaves.

She glanced up at the broken window of the white cupola that towered above the house. On rainy days, she used to climb its winding staircase and paint for hours on her wooden easel, capturing the gardens and fishpond and the path of trees that led down to the cemetery. She had been Rapunzel. Cinderella. Queen Guinevere reigning over her kingdom below.

Vibrant color bubbled up at the base of the manor, and Camden swept her palm across the petals of her grandma's prized tulip garden. Bright swatches of violet, apricot, and magenta shone through the weeds—her grandmother had never met a color, or a flower, she didn't like.

To the left of the house was a detached garage, and through the filmy glass, she saw the roof of the Chrysler Imperial that Rosalie drove.

Camden rushed toward the cement steps in front of her, climbing them to the lofty front doors. White paint was peeling off the wood, and on each side were sculptures of a lion's head. She lifted the brass knocker and pounded three times.

No one answered so she rang the doorbell.

Wind blew over the hillside again, and last fall's leaves whirled in the yard. She shivered in her jacket, the horrible feeling of déjà vu washing over her. She was back at the *Fount Magazine* office, knocking and knocking, but no one answered.

She jogged back down the steps. Perhaps her grandmother was down at the beauty shop or visiting a friend. Or maybe she was living at a local retirement home now. Surely, her stepmother would have called her if something had happened to her . . .

The overgrown path led her along the side of the house. One of the columns on the arcade looked like it was about to collapse, and the roof looked like it was drooping as well, probably tired from years of hard labor. If her grandma wanted to renovate, a contractor would probably recommend they tear it down and start from scratch.

At the back of the house, Camden stepped up onto the long patio that overlooked the trees and farmland below. She could see for miles and miles from here, not a single skyscraper in sight. Her shoulders relaxed as she leaned against a column, breathing in the clean, fresh air.

It was good to be back.

The sound of tires rumbling up the driveway interrupted the tranquility. Rushing to the front of the house, she coughed in the cloud of dust. A minivan had whipped up the gravel, and Camden squinted at the dark green vehicle to see if her grandma was inside. Instead, a woman in a pink sweatshirt and pants hopped out and opened the door for a girl aged four or five.

Like a beach ball, the girl bounced all the way to the front stoop, her pigtails fluttering. The woman rested her hand on the girl's head, but that didn't stop her from hopping up and down.

"We were driving by, and I didn't recognize your car." The woman pushed her sunglasses back up her nose. "Can I help you?"

"I'm not sure . . ." Camden's gaze fell from the woman's brown ponytail to her feet. She couldn't stop the smile spreading across her face. The woman wore two different colored Crocs—one pink and the other purple.

The woman glanced down at her feet and groaned, pointing to the bouncy child beside her. "I have three more kiddos," she attempted to explain. "All of them six and under."

"So you're lucky to be wearing shoes."

"Exactly." The woman stuck out her hand. "My name's Jenny, and this is Hailey."

Camden shook Jenny's hand, and then reached her hand out to Hailey. Instead of shaking her hand, Hailey licked it. Some days Camden wanted to have children—and some days she didn't.

"I'm so sorry . . ." The woman picked up her daughter. "She thinks she's a puppy dog today. A labradoodle."

Camden wiped her wet hand on her jeans. "At least she's not a rottweiler."

Hailey whimpered and batted her mother's hair while she tried to talk. "This month I've lived with a gorilla, a lion, and a chimpanzee, and not one of them was tame. At one time, I thought it was funny."

"Where are your other kids?"

"Two are with my sister, and one, thank God, is in school." Her laugh sounded more like a girl than an adult, and it reminded Camden of someone she once knew.

Camden squinted at her. "Jenny Nixon?"

The woman laughed again, taking off her sunglasses. "It's Jenny Sprague now, but it's nice to meet someone who remembers me when . . ."

"We used to play flashlight tag together." Camden nodded toward the forest. "Down by the cemetery."

Jenny set her squirming daughter back down on the ground. "Camden?"

"It's still Camden Bristow."

The smile vanished from Jenny's face. "Oh, Camden . . ."

"It's not so bad . . . I like being single."

"Single? No . . ." Her voice trailed off as she glanced over at Hailey who was chasing herself around a pine tree. She looked back at Camden. "What are you doing here?"

Camden stuck her hands in her pockets. She didn't really have a good reason to come back except she needed a place to stay . . . and she wanted to see her grandma.

She took a deep breath. "I came to see my grandmother."

Jenny blinked several times, and for a moment, Camden thought her childhood friend was about to cry. "What's wrong?"

"Someone should have called you."

"Why should—" she started. "What . . . what happened?"

"She passed away," Jenny said softly. "From bone cancer."

"Cancer?" Camden repeated. She pulled her phone out of her pocket like somehow she'd missed the call telling her Rosalie was sick, but there were no messages.

"When did she—?"

Jenny bit the side of her lip. "Friday."

Five days ago.

"She died in her sleep."

Camden blinked. "On Friday?"

"I thought someone called you . . . or I would have tried to track you down."

"Thank you," she tried to say, but her words slurred.

"The memorial service was yesterday."

If only she'd left New York last week. She could have told her grandma how much she loved her, how much she cherished the summers they spent together. And she could have told her that she was sorry for not visiting sooner.

"Come home with me." Jenny tugged on Camden's sleeve, urging her toward the minivan, but she didn't move. "We can talk over tea."

She stared at the vehicle.

"Are you okay?" Jenny asked.

A tiny palm pressed into hers, fingers wrapping around her hand, and Hailey grinned up at her.

"C'mon, Hailey." Jenny tried to draw her daughter away, but Hailey refused to let go.

"Ahhroo," the girl howled softly and nudged Camden's arm with her nose.

Camden followed the child's gentle prodding, all the way to the van.

Hidden behind pine branches, Jake Paxton watched Jenny Sprague and the blond chick gab like they were pals. Jenny and her kid had driven up the lane ten minutes ago like her tailpipe was on fire. He never expected to see her here—usually, her husband was the one meddling.

He didn't trust Jenny. Not one bit. No one would trust her if they knew what she'd done to him.

Now she was too good to even acknowledge him when he saw her around town. She didn't even wave at him, like he didn't exist.

It was no big deal if Jenny ignored him. He had a better girlfriend now. A much prettier one and a whole lot younger too.

Jenny was stuck with Lawyer Dan.

It didn't matter whether or not he trusted her. Jenny wasn't bright enough to know what was behind those mansion walls anyway, but he wasn't sure about the blond. He'd watched her knock on the front door and peek inside the windows like she was searching for something. Then, when she thought no one was looking, she'd wandered around to the back of the house.

Did she know what was inside?

Edward swore no one else knew the secrets of the house except the two of them. But if the blond didn't know, why was she here?

Maybe she wanted to buy the place.

Jake laughed at the thought. *Like someone would want to buy this dump.* The walls wouldn't last another five years, a decade at most. A few of his buddies down at the pool hall speculated that the roof would cave in by the end of the year, but he'd bet the house would still be around come New Year's. If the house didn't collapse, he'd win a hundred bucks.

As the women sped away in the van, he released the branch he'd been holding. Pinecones smacked his face, and he stumbled backward, grappling for another branch. When he was upright again, he straightened the bottom of his bomber jacket and crammed his hands into his pockets.

If the blond was just snooping around, he would hold off for a day or two, but if she was going to buy the place, he'd best get himself right inside those doors before she—or someone else—stumbled onto the treasure before he did.

CHAPTER FIVE

Heat emanated from the stone terrace, soaking every pore on Stephanie Ellison-Carter's skin. The temperature at one o'clock was pushing a hundred with a hundred percent of humidity. And it was only May. Every year, it felt like the equator was inching closer to South Carolina. By the time she was forty, it would probably be freezing in Brazil and blazing hot in the Carolinas.

She dabbed her forehead with a tissue. It seemed crazy to sit outside in this heat, but Aunt Debra's air conditioning was broken. Sweltering inside, on an afternoon like this, was even more crazy than soaking up the sunshine.

On the other side of the table was a newspaper, and Stephanie reached for it. The *Etherton Daily News*. She twisted the paper around and skimmed over the mast. The town was in Ohio. Population 10,895.

Instead of reading the headlines, she fanned the paper in front of her face with one hand, and with the other pulled her cotton skirt over her knees and tucked her sandaled feet under the chair so the sun wouldn't fry them. One would think, growing up in the south, that the UV rays wouldn't affect her, but no matter how much sunscreen she applied, her skin always burned and peeled in the spring.

Driving down to Columbia this morning, she hadn't even thought to bring sunscreen. She'd been too distracted getting ready to visit her aunt, too distracted thinking about her wretched term paper that wouldn't come together.

She flapped the *Etherton Daily News* even faster.

Her term paper hadn't started out wretched. Her American history professor wanted a paper on an unsolved mystery in the history of the United

States, but Stephanie didn't want to write a paper on just any mystery. She wanted to write one about the legends she'd heard growing up. The unsolved mysteries in the Ellison family.

Her professor agreed to her idea—was excited about it, really. A few hours after she proposed the topic, she walked into the library and began digging in the archives. When she didn't find much about the Ellison family at the university library, Stephanie called her mom, who suggested she visit Aunt Debra. Other relatives had moved on to other parts of the country, but Debra Ellison had stayed in Columbia, South Carolina, along with her collection of family papers and memorabilia.

That had been two months ago. Two months of searching through every historical archive she could find online. Two months of avoiding a call to her aunt.

In the next month, she was supposed to turn in the paper so she could graduate from Clemson this summer, but so far, she hadn't written a single word. She hadn't found any facts to collaborate the stories passed down through her family. On Monday, she'd been preparing to meet with her professor and grovel until he let her change the topic of her paper to anything except the Ellison family mysteries. Her mom, however, insisted that she visit Aunt Debra before she reneged on the term paper, and so here she was, down in Columbia. Ready to talk.

She should have come visit her aunt over a year ago, long before she needed information for a term paper, but she'd done everything possible to avoid traveling to Columbia. Not because she didn't love Aunt Debra—she loved the woman dearly—but because of what happened last year with her cousin. Debra was still grieving the loss of her son. Stephanie and her parents felt bad for her aunt, but none of them felt bad for Trent Ellison.

"Here you go, honey." Debra handed her an icy Coke and sat down on a wicker chair, careful not to spill her drink. A white straw hat hid her aunt's auburn hair, and her arms and neck were much thinner than Stephanie remembered. The last time she saw her was more than two years ago, at Thanksgiving.

The cold glass chilled her hands as she drained the liquid. Then she began crunching on a piece of ice.

Debra tucked a strand of hair back under her hat. "So your mama says you're writing a research paper about the Ellisons."

Stephanie opened her laptop, and the screen slowly came to life. "My history professor asked us to research an unsolved mystery."

A smile lightened her aunt's eyes, and Stephanie was glad to see a bit of the joy that used to bubble out of her aunt's heart. "Then you've come to the right place."

"I'm sorry I didn't come sooner . . ."

Ice clanked on the sides of Debra's glass as she swirled it, watching her niece. Then she put the glass down and reached over, patting Stephanie's knee. "I've spent the last two years filled with regrets, Steph, honey. You don't need to feel bad as well."

Swallowed by guilt, she nodded. What do you say when your aunt's son—your cousin—had been locked away in prison for the rest of his life? She hadn't known what to say to her aunt when her mom called with the news that the jury found Trent guilty, and she didn't know what to say now. In the days after Trent was convicted, she figured it was better to avoid the conversation than bumble her words in attempting to be considerate when really she was furious—and heartbroken—at what he'd done.

When Trent was on trial, she'd been at college, deep into her studies for a week of tough finals, but she didn't have a good excuse to skip his sentencing. She knew in her heart he was guilty, and she couldn't bear to watch her cousin be convicted of murder.

Her mom and daddy were in attendance every time Trent was in the courtroom, for Aunt Debra's sake. According to them, Trent seemed remorseful, but Stephanie wondered how much of their perception was wishful thinking. Even if he were sorry for what he'd done, it was too late to undo the pain he'd caused his mother and himself and most of all, the family of the woman he'd claimed to love.

A tiny part of her felt sorry for Trent. He'd never known his daddy, never known what it was like to grow up with a father, and from the very beginning of his life, he'd been a frightening mixture of charm and violence. He was four years older than her, and when he'd come for a visit, she was never quite sure which Trent would show up at their door. Often the charming Trent would knock but minutes later the scary Trent would emerge, throwing things and threatening to kill her with his toy gun.

When he turned twelve—and attempted to microwave her kitten—her parents called Debra and told her that they loved both her and Trent, but he was no longer welcome at their house. That was the last she had seen him. Debra came for the occasional holiday, but never with her son.

Her parents' stance hurt Debra, but as the years rolled past, even she recognized that Trent had problems. By the time Debra was willing to admit that her son was dangerous, it was too late. Stephanie couldn't imagine how the regrets must have heaped up for her aunt. The questions and the "what ifs." She'd been hurting, and most of the time, she was hurting alone.

She pushed back her laptop a few inches on the patio table. "How are you doing?"

Her aunt managed a weak smile. "A little better."

"And how is he?"

"Not so good." Debra reached for a canvas bag in the chair beside her and pulled it to her lap. "But I don't want to talk about that today. I'm just glad you're here."

"Me, too," Stephanie whispered.

Her aunt reached in the bag and pulled out a binder. "What can I tell you about the Ellisons?"

"We don't have to talk about this."

"But I love to talk about it." Debra opened the binder. "I'm just not sure where to begin."

Stephanie leaned forward. "Grandpa used to talk about the wealth of the Ellisons. The prestige."

"That was before the Civil War."

"I'd like to know what happened to our family."

Debra picked up her drink and sipped it. "No one really knows what happened to them."

"Grandpa said the Yankees stole our money."

Debra shook our head. "They didn't take all of it."

Before her grandfather died, Stephanie remembered listening to him talk about his family with pride. The Ellisons had been one of the first families to come over to the New World, and with plenty of hard work, they turned the soil outside Columbia into a wealthy plantation.

By the mid 1800s, Arnold Ellison married a woman named Miriam and had a half dozen children, most of whom had died during the Civil War. They lost their children, their property, and as Southern stocks plummeted, their wealth disappeared as well. Whenever Stephanie's grandfather began to talk about their heritage, he'd drone on for hours. Usually, when he started losing himself to the past, she'd run outside and play with Trent, but she remembered a few bits of his conversation.

"Grandpa used to say the Ellisons left some sort of treasure on the plantation."

Debra smiled. "My father also thought aliens would attack us."

"But why did he think there was a treasure?"

Debra paused, and then turned the pages of the binder until she stopped. "Because of what went missing before the Civil War."

Stephanie leaned over her aunt's shoulder and saw a page filled with pencil sketches of jewelry. There were several necklaces with jewels. A ring. An oversized pendant. "What are these?"

"They were heirloom pieces, made in Britain."

Stephanie's mind wandered as she envisioned one of the necklaces dangling from her neck, bright and sparkling in the sunlight. "These were the Ellison jewels?"

"For a season."

She typed her aunt's words into her computer. "How did our family get this jewelry?"

Debra set her glass on the table and wiped her forehead with her sleeve. "The Ellisons were quite loyal to the Crown in the 1700s."

"The Crown?" Stephanie squirmed in her seat as she typed *quite loyal*. "But our family were some of the original colonists."

"That didn't mean they were revolutionists."

She winced. Her ancestors—she'd assumed they fought for freedom alongside the other colonists. "So the Ellisons were rewarded for their loyalty?"

"Quite well," Debra said. "Before the Revolutionary War, King George lavished gifts on them and other prominent families for their cooperation."

"Bribery."

"Something like that." Debra took another sip of her Coke. "He bought their faithfulness to England, and they remained in his service until after the war."

"Then they began to enjoy their freedom," she commented as she typed. Not once did she recall her grandfather mentioning the fact that her ancestors had opposed the American Revolution. "What happened to the jewelry?"

"That is the mystery," Debra replied. "No one remembers where it went."

"If they found it today . . ."

"Each piece has the hallmark of royalty," Debra explained. "They would be worth millions."

Stephanie stared at the word *millions* on her computer. One could do a lot of things with that kind of cash.

Debra pulled an old book out of her bag and held it in her lap. "This is the journal of Miriam Ellison."

Stephanie reached out and brushed her fingers over the soft leather on the cover. "How did you get this?"

"My father gave it to me when I was about your age. It's been passed down to the oldest child for generations."

"I'm sorry—"

Debra patted her knee. "Trent wasn't interested in this stuff anyway."

"I want to find out the truth."

"I learned a lot of things about our family from Miriam," Debra said, "but I never discovered what happened to the jewelry."

"What did you find out?"

Debra held out the old book to her. "You read it first. See what you think."

Stephanie took the journal and cradled it in her arms.

CHAPTER SIX

Light streamed through the breakfast nook in Jenny's blue and yellow kitchen. Dishes overflowed from the sink to a tile counter speckled with crumbs, glue sticks, and several pieces of what Camden assumed was artwork.

The backyard was littered with bikes, scooters, and a doghouse that Hailey disappeared into when they arrived. Camden inquired about a real dog, but Jenny shook her head. Their dog was given to a single woman after Sprague kid number three was born.

Jenny's younger sister ran out the door minutes after they arrived, and a baby crawled across the linoleum, her diaper sagging under a pink sundress. A toddler zoomed an oversized fire truck into the room, and the boy tipped his hat to her. Camden lifted her hand to say hi, but the boy flew past her.

Jenny didn't seem to notice the diaper or the toddler blaring his siren as he rounded the bend into the living room. She set a plate of brownies on the breakfast table, followed by two steaming mugs of tea.

As her childhood friend sat down across from her, Camden wrapped her hands around the ceramic mug and watched the steam dissipate into the air. How long had her grandmother been sick? Where had she lived her last days? Who had helped her eat? Bathe?

Jenny leaned toward her. "She asked about you last week."

Camden's head jerked up and met Jenny's eyes. "What did you say?"

"I told her you were probably traveling in some exotic place, taking pictures."

She shook her head. "I was in New York."

Alone.

"Rosalie loved telling people that her granddaughter was a famous photographer." Jenny shook sweetener into her tea. "I think she told everyone she met."

"I thought she lost her hearing."

Jenny smiled. "She couldn't hear much, but she had no problem talking."

"I should have been here with her."

Jenny swooped a brownie onto a napkin and pushed it toward her. "Eat."

"How long did she have cancer?"

"About a year."

The baby crawled back toward the table and held out her arms. Jenny reached over and picked up the child, bouncing her in her lap.

Camden twisted the mug in her hands. "Was she in much pain?"

"Hospice helped her manage it, but even when she was in pain, there was joy, Camden. We all knew she was on her way to heaven."

"Was Eloise with her?" she asked, even though she hoped for her grandmother's sake that her stepmother had stayed away.

Jenny held up a piece of brownie, and the baby devoured it. Brown crumbs covered the girl's cheeks as she reached for another piece. "I didn't see her, but Liza visited almost every weekend."

Envy pierced her heart. She should have been alongside her half-sister to comfort Rosalie during her last days.

"So she was at home . . ."

Jenny chewed a bit of her brownie, swallowed, and dabbed at her lips. "She didn't want to go to a hospital."

Camden understood. She couldn't stand the smell of hospitals . . . or being confined in one space.

"She's happy now," Jenny smiled. "And healthy. I keep imagining her dancing the Charleston down those streets of gold."

A telephone rang on the kitchen counter, and with the baby on her left hip, Jenny hopped up. Before she answered the phone, she turned back to Camden. "And you know Philip was waiting beside Jesus to welcome her home."

She smiled at the memories of her grandma, watching her glide across the ballroom floor with her son, Camden's father. She could almost see Rosalie dancing through heaven's gates as well, probably right into the arms of Philip Bristow—the husband Rosalie had lost three decades earlier.

Jenny wandered down the hallway with the phone. "You'll never believe who's here."

As her friend's voice trailed off, Camden sat in silence. Her stomach rumbling, she eyed the brownie in front of her. She hadn't eaten since she'd devoured a Hardee's biscuit along the Ohio-Pennsylvania line. Nine hours ago.

She swallowed a small bite without tasting it.

Liza probably cared for their grandmother and told her how much she loved her. Probably brought her flowers and plumped her pillows and asked to hear more stories about their family before she passed away.

Thank God, Rosalie had a grandchild who stayed with her until the end.

Through the window, Camden saw Hailey peek her head out of the doghouse and sniff the ground before crawling toward a tricycle and beginning to gnaw on a tire. Camden didn't want to think about where that tire had been.

Minutes later, Jenny set the phone back on the counter and walked over to her. "Sorry about the interruption."

"Don't worry about it."

"My husband's a lawyer." Jenny scooted back into the chair, patting the baby on the back. "And he's on his way home for a late lunch."

"I guess I'd better head out."

"Oh no." Jenny moved the baby to her knee. "He said he needs to talk to you right away."

She blinked. "Why does he need to talk to me?"

Jenny shrugged. "He pulled the old attorney-client privilege card with me."

"I'm not his client."

"That's true." Jenny picked up a spoon and stirred her tea. "But your grandmother was."

Stale cigar smoke permeated the living room of the house Jake shared with Edward. He sneezed when he snuck into the back door and then he swore. At least a dozen times he'd asked the old geezer to step outside to smoke, but ever since Mariah left, the man lit up a cigar whenever Jake walked through the back door.

It wasn't like he couldn't go outside. His grandfather left the house almost every day to drive his Mercedes a mile down the road to visit his cousin Dotty over at the old folks home. Edward forked out the cash each month to pay for his cousin's care, and then pretended he was doing it for her own good.

When Edward wasn't out at Beaverdale, he was checking in with his two employees at the Paxton Antiques Shoppe or stopping by town hall to harass whoever happened to be trying to run their town. Edward could smoke in his blasted shop if he wanted—or light up a cigar in front of town hall.

He sneezed again.

Technically the house was Edward's, but one day the shack would be his and Mariah's place . . . if they didn't escape Etherton before then. He didn't want to breathe smoke now nor did he want the foul smell permeating the furniture and carpets after his grandfather kicked the bucket.

When Jake stomped into the study, Edward was reclining in his La-Z-Boy, feet crossed on the leg rest. He was dressed in his signature navy vest and black pants, and what remained of his gray hair bristled from his head like a wire brush. No one bothered to remind Edward that his eightieth birthday was on the horizon. In his mind, he would always be a distinguished sixty or so except, with his pointy ears and wrinkly skin, he looked more like the house elf in the Harry Potter series than a distinguished gentleman.

The next puff released into the air and settled over Jake's face. "Where did you go?"

He tried to fight off another sneeze, but lost. "I told you not to smoke in here."

"A little smoke is good for you, Jakey. Might even make a man out of you."

Queasiness rocked his gut, and he waved his hand in front of his face like it would clear the air. "It doesn't make me anything but sick."

Edward recrossed his loafers, his tone as calm as his demeanor. "You didn't answer my question."

Jake plopped down on the couch beside him. "There was a woman up at the Bristow house so I went to check it out."

He didn't have to mention the woman was with Jenny. His grandfather would start badgering him again for letting Jenny dump him.

A bitter smell ballooned into the room as Edward crushed the tip of his cigar in the ashtray. "It was probably Liza Bristow."

He blocked the stench from his mouth and nose, shaking his head. "This woman was a blond."

"So she dyed her hair . . . or maybe it was Liza's mother?"

Jake shook his head again. "Too young."

Edward collapsed the leg rest with his heels and sat up like the professor he used to be. "What was this strange woman doing?"

"Peeking in all the windows, like she was searching for something."

Edward paused. "Was she from Etherton?"

"The plates on her car were New York."

"New York . . ." Edward's voice trailed off.

Jake covered his mouth with his flannel sleeve, but it didn't stop his sneeze. "We should probably wait to go inside the house."

"On the contrary." Edward drummed his fingers together and then smiled. "We shouldn't wait another moment."

"But what if she comes back—"

"There's no way she'll get inside."

CHAPTER SEVEN

Dan Sprague nodded toward the hallway. "Follow me."

Clutching her mug, Camden navigated the minefield of wooden blocks and brightly colored Legos behind Dan and the aspiring young fireman who expertly dodged the toys like he and his truck had practiced the course. When they reached the last door in the hallway, Dan kissed his son, and then motioned Camden into the den.

Dan locked the French doors against the fire truck and driver, and plopped his briefcase on the desk. The doors quaked as the boy rammed into them.

Dan's brown hair curled over his collar, and his striped tie was smeared with ketchup. "Sorry about the background noise."

"I live in New York," she said, like that explained everything.

"Lots of racket?"

"Plenty of trucks and sirens to keep me awake." Though no one ever tried to break down her door.

He unzipped his leather case. "We never lack for drama around here either . . . especially between about two and four in the morning."

The doors beside her shook again, and she wondered if the boy ever crashed through them. "I bet not."

Dan sat down on the leather chair behind the desk, and she slid into one of two plush chairs across from him. He clapped his hands together. "Are you doing okay?"

"It's been a rough day."

"Jenny told me you didn't know Rosalie had passed on."

She shook her head, turning the mug in her hands.

"Your timing's kind of interesting, isn't it?"

Her head jerked up, and she met his gaze. "What are you implying?"

"When was the last time you were here, Miss Bristow?"

She straightened her shoulders. "It's Camden, and I was here eighteen years ago."

"And now you decide to come for a visit?"

"It's complicated."

"I bet it is."

She sprung off her chair and stepped toward the door. "I'm sorry, counselor, but it's been a long day."

"Please sit down." His smile was forced. "I'm not accusing you of anything. I'm just wondering why you didn't come to the memorial service."

Slowly, she lowered herself back into the seat, but she perched herself on the edge, trying to remind herself that this was Jenny's husband . . . and he was an attorney. He was supposed to ask questions. "No one told me about it."

"Liza didn't call you?"

"She doesn't have my number." Even if Liza knew she was in New York, she probably wouldn't have called. "I would have come if I knew she was sick."

He plucked a folder out of the case and laid it on the desk beside him. "She'd been sick for a long time."

Camden tapped her boots on the carpet, ready to exit. "Jenny said you needed to talk with me."

A skirmish rattled the doors, and she heard Jenny's voice. Apparently the firefighter lost the battle because the banging ceased.

Dan opened the folder and slid the clip off a stack of paper. "Rosalie Bristow cared about a lot of people . . . but she had a special place in her heart for you."

She blinked back tears, scooting back into her chair again.

"And Rosalie trusted you."

In the quietness, she glanced down at the stack of papers on the desk in front of her. Bold letters on the title page read, ROSALIE STULL BRISTOW'S LAST WILL AND TESTAMENT.

Had her grandma left something for her? Maybe one of her beautiful glass pieces to commemorate their summers together. Whatever the gift, she would treasure it.

"Shouldn't Liza be here for this?"

Dan flipped back one of the pages. "I already gave her the details."

Her hands trembled as she set her mug on the desk. "Did Rosalie leave me something?"

Dan pulled out a flecked envelope from under the will, and she reached for it. Perhaps her grandmother left her a letter.

"Thank you," she said, tugging the envelope to her chest. She may have missed her grandmother's final days, but she would find a quiet place to be alone with Rosalie one last time.

"That's not all," Dan replied. His voice sounded strained, and she swallowed, wondering what was so difficult for him to say.

She smoothed her fingers over the envelope. "Is something wrong?"

Instead of answering her question, he reached into his pocket and pulled out a key.

Alex drove past a huge billboard promoting Louise Danner's bid for reelection, his boss's smiling face trying to convince residents that they could count on her during the next four years to bring them out of the mire. The mayor's hands were tied, though, if she couldn't persuade the council to begin revitalization. And begin it right away.

Instead of continuing down Main Street to town hall, Alex turned right, left, and then slowly crested the hill. He scanned the driveway in front of the Bristow mansion until he spotted the blue Miata with a duffel bag strapped across the trunk rack. Camden Bristow had found the place.

Pulling into the driveway, he wondered if he should check in on her. But as quickly as the thought came, he realized the real reason he was here—he was intrigued by Camden's smile and her fiery blue eyes. Being intrigued was not a good reason to knock on her front door though. In fact, it was plain dangerous.

It was strange that she'd asked him about Crescent Hill, like she didn't know the town celebrated her grandmother's life yesterday. Either she didn't have a clue or she was as heartless as Rosalie's other grandchild.

He'd begun to ask her about Rosalie's memorial service, but the Holy Spirit checked his tongue. If she didn't know that her grandmother was gone, he wasn't the one to tell her.

He'd met Rosalie Bristow at Community Bible Church last fall, and she talked about her granddaughter with such pride—not only was she a gifted photographer from New York, but according to Rosalie, the woman could capture pain and love and regret with her photo lens in a way that made you experience every emotion.

Rosalie told him all about Camden, but she never mentioned Liza Bristow, her other granddaughter.

Alex met Liza for the first time last month, and it hadn't been a privilege. The woman arrived in his office without an appointment, sipping a lime Perrier and asking what inspired him to move to this god-forsaken town. He assured her that God had not forsaken Etherton or its residents, and his comment abruptly ended their discussion about spiritual matters.

Liza proceeded to ask him what it would take for the city to buy Crescent Hill, and his jaw dropped. Rosalie wasn't gone yet, and already Liza was trying to sell the property. He doubted Rosalie knew her granddaughter was at his office, and he also doubted that Liza planned to care for Rosalie if the city bought the property. The instant they'd made their deal, she'd probably ship her grandmother off to a nursing home.

Still, it was his job to talk about acquiring new property in Etherton so he'd thrown out a number that City Council might agree to if he twisted their arm.

Liza froze momentarily at his offer before she tossed a ridiculous number back at Alex. He showed her to the door.

Crescent Hill was forty-five acres, on a prime piece of land, but the town was bleeding money—almost as fast as its citizens were losing their jobs. It would be the perfect property to develop into new business, but the town would need to pass a bond to pay what Liza Bristow asked. City Council said they wanted something bigger from him than the Truman community center and park, but locals would never agree to a tax increase.

Now that Rosalie was gone, Liza probably inherited the house, and he had no doubt she would be back with another offer. If he could persuade her to lower her price, and the council to let him acquire it, he could find someone to develop it.

He scanned the house and then the trees around him to look for Camden.

Was she sniffing around for an inheritance as well? It would be a tragedy if Rosalie's death snowballed into a family brawl.

Plenty of people dreamed about receiving a large inheritance—like money would be the answer to their problems. Money almost destroyed what remained of the tepid relationship he had with his parents and brother, and money destroyed the relationship with his fiancée and sent him packing from Columbia.

He'd never wish an inheritance on anyone.

Glancing up at the windows, he wondered if Camden was boxing up what she wanted before she ran back to New York. On the third floor, he caught the shape of a face in a window, watching him. He lifted his hand to wave, but instead of waving back, Camden slipped away from the glass. Alex waited several minutes, thinking she might come down to speak with him, but she didn't open the front doors. Nor did she reappear at the window.

He almost knocked on the door, but he didn't have a good reason to visit and she didn't have any obligation to speak with him. Backing up his car, he drove out into the street instead and down the hill.

Halfway down Crescent Hill, Alex passed a green and white house with wide columns along the porch and a white cupola overhead. Jake Paxton's truck was parked along the curb, the same place it was parked every time Alex passed the Paxton home.

Louise warned him about the Paxton family his first day on the job. Edward Paxton, she explained, was going to be the thorn in their side, and she was right. Edward was the one city councilor who refused to concede and refused to retire. Louise tolerated him, but Alex was convinced that Edward was the main reason he couldn't do his job.

No matter what Alex proposed, Edward turned it down, and a majority of the other councilors followed. According to Louise, the Paxtons were one of the first families in Etherton, and in Edward's mind, he owned the entire town instead of one antique shop. Alex thought the man would want new business, but Edward was happy with his town just the way it was.

During his eight months in Etherton, Alex had seen Edward's grandson only once, at an Etherton High football game. Louise told him Jake's mother had left him with his grandfather when he was a kid and moved to California. He'd been a decent linebacker in high school, but dropped out his senior year. Louise said Jake turned thirty-one recently, but he'd yet to pursue a profession.

Alex stopped at the base of the hill and turned right toward town hall. His phone rang, and he reached for it, but when he answered the call, all he heard was crying.

Alex pulled to the side of the road, flashing back to the last time he'd received a call from a crying woman. His life was never the same.

"Who is this?"

"Alex?"

"Who is this?" he repeated.

"Liza Bristow."

Why was this woman calling him, crying? He hadn't seen a single tear fall from her eyes at the service yesterday.

"Okay . . ." he muttered, not knowing exactly what to say. He never had understood women.

"I need to talk to you," she said.

"What's wrong?"

"I just found out . . ." Instead of finishing her sentence, another sob rocked his ear. "Can we meet someplace?"

He edged back into the street and continued his drive back to the office. "I don't have any plans to be in Columbus."

"Not Columbus, silly." A strange giggle replaced her sob. "I'm at the Zandorf Inn."

His car bumped over a hole in the brick street. "I'll be at my office in ten minutes."

"I'll be there in five."

CHAPTER EIGHT

Crumbled brick littered the floor of the tunnel like decaying war rubble. Water trickled down the curved walls, soaking gaps left behind by the fallen bricks. The air was cold, dank, but much better than the smoky room he'd left behind. At least he wasn't sneezing.

A flashlight clutched in his hand, Jake trudged down the dirt path toward the Bristow mansion. It was stupid for him to go inside this afternoon with that woman sniffing around the place—he didn't know what she was after and neither did Edward. Yet his grandfather insisted they proceed.

Jake grew up in the house midway down Crescent Hill, and he never even knew about this tunnel, not until last week when Edward let him in on the little secret he'd been harboring for sixty years. Jake waited to go into the tunnel until most of Rosalie's visitors were gone . . . and before someone else moved into the dump.

Edward told him the path might be a little tricky, but it wasn't tricky. It was treacherous. The brick ceiling and walls looked like they could collapse at any moment, and if they did, they'd bury him alive.

Sweat beaded on his forehead, and he wiped it away with the sleeve of his flannel shirt.

When he was a kid, Edward used to tell him the most horrific stories before he went to sleep, stories about corpses coming back to life to haunt those who once tormented them. In Edward's bedtime stories, the corpses always succeeded in their revenge.

The nightmares that followed these stories had been terrible, but Edward wasn't the least bit compassionate. He laughed whenever Jake cried out in fright—like he enjoyed terrifying a child—and said the nightmares would make Jake stronger.

The flashlight shook in Jake's hand, and he berated himself. Ghosts may be real, but there were no ghosts or graves in this tunnel. Or anything else except bricks and mud. Panicking was for cowards, and he wasn't a coward . . . nor was he a criminal. He was only going in for what was rightfully his . . . and Edward's. All he had to do was retrieve the box and get out of the tunnel—if the brick walls didn't bury him first.

The air chilled his lungs, and he shivered, wondering if the smoky house might be better after all.

But it was too late to turn back now. Edward had disclosed his secret, and he'd done it with plenty of strings attached. After the week in jail a few years ago, there was no way he'd go back again. Whatever it took to get in the house, he would do it.

A loud slurp erupted from the quiet when he tugged his foot out of the patch of mud. Water dripped on his hair, down his ears. He should have worn a raincoat, but Edward hadn't bothered to warn him about the dripping water.

The tunnel bent left, and in front of him, the ceiling had caved in, leaving behind a pile of bricks and dirt with a jagged hole in the center. He reached up, fingering the cracks along the ceiling. The whole blasted thing was about to tumble on his head.

The Bristows probably hadn't built this tunnel to last more than a few decades—forget one hundred and fifty years. Once their work was done, they wouldn't care if it collapsed. According to Edward, the upstanding Bristows didn't even record the tunnel with the city.

If the tunnel did collapse, Edward would probably shrug his shoulders and say he didn't have a clue where his grandson went. The tunnel would bury Jake and any hope of his finding the treasure . . . if there really was a treasure.

Thrusting the flashlight in front of him like it was a sword, he snaked his right foot through the hole and then his head and torso. The jagged edge of a brick snagged his shirt, and the flannel ripped when he yanked it away.

His left hand clinging to the edge of the hole, he pulled his other leg through until his foot touched ground. His shoe slid across the mud and bricks, and he stumbled forward, cutting his fingers. When he reached over to stop the pain, his flashlight flew out of his hand.

In the darkness, he eased to his knees and brushed his good hand across the floor. It might take hours to get out of this tunnel without a light . . . if he could even find the entrance where he started.

This was Edward's obsession, not his. He didn't really believe there was a treasure hidden in this house anymore—the Bristows would have uncovered it long ago. But Edward believed it was still there, and the only way for him to avoid jail was by scouring the house and then convincing his grandfather that the legend was a farce.

Frantically, he sifted through the brick and mud until his fingers grazed the edge of a wooden box. His hand recoiled, and the trembling started again.

He shook his head to stop the tricks playing in his mind. Edward would have told him if someone were buried in here. But perhaps . . . perhaps it was the box with the treasure. It could have been hidden in the tunnel a long time ago.

Tentatively, he stuck out his hand again and sighed in relief. It wasn't a treasure box, but it wasn't a coffin either. It was a wooden step.

He'd made it to the end of the tunnel.

The steps creaked as he climbed upward through the inky black. Fifteen. Sixteen. Seventeen steps. The walls narrowed until his shoulders brushed the sides. Another step, and his head bumped the ceiling. He was almost inside the house.

Groping above his head, his fingers found a hatch in front of him, and then the metal latch. He slipped up the latch and then pushed on the door with his good hand.

It didn't budge.

Throwing his shoulder into it, he shoved the door several times, and when it didn't move, he kicked the wood.

Leaning back against the rugged wall, he wiped the sweat off his forehead with his sleeve. He'd managed to get all the way through the tunnel, but if he didn't get through this last door, Edward would berate him like he was an idiot. And he wasn't an idiot.

His good hand searched the door until he found a leather handle. He jiggled it as hard as he could, pushing and then tugging it right and left. Propping his left elbow and leg against the wall, he pushed again. This time dust showered down on his head.

Camden's hands trembled as she walked back up Crescent Hill. Clasped in one hand was the sealed envelope—Rosalie's letter. In her other hand was a key.

Her Miata was still parked beside the garage, a blue dot against the reds and browns of the mansion. The overgrown gardens were still there along with the broken glass in the cupola. The view was exactly the same as when she'd arrived three hours ago . . . but everything else had changed.

Her grandmother was gone, and now she—

Camden broke her gaze away from the house and stared at the key in her hand. The edge was jagged, the brass tarnished. It was probably the same key her grandparents used when they inherited the property. And perhaps the same key her great-grandparents used as well.

And now it was hers. The key, the Chrysler, the tulip garden, and the dilapidated mansion. Yesterday she had no place to sleep and now she had ten thousand square feet in which to rest her head.

Wind lashed over the hill, but instead of shivering, she smiled. For the first time in a year, she would be able to pay all her bills. She could pay cash for hot water and lights and food. She didn't know how much the house was worth, but surely it would pay off her debts with a little left over for lean years ahead.

She couldn't believe her grandma willed the property to her instead of to Liza or a charity. Dan assured her that Liza had inherited several items to remember Rosalie, but still . . .

She and Liza inherited her grandma's house and possessions, but there was no money left—Dan said Rosalie gave it all away years ago. When Timothy Bristow—Camden's father—died, his will stipulated that his estate would care for his mother until her passing. The estate paid the property taxes and utilities for Crescent Hill, and Dan said it even provided for some repairs, but Camden couldn't see any improvements made on the exterior of the mansion or the property around it.

Now that Rosalie was gone, the estate would no longer pay for the house, but it didn't matter either way. Camden couldn't keep it.

She tucked her grandma's letter into her handbag and climbed up the cement stairs to the mansion's mammoth front doors. Poking the key into the lock, she jostled it until the double doors swung open with a bang.

Inside the entryway, she stopped. Her heart longed for Rosalie to rush down the stairs and kiss her cheeks like she'd done the last time Camden visited. For an instant, she thought she heard something shuffle overhead, but then the house was silent. No one to hug her or offer her a mug of apple cider or sweep the jacket from her hands and hang it in the closet.

Black and white marble dotted the entrance floor, all the tiles smeared with mud. Cobwebs drooped from stained plaster molding that decorated the ceiling like stale icing on a wedding cake. At the side of the great hall was a staircase carved from dark mahogany. The wall along the steps was lined with pictures of her Bristow ancestors as well as a prized picture of Abraham Lincoln and one of Harriet Beecher Stowe.

The interior of the house was even more worn than she remembered. And dark. It had grown old alongside its owner.

Former owner.

The thought of owning such a place almost overwhelmed her. Besides her car and equipment and a few duffel bags worth of clothes, she'd never owned anything in her life. And now all of this was hers.

She peeked into the drawing room at the left. On the far side of the room was a grand piano and a marble fireplace topped with a bronze mirror. Swirls of sage, tan, and gold colored the Victorian wallpaper, and a crystal chandelier hung eighteen feet above the collection of sofas and chairs. A walnut hutch displayed silver bowls and china and pieces of beautiful glass. Each generation of Bristow women added artwork to the house's collection—bronze sculptures, oil paintings, and elaborate quilts. Her grandmother's addition had been the glass.

Camden stared at a vase inside the hutch—tinted blue and silver. It was only one of her grandmother's many fine pieces. One that she would never sell.

In the next room, hundreds of leather-bound books filled the walls of the library, on both the first floor and in the balcony above. She climbed the spiral stairs to the balcony that overlooked the library and crossed the carpeted floor alongside reading alcoves with lamps and chairs.

Rosalie preferred entertaining instead of retreating to the library with a book. Camden, however, would sometimes sneak into this room and hide in one of the alcoves to look at pictures of castles and old churches and art. But today the only thing she wanted to read was the letter in her bag. Up in the solitude and light of the cupola, she would savor the last of Rosalie's words.

At the far end of the balcony was a stairwell. When she reached the doorway, she turned the knob and shivered as cold air poured out from the darkness. Dust flew in her face with her first step, and a tremor of fear sparked at her skin. Years ago, she would bolt up this staircase, across the floor, and up the last set of circular stairs to the cupola in under a minute. It wasn't until she was up in the light that she stopped being afraid.

With her second step, Camden wondered how long it had been since someone had traveled up these stairs. There wasn't much up on the third floor—just a small theater and a study and several storerooms filled with boxes and trunks. She couldn't imagine that Rosalie had come up these narrow stairs in a long time.

The door at the top creaked in greeting as she opened it, and on the other side of the door, she paused at the arched entrance and looked into the theater.

Two windows faced the town on the right, the glass smeared with dirt. A layer of dust coated the white wainscoting and crystal sconces, and stern-faced oil paintings hung crooked on the yellow wall. There was a grand chandelier in the middle of it all, dozens of crystals glistening in the sunlight.

Before her parents divorced, she remembered her mother bringing her up here for a Christmas celebration. White lights had twinkled from the ceiling, and a barbershop quartet sang carols from the platform. Beside the stage, the grand fireplace had glowed with red and green lights instead of flames.

The memories were hazy but she remembered sipping thick hot chocolate and belting out Christmas carols along with the quartet. Magical.

At the left of the room were frayed curtains that hung like honey-colored braids on each side of the stage. Sweeping past the curtains, Camden slid down to a bench that had been used as an orchestra seat. If she designed the house, she would have put the stage to the right of the room and a long picture window to the left so all the guests could enjoy the natural beauty of the fields and pond on the east side of the house. And she would have exchanged all the harsh oil paintings along the wall for elegant watercolors and mirrors.

She pulled her knees to her chest and rested her head on top of her knees.

The strange thing was—if she had the money—she could replace everything in this room. Everything in the house. With extra income to restore the place, she could stay and live in the Bristow mansion when she wasn't traveling. She'd always prided herself on being a nomad, but at this moment, all she wanted was a place to belong.

It was wishful thinking, of course. She could never stay here. Even if she sold some of the more valuable items and artwork in the house, she'd never have enough money to restore or even renovate the house, but it was nice to dream about having a home.

Stepping out of the theater, she turned down the hallway toward the cupola entrance. In the silence, she heard the slightest sound ahead of her, almost like a footstep, and she shook her head. The house made all sorts of creaks and groans. As a kid, she would hide from the scary sounds, but she was an adult now and she knew that there was no one here except her.

Her fingers brushed over her handbag, her grandma's letter safe inside. The staircase at the end of the hall would take her up to the cupola, but instead of going up another flight of stairs, she couldn't wait another moment to read the letter. Edging down the wall, she sat on the floor in the hallway. Even though her grandma's presence was gone, she felt close to her here.

Reaching into her bag, she pulled out the envelope and slowly opened it. Two pieces of paper fell onto her lap, and she saw her grandma's handwriting on the first sheet. She smiled when she saw the letter addressed to her.

> My dear Camden,
>
> I've finally gone home, straight into the arms of my sweet Jesus. Please don't be sad. I'm rejoicing, and I want you to rejoice for me and for the many blessings in your life.
>
> My prayer is that you embrace the future and the purpose that God has planted in your heart. You love people, Camden. I saw it in your eyes as a child, and I see it today in your work. Don't be afraid to love. Or serve. Even when it hurts, I pray you will open your arms to the least of these. Protect them. Love them. Fight for them. And give them back to God.

Something rustled in one of the storage rooms along the hallway, and goose bumps spiked across her arms. Surely it was just the wind, rattling windows . . .

But what if it was something else? What if someone was in the house?

She folded the letter and slid the papers back into her bag. She would read the rest later.

Another board creaked, and she jumped up.

"Who's there?" she shouted.

No one answered, but glass shattered on the floor.

CHAPTER NINE

Camden hustled back down both staircases and across the entryway. Her heart racing, she fumbled with her handbag until she found her phone and punched in 9-1-1. She kept moving toward the front doors as she brought the phone to her ear.

"Someone's in my house," she panted, trying to stay calm.

"Are you injured?" the operator asked.

"No."

"What is your location?"

"Crescent Hill . . . in Etherton."

She could hear the man type on his keyboard. "I need the street number."

She jogged down the cement steps, and dry grass crunched under her boots as she fled into the yard. "There is no street number."

"Can you get outside the house?"

"I'm out."

"Very good," he said before placing her on hold to call the police.

Sliding into the safety of her car, she punched the lock. She was well versed in self-defense, had to be in order to photograph impoverished and war-torn areas of the world, but when she armed herself with her camera, people rarely threatened her.

There was no camera for her to hide behind now. The equipment that hadn't been stolen in Indonesia was in her trunk, and she wasn't getting out of the car until the police arrived. She told herself she wasn't afraid of the intruder, but she had a healthy fear of any weapon an intruder might carry with him.

Holding her phone up in front of her, she aimed it at the door, ready to snap a picture if the man decided to take off before the police arrived.

Of course, if the person inside was familiar at all with the mansion, he wouldn't come through the front door. There were too many ways to get outside the house, too many places on this hill to disappear. He was probably long gone, hidden in the trees or down at the cemetery.

Sirens blasted up the hill, and gravel spewed from the tires of three cop cars. Dust erupted above the cars as the officers parked haphazardly in the grass.

Opening her door, Camden climbed out at the same time an officer stepped out of the first car. His eyes rapidly scanned the yard until they homed in on her. As he advanced, she glanced at the badge. Sergeant Kelley. The man's black face was lean; his nose slanted left. The short sleeves of his uniform barely fit around his bulky arms.

She'd bet most criminals ran from this man.

The sergeant didn't bother with pleasantries. Instead he grilled her, and she tried to answer his many questions. Yes, she was from New York. Rosalie Bristow's oldest grandchild. Yes, today was the first time she'd been back on the hill since Rosalie passed away. No, she hadn't seen anyone in the house, hadn't distinctly heard anyone either, nor did she hear voices. Only footsteps . . . and the splinter of glass.

One of the officers laughed when she mentioned the footsteps, and the sergeant whipped his head toward the younger man. "Zip it, Reeve."

The officer shut up, but she could see the amusement playing in his eyes. It did sound a little silly when she repeated the story. Her nerves were shot, and at the first hint of threat, she'd hit the panic button. Usually, she was more levelheaded than this. What she needed was a good night's rest and a few hours to digest all that happened since she arrived in Etherton this morning.

The sergeant asked her again about what she'd heard. As she described the sound of glass breaking, she braced herself for another laugh, a joke about her paranoia, but the sergeant neither laughed nor teased. Barking out instructions, he told her to wait with Reeve in a police car, and then he motioned for two of the men to check the back of the house. Sergeant Kelley and his partner entered through the front door.

Camden inched toward the police car, but didn't get inside. Her fear slowly dissipated as she imagined the officers scouring the house for signs of intrusion. She would be embarrassed if they found nothing. And relieved.

As she waited, she realized that she needed to find a place to take a hot shower and spend the night. Dumping the little credit she had left into a hotel room seemed like a bad idea. She'd need her card for food and gas until she could figure out how to sell a few of Rosalie's things. And there was no way she could sleep at Jenny's house, not with all her cute critters climbing walls and banging on doors. Her car was another option, albeit a bad one. She hadn't slept well last night at the rest stop, and her neck was still angry at her for even trying.

Maybe she should ask Jenny if she could spend one night at her house, until she could figure out a better option. Little intruders may bang on her door at Jenny's house, but at least no one would be stomping around the attic above her room.

The mansion doors burst open, and Sergeant Kelley hustled down the stairs, followed by his officers. When the sergeant reached her, he held out a plastic bag filled with orange- and red-tinted shards.

"We found a vase broken on the third floor."

Her hand flew to her mouth. She recognized the pieces of glass—it was from a vase her grandmother had blown as a gift for her husband, Camden's grandfather, long before Camden was born.

"Do you recognize it?" the sergeant asked.

She opened her mouth, the words struggling to come out. "My grandmother made it."

Sergeant Kelley pulled the bag back to his side and eyed her warily. "Before we continue, I'd like to see some ID, Miss Bristow."

She tilted her head. "What?"

"Your driver's license, please."

She slinked back toward the car to get her ID. It was a reasonable request, she supposed, to prove she was Rosalie's granddaughter, but it felt like everyone was doubting her today—her identity and her motives. All she'd wanted to do was to arrive quietly and visit her grandma, maybe stay a few weeks and help her clean up the house in exchange for a bed. Now she was answering to everyone except Rosalie.

She reached for her handbag on the front seat of the car. As she pulled out her wallet, her fingers swept across her grandma's precious letter. She would finish it tonight, before she slept.

Sergeant Kelley examined her license without comment before handing it back to her. "There was no sign of forcible entry, but there was a cracked window in the room where we found the glass. We think the wind blew the vase over."

"But I heard . . ." she started, and then stopped. Had she really heard footsteps or was it just the floorboards groaning with her arrival? She remembered the loud creaks in the attic when she was a child, the noises that would make her pull the covers over her head and hope the ghosts wouldn't find her. "I probably heard wrong. It's been a long day."

The sergeant wrote another note on his tablet, and then scribbled his cell phone number on the back of a business card before he handed it to her. "Let me know if anything else is missing."

She stared down at the blue and yellow logo on the card.

"I'm real sorry about your grandmother," he said as he flipped his tablet closed and pocketed it. "She was a fine lady."

Camden deposited her wallet and the card in the pocket of her coat. "Did you know her?"

He nodded. "I've been going to Community Bible my entire life."

She tried to remember the sergeant from her summers in Etherton, but couldn't recall his face. Going to church with her grandmother had been an overwhelming experience for her as a child. She'd loved listening to the fun music each week. The stories. When she was nine, she walked down the aisle and told the pastor she was ready to believe in Jesus.

When Camden arrived back in the States, she'd wandered into a few New York churches, but she never felt at home. She'd found God in Etherton, and it seemed she'd left Him there.

The radio squawked in the patrol car beside them, but another officer responded to the call. "Rosalie mentioned your name," the sergeant said.

"Really?"

Sergeant Kelley looked like he was about to say something else, but Reeve leaned his head out the window. "It's a traffic accident."

Sergeant Kelley reached out to shake her hand. "I'll try and keep my eye on the house for you."

~

Liza Bristow stopped crying. Finally. Alex didn't think it was possible to dispense that many tears, but Liza proved him wrong. She'd opened the gates and flooded his office floor.

He handed yet another tissue across the divide of his desk, and she blew her nose.

When she'd followed him into his office earlier this afternoon, he'd intentionally set himself up behind the mahogany partition to keep her from trying to spill her grief on his shoulder . . . if you could call it grief. He'd grieved not long ago, from the depths of his gut, but in his grief, he'd only cried once. And it was nothing like this. More agony . . . and a lot less drama.

What kind of person grieved over a house? He could understand if Liza was mourning her grandmother's death, but this had nothing to do with her grandmother. It was all about expectations. Liza thought Rosalie would leave her the house, but apparently her grandmother had other plans.

It was all wrong, Liza mumbled between her tears. She had loved Rosalie. She'd cared for her grandmother even when Rosalie didn't recognize her anymore, and she deserved a little payback for all she endured.

Endured?

Alex choked on the word, but Liza didn't seem to notice. Rosalie's face came into his mind, her crystal blue eyes and the pink bow on her fancy Sunday hat. And especially her smile. Even with cancer, she never stopped smiling.

He'd felt sorry for plenty of people in his lifetime but didn't feel the least bit sorry for Liza Bristow. She hadn't suffered a thing. Hers were tears of anger, not of sorrow. Liza didn't want the pieces of art Rosalie left for her. She wanted money.

Liza's perfectly manicured hands reached across the desk, like she expected him to take them into his own hands and comfort her. His fingers drummed the edge of his armrest instead. He didn't want to hold her hands or even sit here another minute.

She'd been here almost two hours, and he was supposed to play basketball with Dan Sprague and a few other guys at six.

Someone else should be listening to Liza, trying to appease her somehow. Anyone but him.

"How can I help you, Liza?"

She dabbed her face with the tissue. "I need to hire a local attorney."

His eyes narrowed. "For what?"

"To contest the will, of course." She blew her splotched nose again.

He sat back in his chair. "Contest it?"

Her lips pressed into a pout, like she was upset that he dared question her. "I only want what's supposed to be mine, nothing else. I need to correct this mistake."

Mistake? Dan rarely made mistakes. He was the type of attorney who checked every fact twice, crossed every T.

"It's his fault . . ." she insisted.

"Whose fault?"

"Her ridiculous attorney, of course. Completely incompetent. Obviously Rosalie wasn't thinking straight when she wrote this will." She flipped her hair out of her eyes. "She was supposed to leave the house to me."

"She told you that?"

From some hidden reservoir, fresh tears started flowing.

"I'm sorry," he said as he stood. "I can't recommend any attorneys."

He lifted his jacket from the back of his chair and stepped around the desk. He was done here . . . almost.

"Liza?" he asked, and she smiled at him with quivering lips. "Did Dan say who inherited the house?"

Her eyes hardened at the mention of Dan's name. "He refused to tell me."

Could Rosalie have left Crescent Hill to the town? After all, she loved the place where she'd spent most of her life, loved its people. It would make sense . . . but if she had done that, Dan would have told him by now.

Then he thought again about the pretty woman at the café. The other granddaughter.

He opened the door, and Liza stood and followed him into the hallway.

In the morning, he'd take another drive up Crescent Hill.

CHAPTER TEN

What did you do?" Edward hissed, his gnarled finger inches away from Jake's face.

Jake backed away from the accusing finger. His shirt was torn, the cuff of his sleeve stained with blood. His cheek was sore, probably bruised, and he felt like he'd been on the losing end of a bar fight.

He didn't have to answer Edward's questions. Not right now. A hot shower was what he needed. And a six-pack. Nothing had gone right, and it was Edward's fault for pushing him to go inside the house way too early.

He curved around his grandfather and limped into the living room. When he was good and ready, he'd explain himself.

The sofa was a formal, uptight affair, but it didn't matter to him in the least. Collapsing onto it, he propped up his feet, and seconds later, Edward's finger was in his face again, wagging back and forth like the tail of a dog—except his grandfather wasn't excited to see him.

Jake closed his eyes. He could break that finger in a heartbeat, and he would if Edward ever tried to hurt him. His grandfather may call him stupid, but he wasn't. Jake knew about the others who suffered when they crossed Edward, and he wasn't about to make that mistake.

But life was fleeting, especially for a seventy-nine-year-old man.

Edward waved his hand toward the window. "Cops were swarming the place."

Jake shifted and looked toward the window. The mansion wasn't visible beyond the fortress of trees, but Edward could have watched the cop cars rush up the hill.

Edward sat down on a wingback chair and straightened his cardigan. "Tell me what the heck happened up there."

Jake closed his eyes—he didn't have a clue what happened. He'd gotten through the tunnel, done exactly what Edward had told him, but the second he lifted the door, he heard a crash and then a scream—about gave him a heart attack.

It was a woman who'd screamed—not a ghost—and she sounded scared. He figured he'd have no trouble shutting her up, and he almost pushed the hatch open again when the thought of going back to jail raced through his mind. Instead of continuing into the house, he'd fled down the staircase and into the tunnel. It took forever to crawl back in the darkness, but it was a darn good thing he hadn't stuck around.

"I didn't find anything." Jake opened his eyes. "And I didn't see the cops."

He didn't need to explain that he never made it into the house.

Edward settled back into his chair, and Jake realized his grandfather had been scared. Not afraid that Jake had been caught, but that Jake had talked. It was a fine line his grandfather was walking, trying to preserve his reputation and chase his dream. Or obsession. Or whatever it was that made Edward so reckless over this supposed treasure.

When Jake did make it into the house, it would take days for him to search the place, and if the blond chick had a key to the house, he had a funny feeling they didn't have days.

"Did you lock the hatch?"

Jake groaned, but he refused to admit failure. "I was running away!"

Edward pressed his fingers together. "The devil is in the details, Jake."

He hadn't been thinking about the details or the devil—only about getting away from the house. Who really cared if he locked the hatch anyway? No one had found the tunnel in almost two centuries. It wasn't like this woman was going to stumble over it by accident.

"You're going back in," Edward explained calmly.

Jake felt anything but calm. "When do you suggest—"

"Tonight."

"But what if she's still there?"

Edward laughed, that awful laugh that meant Jake was naive. Stupid. "She'll be too scared to sleep there."

"You don't know that," Jake replied, but his mind began to wander. What if the same woman who screamed in the house was the blond he'd seen wandering around the property? It might be interesting to find her in the house. Alone.

But he didn't want to go back through that tunnel—most people didn't mess with him, but the supernatural didn't frighten as easily. Nor were they bothered by a little muscle. He couldn't control a ghost, but if the blond was still there, he could control her. He'd never been afraid of women.

"Don't touch her, Jake." It was like Edward could read his mind. "Just find out who she is."

He inched up and stared at his grandfather. "But the cops?"

Edward nodded toward the window. "They're gone now."

"What if they catch me . . ."

Edward's eyes darkened. "Then you won't say a word."

Jake rolled each shoulder and stood up. He was used to being in charge—of Mariah and the other women in his life—and he didn't like anyone bossing him around, especially not an old man who thought he was better than everyone else.

Looming over his grandfather, Jake balled his right hand into a fist. He'd like to use it right now, show Edward that he wasn't afraid. He punched his fist into his left palm, and his grandfather glanced up, but he didn't cower. Instead he gave Jake another eerie grin.

"Anger is good for you, Jakey."

Beaten, he turned away and reached for his lined rain jacket.

Ten minutes ticked by slowly. Then fifteen. In her car, Camden keyed Bryce Kelley's number into her phone, and then tossed his card onto the floor mat. As the colors in the sky faded to black, her eyelids started to droop. The wind wasn't going to scare her away from the house, at least for the night. Sleep was what she needed. And a fresh perspective. After a little rest, she'd try and make sense of everything that had taken place today.

Untying the duffel bag from her luggage rack, she propped open the trunk to grab a smaller bag that contained her laptop and what was left of her photo equipment. She left several boxes of her things in the trunk and on the passenger seat, but she slung the strap of her handbag over her shoulder and strutted toward the house.

There was no intruder inside these walls. No reason to be afraid. She'd sleep here tonight, and then she'd determine her next step in the morning.

The breeze wrapped hair around her face, and she brushed it away as she stepped into the house. After she double-bolted the front door, she checked the locks on the other doors and first-floor windows. Everything was secure.

Instead of walking back through the library, she climbed the wide staircase at the front of the house, two steps at a time. As she crossed the landing, she passed matching ivory sofas and a grandfather clock. At one end of the hallway was her grandma's bedroom and on the other side were four guest rooms.

She turned right and walked toward the room where she used to sleep. Standing in the doorway, she flicked on the lights, and for a moment she was a kid again, running up the steps and flinging herself across this bed.

The room was large with a bay window to the right and an oversized armoire in the opposite corner. There wasn't a single wrinkle on the yellowed bedspread although a balloon-shaped watermark stained the wallpaper and the room smelled faintly of spoiled milk.

She leaned against the doorpost. Before she sold the house, the floors would need to be cleaned, the walls repaired, windows washed.

The thought overwhelmed her.

Setting her bags on the floor, she unzipped her boots and propped them beside the bed. Then she collapsed onto the bedspread. Her two or so hours of fitful sleep at the rest stop had caught up with her, not to mention the complete drain of adrenaline after she'd heard the sounds upstairs.

She yawned. She wouldn't think about the third floor right now. Except for the wind rattling the bedroom's dark window, the house was quiet. She was alone and grateful for a bed.

Her arm draped over the mattress, feeling for her handbag along the ground. When she found it, she pulled it up to the nightstand to find the letter and finish reading her grandmother's words.

Hanging on the wall across from the bed were three worn quilts, all made by Bristow women in the last century . . . or the one before. The one in the middle was the most intriguing. The faded blue and green and tan squares were filled with random objects—stars and triangles and circles and what looked like a boat.

She blinked and tried to focus on a square toward the bottom, two ragged lightening bolts crossing paths.

The square blurred in front of her as she struggled to stay awake. She would finish reading her grandmother's letter before she succumbed to sleep.

CHAPTER ELEVEN

Hot water streamed over Alex's head and shoulders in the YMCA's locker room. The other team had creamed them by eighteen points. Annihilation . . . again. He should have blocked that last three-pointer. Dan should have made both his foul shots. And their team should have sunk that ball into the basket seven more times. A little more effort, and they could have won.

He shook his head under the water. It didn't matter that they lost, not really. Or at least that's what he tried to tell himself. His mother's voice rang in his head.

It's only a game, Alex. It doesn't matter if you win.

His mother said the same words every weekend he moped around the house, sulking after his JV team lost yet another basketball game. It was only a game, but it was a game he really, really wanted to win. Of course, that was back when he thought losing another Friday night game was the worst thing that could happen . . .

Lately, he'd become an expert at losing. He couldn't win with his family. Couldn't win with City Council. Couldn't even win a stinkin' game of basketball. God, in His mercy, was probably trying to teach him a lesson, but learning to be content in the midst of loss was painful.

He turned off the shower, and minutes later, rushed out to the hallway in jeans and a sweatshirt. The only thing he seemed to win these days was beating his buddy out of the locker room, as if Dan was competing with him to see who could get dressed first. Alex groaned at the competitiveness he should have left behind with his JV years.

Glancing out the windows beside him, he watched other players running back and forth down the court, shooting hoops. He'd spent most of the evening on the wrong end of the court, trying unsuccessfully to steal the ball. It was pathetic. A thirty-two-year-old man getting all worked up over a silly pickup game.

The door to the locker room swung open, and Dan snapped Alex's leg with the end of a towel. "Good game."

Alex snorted. "We stunk."

"It's only a game."

He turned toward the lobby. "Shut up."

His friend laughed, following him. "Maybe I can get in here a few times this week to practice."

"Right . . ."

Wednesday was the one night Dan left the house to play. Or maybe the one night Jenny kicked him out. Alex wasn't sure. Either way, Dan wanted to spend most of his evenings at home with his four kids, and Alex couldn't blame him. If God ever blessed him with kids, he'd want to be home as well.

Alex was first into the lobby. "Liza Bristow showed up at my office this afternoon."

"What did she want?" Dan asked.

"Apparently, a good cry . . . and an attorney to contest the will."

Dan rolled his eyes. "I saw her this morning too, but I was besieged with words instead of tears."

Alex held open the door, and his friend walked through. The parking lot was brightly lit against the dark. "I heard you were the bearer of bad news."

His friend shrugged. "Bad for Liza, perhaps."

"Liza was surprised."

"She shouldn't be." Dan's voice fell to a whisper. "Rosalie never intended for her to have the house."

"Did she leave it to charity?"

Dan shook his head. "She willed it to her other grandchild."

Alex stopped walking. So that's what Camden Bristow was doing in Etherton. She'd come to claim her inheritance. What would Liza do when she found out the truth?

"Camden's been away for a long time," Dan said as he hopped off the curb, onto the asphalt. Alex followed him into the lot.

"She's blond, right?"

Dan flashed him a curious look. "How do you know?"

"She asked me for directions at the Underground this morning."

He laughed. "Don't let Jenny know . . ."

Alex cringed. If Jenny knew he'd met Camden—and he thought she was attractive—she would concoct some sort of weird, blind date before the day's end. Camden may be pretty, but he didn't know anything about her, except she was Rosalie's granddaughter, and, as he explained to Jenny multiple times, not only did he hate casual dating, he was nowhere near ready to start pursuing another relationship.

He dug his keys out of his pocket. "You won't tell her, will you?"

Dan stopped beside his car. "Of course not."

"Good." Alex took a step toward his car and then turned back. "And please don't tell her that I'm going to go visit Camden in the morning."

The lights on Dan's car flashed. "You're what?"

"I'm going to visit her." He hesitated as he saw a smile creep up his friend's face. "About the house."

Dan opened his car door and threw in his backpack. "Right."

A breeze gusted through Stephanie's bedroom window as she leaned back against the headboard and tugged a comforter over her chest. The hot temps had finally cooled, but she didn't want to put down Miriam Ellison's journal to close her window.

Running her fingers over the rough edges of the pages, she poured herself into the story that transported her to the 1800s, to the days when her ancestors lived on a thriving plantation near Columbia. Back when her family was preoccupied with parties and banquets and managing the slaves who worked the house and fields.

Miriam Ellison's cursive writing was faded and difficult to read, but the fluid script was like gentle waves drifting over a shoreline. Stephanie lost herself in the movement, swept away in the world of her grandmother.

The daily rituals of plantation life fascinated her, at least the nuggets hidden in Miriam's writings. Ordering supplies from England. Chasing the constant swarm of mosquitoes out of the house. Overseeing the laundry and other housekeeping work. Miriam mostly focused her writing on the parties she was planning at Ellison Manor. And she wrote extensively about her four boys and two girls, along with the houseful of domestic slaves—Miriam called them *servants*—who helped care for the children and the main house, slaves whom she cared for like they were part of the family. Stephanie wondered who cared for the children of the slaves.

Miriam's favorite servant was a mulatto woman named Rachel, though Miriam wasn't fond of Rachel's husband, William. *Pride would be his demise*, she wrote plainly after her husband punished him yet again. His pride and unrestrained notions about freedom from slavery had cost them two slaves already.

Miriam noted how every time William's behavior forced Arnold Ellison into beating him, Rachel's demeanor would crumple. The smiles that once came quickly to her lips came more slowly, or not at all, and Miriam blamed it on William's rebellion. She'd never tell her husband, but she almost wished that William would run away so Rachel's cheery disposition would return. His dissatisfaction for their way of life was souring every soul on the plantation. If he didn't run, perhaps she could talk her husband into selling him to another plantation. Sending him far away from her Rachel.

Irritation trickled through Stephanie as she read her ancestor's words, followed by a flood of anger. All the Carolina plantations were worked by slaves in the 1850s, yet Stephanie couldn't help the fury rising inside her, spurred by the callousness of Miriam's words along with the gross negligence of the human spirit and soul. Not only had her ancestors owned slaves, they'd beaten them into submission. And they'd denied doing anything wrong.

The clock clicked past two in the morning as she continued to read, turning the pages slowly as the minutes passed, both horrified and mesmerized at what happened more than a hundred and fifty years ago in the Ellison house. These were stories written by her ancestor's own hand, a woman who thought owning slaves was upstanding. A woman who thought it was moral to control their family's possessions by beating them.

Engrossed in Miriam's life—and Rachel's life—Stephanie squinted again in the lamplight as she deciphered the slender curves in the letters, the old English words. Rachel had a baby boy, a curly haired child who played at her feet as she cleaned and sewed. Initially Miriam was concerned the child would take Rachel's focus from her duties, but as Stephanie turned the pages, Miriam fell in love with the boy. And then, a year later, Rachel's second child was born, a daughter, but the girl wasn't well. Something was wrong with her legs, and she cried and cried, disturbing the entire house.

Miriam insisted that Rachel leave the child with one of the slaves who worked the fields during the day, where the girl's cries wouldn't bother those who were trying to eat or read. Rachel did as she asked—probably had no choice—but after Miriam wrote about her relief at the ill girl leaving their home, for the good of both her and Rachel, she never wrote another kind word about her housekeeper. The following pages were filled with harsh criticisms, frustration at all of her servants and those white people who were trying to rile up the South.

Not until she reached the end of Miriam's writing did she stop reading. It was the day everything must have changed for Rachel and the Ellison family.

The day William ran away.

CHAPTER TWELVE

Camden's eyes blinked open, and she stretched her arms, grateful she'd slept all night. Her mind felt much more clear. Calm. The wind seemed to have calmed as well, although clouds had replaced the blue in the sky. A grayish light mixed with the cold air that crept through the window.

Shivering, Camden pulled the blankets over her. Her mind was clear, but her body was freezing. In her stupor last night, it never occurred to her to make sure the heat was on. Hopefully, the hot water still worked. She would thaw in the shower and then rummage through the kitchen to see if there was anything left to eat. Dan Sprague said everything in the house was hers, including the groceries. Right now, she was more thrilled about inheriting food than anything else.

Until the city turned off the utilities, she would have a place to sleep and food to eat for a few days, maybe even weeks if her grandmother had continued to can in her later years. She could almost taste her grandmother's sweet strawberry jam . . . and her canned peaches.

She would eat first and then test the hot water.

Scooting her feet over the edge of the bed, she suddenly remembered the letter tucked away in her handbag.

How could she have fallen asleep before she read it? She rubbed her eyes. Before she scavenged the pantry—or took a shower—she would find out what else her grandmother wrote.

Turning to the nightstand, she reached for her handbag and then pulled her arm back to her chest. There was nothing on the stand except the lamp.

Strange. She thought she left her bag on the stand before she fell asleep. But she had been so tired. Disoriented. Somehow, she must have pushed the bag off the nightstand in her sleep. Or maybe it had fallen off.

Hopping off the mattress, she flipped back the bedspread to search under the bed, but the handbag wasn't there either.

She sat cross-legged on the floor and sorted through the blurry details of last night. The glass broke in the attic, and the police arrived. She put the letter in her handbag, her wallet in her pocket, and climbed up the stairs before she collapsed onto the bed.

Reaching for her jacket, Camden slipped her hand into the pocket and sighed with relief when she felt her wallet. Her driver's license was in the wallet. Two credit cards. No cash. Maybe she'd dreamed she put the handbag on the nightstand. Maybe she'd put it in her duffel instead.

Tossing clothes on the floor, she rummaged through her duffel until there was nothing left inside. There was no handbag. And no letter.

For a moment, her mind wandered back to Indonesia when she searched everywhere for her camera equipment and clothes and silly stuffed dog. Her guide had taken her duffel then, but now . . . ? Had someone been in her room while she was asleep?

She shook her head to clear her thoughts. Surely not. She'd locked all the doors downstairs so she'd be safe . . . but it hadn't occurred to her to lock the door to her bedroom. The wind may have blown over the vase upstairs, but it didn't blow away her bag.

She hopped up and ran toward the armoire in the corner of the room. Perhaps in her sleepy state, she'd tucked her handbag inside it.

With a quick jerk, she pulled out the top drawer, but instead of seeing her handbag, she found a mound of printed T-shirts along with a pair of pricey jeans. And a red and white hoodie. She whipped out the sweatshirt from the top of the pile—Ohio State.

She rubbed her eyes. Today was supposed to be a day of calm, time to sort out all that had happened to her in the last two days. Not be bombarded with new questions.

Yet, she couldn't help wonder—who had stayed in this room before her?

Turning, she rushed back to the nightstand and opened the top drawer to find a pink-covered Bible and a copy of *What to Expect When You're Expecting*. The Bible could have been her grandmother's but the other book . . .

Was her half-sister pregnant? Liza could have stayed at the house with their grandmother until the end. But why hadn't she retrieved her things after Rosalie died? Surely Dan would have let her back inside to collect her clothes.

Perhaps a nurse moved in with Rosalie before she passed away.

Camden fell back down on the bed. Did the person who'd been living here come back into her room last night? If so, she must have been shocked when she found Camden in her bed.

Maybe whoever had moved in here needed money, and they'd taken her purse hoping to find some cash. But instead of money, they'd stolen an even greater treasure from her. Rosalie's letter.

Someone shook Jake, and he shoved away the hand. Sleep was what he needed, about eight more hours. Or ten. Mariah knew not to bother him when he was trying to get some shut-eye.

"Get up!" Edward barked, and Jake cracked his eyes open.

It was downright wrong, waking a guy after he spent all night searching for some sort of treasure. After all, he hadn't messed with his grandfather when he found him a couple hours ago snoozing in his chair, like he didn't have a care in the world.

Jake was the one taking the risks. If he wanted to sleep all day, Edward shouldn't care.

He cracked his knuckles, and the sound reverberated around the room. Too bad he couldn't give his grandfather a good reminder not to mess with him in the morning.

"What happened?" Edward said, and Jake inched up on the couch with his elbows. The instant he glanced down at the red and black purse he'd dropped on the floor, Edward dove for it.

He hadn't found any treasure, but he'd found the girl.

Edward dumped out the purse. Lipstick rolled onto the rug. A medicine bottle. Kleenex. A couple pens. A notepad.

Jake suppressed a grin as Edward scoured through the stuff. His grandfather could search all he wanted. The only valuable items he'd found were zipped up inside his jacket for safekeeping. Edward didn't need to know about the letter or the birth certificate—at least not right now. It was the smoking gun Jake needed when he was ready to get out of this deal.

"You took an empty purse?" Edward demanded, shaking the purse upside down.

Jake swung his legs off the couch and sat up. "It wasn't empty."

Edward's eyes narrowed, like his glare would bully the truth out of him. "We need a driver's license or a credit card. Something with her name."

There was no wallet, but he knew her name. Camden Bristow—or at least, that's what she thought her name was. The truth was much more thrilling. If he played it smart, he would have the upper hand.

"How did you get her purse?"

"She decided to spend the night after all." Jake brushed the dust off his pants. "I suppose I could have woken her up and asked her name, but I thought it would be better to take her purse and run."

"You went into her room?"

"The purse was right beside her. She never even knew I was there."

"But what if she saw you?"

Jake snorted. He wasn't stupid—he wore a ski mask this time. Even if she did wake up, she'd never be able to identify his face. And he certainly wouldn't let her catch him.

Edward paced the room. "Now she'll call the cops again."

Jake kept his shoulders high. "You told me to get information."

"Information!" Edward pounded his fist into his other hand. "Not her purse."

"How else was I supposed to do that—"

Jake marched toward the kitchen to brew a pot of coffee. He didn't know what Edward was so peeved about—he'd done exactly what his grandfather asked him to do, although he'd gotten more information than he bargained for.

The woman already thought someone was in the house. What difference did it make if her purse was gone? It wasn't like he'd stolen anything valuable. There wasn't any money in the bag—he'd looked before he opened the envelope.

Dumping coffee grounds into the filter, he decided he'd continue helping his grandfather chase this treasure . . . just in case it did exist. When Edward tried to double-cross him—as he surely would—he'd hand over a copy of the letter.

It would be enough to convince even Edward Paxton to play it fair.

The doorbell gonged under the pressure of Alex's thumb, and he heard it echo down the entryway, vibrating the wooden doors. Even though he spoke to Rosalie Bristow several times at church, he'd never been inside her elaborate mansion. By the time he'd arrived in town, she was much too sick to invite company into her home.

This mansion was a beautiful work of Italianate architecture—a masterpiece, really—but it needed a whole lot of TLC. Who would want to sink money into fixing the roof and yard and probably the foundation? It may be a beautiful home if it was restored, but it would be a terrible investment.

The property around the house was much more valuable than the structure, and it would be the perfect location for a rec center or some sort of hotel. Maybe, when their town's economy began to improve, the council could resell or even rent the land to an upscale resort or retail center that would bring both jobs and tourists to their town.

He rang the bell again, and the door opened slowly. Camden Bristow wore a black T-shirt and jeans. Her wet hair was draped over her shoulders, and her feet were bare. He had to remind himself—twice—why he was here.

"My . . . my name's Alex," he said, hoping she would remember him from the coffee shop, but there wasn't a hint of recognition in her eyes. "You asked me for directions yesterday."

Her gaze wandered over his shoulder, out to the trees. "And your directions were impeccable." She glanced back at him. "Thanks for getting me here."

The door crept shut a few inches as he fumbled for his next words . . . words that seemed to elude him. He should have waited and had Dan or Louise introduce him instead of showing up like some vagrant on her doorstep.

"I was hoping to talk to you," he tried to explain.

The door didn't budge. "About what?"

The honk of a horn interrupted his answer, and he turned to watch the Sprague's green minivan fly up the driveway. The honking didn't stop, making it quite clear who was at the wheel.

He shoved his hands in his pockets and wished he could disappear.

Jenny Sprague was the absolute last person he wanted to see at Camden's house. She would never believe he was here to talk to Camden about purchasing the land.

Jenny hopped out of the car, juggling a disposable cup in each hand. And she was grinning.

"Alex Yates," she said, her smile so wide that he thought her face might crack under the pressure. "Fancy meetin' you here."

He tried to return the smile. "Nice to see you, Jenny."

One of her eyebrows slid up, and he wished she would nix the drama. They were all adults here. Civilized. "I'm not interrupting anything important, am I?"

Camden glanced back at him. "I'm not sure . . ."

"We were just discussing her property."

Camden's eyes widened. "We were?"

"Well, we were starting to . . ."

If Jenny got the hint, she didn't act like it. She sprang up the steps like she was Bugs Bunny, flinging brown liquid around her. Obviously, she'd already had enough to drink that morning, and it wasn't like she even needed it—the woman had a boatload of energy without adding caffeine.

She handed one of the drinks to Camden. "I thought you might need a little something to getcha going this morning."

Camden sniffed the drink and then hugged Jenny's neck. "You're a godsend."

"It's a good excuse for me to escape the insanity," she laughed. "I've got at least an hour to hang out before my sister goes all crazy on me." Jenny walked through the door and motioned for Alex to join her inside. "C'mon, Alex. No sense talking business on the front stoop."

He glanced between her and Camden before Camden moved back into the depths of the house. There was no way he was going through those doors, not alongside Jenny Sprague. Any hope of him getting this property would be decimated the moment she started playing matchmaker. Not to mention Camden would probably never want to see him again once Jenny worked her black magic.

He took a step down, away from Jenny and her goofy grin. "I've got to get back to town hall. For a meeting with Louise."

"C'mon, Alex," she insisted. "Surely, you can take a couple more minutes off work."

He shook his head. "Not this morning."

"Then we'll just have to do dinner this weekend. Maybe tomorrow night?"

"I don't think . . ."

"You have plans?" she asked innocently, like he might have another date on Friday. "We could do it on Saturday night. Or maybe Sunday."

He stifled his groan, glaring at Jenny. He didn't have plans this weekend, and she knew it.

"Friday night would probably work."

"Oh, good." She clapped her hands. "I'll make crepes and my special sauce and a big salad and . . ."

He turned and rushed back to his car before she finished the menu. He'd come to talk to Camden about purchasing Crescent Hill, but instead of talking about the property, he'd somehow gotten roped into a dinner date.

CHAPTER THIRTEEN

Camden laughed at her friend peeking out the window, watching Alex Yates drive down the hill. "I think you scared him off."

"Nah." Jenny stepped back from the curtain. "He'll be back."

Camden collapsed on one of the couches and a cloud swirled up around her. She blew away the dust in her face and savored a long sip of the chai latte.

Jenny sat on a chair across from her and propped her tennis shoes up on the glass table. "He's cute, isn't he? All dressed up in his suit and tie."

"I suppose so . . ."

"Oh, please. Don't get all noncommittal on me."

She took another sip. "I'm sure he's married."

"Oh, but he's not, although about every single woman in the county would like to change his status."

"So maybe he doesn't like women . . ."

"Nope, he likes them. Had a fiancée down in South Carolina before he moved here last year."

Camden didn't need to hear about this man's personal life, yet she couldn't seem to help herself. "They broke up?"

"Uh-huh." Jenny drummed her fingers on her jogging pants. "Though no one will tell me what happened."

"I can't imagine why not."

Jenny stuck out her tongue, and Camden laughed again. "He wasn't here to see me, anyway. He said he wanted to talk about the property."

"He works for the mayor," Jenny said. "He probably wants to talk you into selling Crescent Hill to the town."

Her head popped up. "Do you think they would buy it?"

"For cheap maybe." Jenny reached down and retied one of her shoelaces. "You aren't thinking about selling it, are you?"

Camden looked away and a wave of guilt washed over her. She would love to keep the house and restore it, to honor her family and their heritage, but her grandmother had left the property to her, no strings attached. And there was no way she could afford to keep it. She couldn't even pay the bills to keep the lights turned on, forget trying to repair the pipes and wiring and floors and roof. Right now she needed cash to help her claw her way out of debt, not a house to push her further under.

"I don't have a choice," she said, her voice resigned.

"Oh . . ." Jenny's voice trailed off. "I just thought . . ."

"You thought what?"

Jenny glanced up at the crystal chandelier hanging overhead and then around at the grand room. "I just never imagined this place owned by anyone except the Bristow family."

Having another family move into her grandma's home would seem strange to her too. Even though her memories of this place were made years ago, there was a peace in these rooms that she'd found nowhere else. And these sweet memories were rooted within her.

"Me neither," she admitted.

Jenny scooted herself up higher on the chair. "Rosalie would want you to keep the property."

Her fingers tightened around the latte. "Then she should have left me some money as well so I could afford to stay."

When Jenny didn't answer, Camden leaned back on the couch, hating the harshness in her tone. "I'm sorry," she muttered.

"No worries," Jenny said with a shrug. "I'm only trying to help."

Camden crisscrossed her legs and pulled them under her. Jenny might not be able to help with the house, but maybe she could help her understand what happened to her handbag. "Something strange happened last night."

"Okay . . ."

"My handbag disappeared."

Jenny leaned forward like she might be able to spot it in the sitting room. "What do you mean 'disappeared'?"

"I thought I put it beside me when I fell asleep last night, but when I woke up, it was gone." She shuddered at the thought.

"So you put it someplace else."

She shook her head. "I searched the entire room."

Jenny reached for her purse and pulled out her phone. "We need to call the police."

"No," she said, waving her hands to stop her friend. "They already think I'm loony."

"What . . ." Jenny started and then stopped like she wasn't sure exactly how to phrase the question. "Why do they think you're loony?"

Camden told her about their visit yesterday. About what she thought were footsteps. The broken glass. Jenny shivered when she explained the police thought it was the wind.

"The wind can't steal a purse."

Camden felt herself smile. "It wasn't the wind."

"Maybe it wasn't a person either."

The smile disappeared. "Then who could it be?"

"It's just that . . ."

One of Jenny's feet tapped on the glass, and Camden knew what her friend was thinking. She'd heard the ghost stories too, dozens of times, told by the neighborhood kids on those dark summer nights when they huddled around a campfire, down near the cemetery. The scariest one was the story about a runaway slave searching for something he'd left behind, pounding on all the walls, checking under all the beds.

Of course the stories weren't true. She'd known it when she was ten. Roaming the house by herself, day and night, she'd never once run into a ghost.

It was only the top floor of the mansion that unnerved her, but it wasn't because of some silly story. It was because . . . well, she couldn't actually recall the reason why she'd been so afraid of going upstairs alone. Maybe it was because one of the kids had told her some dark tale, passed along by their parents or grandparents.

She took another sip of her latte. "You can't believe those ghost stories."

"I wouldn't believe them except . . ."

"Except what?" Camden pushed.

"Except I've seen the lights."

She sighed. "What lights?"

"On the top floor, at night."

"Oh, please." She laughed. "It was probably my grandmother, looking for something."

Her friend shook her head. "Rosalie couldn't walk around like that at the end. She needed help getting out of bed."

"So maybe she asked her caregiver to get her something."

The look Jenny flashed her was filled with sympathy. "Perhaps . . ."

"There aren't any ghosts in this house," Camden insisted.

"Then we should tell the police about your handbag."

She pushed herself off the couch and stood up. If the police came, they'd probably find her bag hidden under a pillow or in a closet, someplace she'd stashed it when she was walking about last night in a stupor, trying to find a place to crash. They'd find her bag, have another laugh at her expense. The next time she called, they may or may not come.

Her bag may be gone, but there was nothing in it she needed anyway . . . except the letter. Her wallet was safe, as well as her laptop. If a thief had taken her bag, he would be sorely disappointed when he discovered the lack of cash.

"Let me show you something else," she said, and Jenny followed her upstairs to the room where she'd spent the night.

Camden showed her the clothes in the armoire, but Jenny didn't seem alarmed. "Maybe it belongs to the ghost," she quipped.

"Very funny."

Jenny ran her hands over the sweatshirt. "It looks like one of Rosalie's caregivers moved in."

"Don't you think it's strange?"

"Not really," Jenny replied. "Maybe she returned her key the day Rosalie passed away, and she hasn't been able to retrieve her things."

"So now I have to call Liza and ask who cared for her . . ."

"You don't have to call her," Jenny said. "The Mansfield Home Agency had someone here 24/7 the past few months. I'm sure they'll send whoever left their stuff over to pick it up."

"Thank you," Camden said with a sigh. As children, she and Liza hated each other, and even though a lot can change in twenty years, she couldn't imagine they'd be friends now. Perhaps they could play nice as adults, but she was still glad she didn't have to make the call.

Jenny turned from the armoire and her gaze landed on the old quilts hanging along the wall. She reached for the one in the middle and gently stroked her hand over it. "This is gorgeous."

Camden squinted at the patches of old fabric. "You think?"

Jenny moved to the next quilt, mesmerized. "It's at least a hundred years old."

"Grandma said all of these were made before the Civil War."

Jenny whistled and examined the colorful squares.

"You're interested in quilts?" Camden asked with surprise. Jenny didn't seem like the kind of person who could sit still for fifteen minutes, forget however many hours it took to make a quilt.

"My mother has always been a quilter."

"And you?"

"She taught me after I quit selling real estate." Jenny grinned. "I had this crazy idea that I'd have time to make a quilt for each of my kiddos."

"That's not a crazy idea."

"I started one six years ago, and it's buried someplace. The closet, I think."

"So you'll resurrect it for your grandchildren."

"I like that idea." Jenny smiled. "A special gift for each grandchild . . . though it can hardly compare to the gift your grandmother left you."

Camden took a deep breath. "Did you keep your real estate license?"

"Sure." Jenny turned back to her. "But I don't sell real estate anymore."

She clutched her hands together. "Would you make an exception for a friend?"

"You're really going to sell it?"

"I don't have a choice."

Jenny's hands swept through the air. "I think you should move back to Etherton, restore this place."

Camden shook her head. "I don't have the money to do that."

"You could get a job here," Jenny said, but her words didn't convince either of them. There weren't any jobs around here for a photojournalist or probably even a photographer. She could get by working at someplace like the Underground Cafe, but she'd never make enough to pay even the utilities for Crescent Hill.

A wide smile crossed Jenny's lips. "Besides, I was hoping you and Alex could get to know each other."

"I'm not interested in getting to know him, Jenny."

Her friend winked. "But you will be . . ."

Before Camden could think up a good retort, Jenny's phone rang, and she dug into her pocket for it.

"What happened?" she asked as she stepped toward the window and listened to whoever was on the other end of the line. "All right, I'll come pick her up."

The phone snapped shut. "I'm sorry, Cam. I'll have to hang out another day."

"What happened?"

"Hailey busted her lip."

"Is she okay?"

"An ice pack and a few hugs should do the trick." Jenny slipped her phone into her pocket and walked toward the door. "But I like to be the one giving the hugs."

"Completely understood."

"If you decide you really want to sell, there are some great realtors around here who'd love, love, love to list this place."

"I don't want just anyone to list it, Jenny. I want you to find a buyer who will restore it."

Jenny crossed her arms. "I don't want to sell it."

Leaning back against the wall, Camden muttered, "Neither do I."

CHAPTER FOURTEEN

There's no way to break this to you gently," Louise said, tapping her pen on a legal pad.

Alex cringed, knowing what came next. He didn't need her to sugarcoat the truth. "They want my job, don't they?"

"It's not your job they want." She scribbled something on the blank yellow paper. "It's your salary."

He slapped his hands on his knees, but he didn't look away from the mayor and the mounds of paper cluttering her desk. The town's coffers may be almost empty, but his salary was a drop in the bucket compared to the type of revenue he could generate if the councilors would let him do his job.

They'd promised him two years to revitalize the local economy, but they'd given him only eight months. Initially this job had been an escape for him, but it had become one of the greatest challenges of his life. Now they were about to boot him out the door before giving him the opportunity to succeed.

He ran his hands over his tie and straightened it. "When did the councilors tell you this?"

"Last night." She hesitated. "After work."

"They couldn't wait and do it during their regular meeting?"

"They don't want to make a big stink about this."

"Of course not . . ." *How terrible it would be if the public got involved.* "Did Edward Paxton lead the charge?"

"He didn't come last night."

"I guess they already knew what he would say."

The mayor set down her pen and met his eye. "I told them we haven't given you enough time to do what we hired you to do."

"Thank you, Louise, but time isn't the only problem." He pushed his heels into the carpet and slid forward to the edge of his chair. "The council doesn't want to do what it takes to generate revenue."

"Now I don't know about that . . ."

"They shoot down everything I propose." His fingers wrapped around the arms of the chair. "It's like the moment I walk through the door, they pull out their guns and begin blowing away my ideas."

Her eyes narrowed. "You've given us a superstore that terrifies local businesses and a community center that no one seems to want."

"Those are just the beginning, Louise. Both of those places would have brought in jobs and revenue and other business."

"But we need something much bigger."

"And flashier," he added with a groan. "It's about the elections, isn't it?"

"Of course it comes back to politics," she said, "and I'm not the only one worried. Some sort of Etherton stimulus package would help all of us who are up for reelection."

"Big and flashy often means a whole lot more debt."

"It's not my job to figure this out," she said with a wave of her hand. "That's why I hired you."

She'd hired him, told him to do whatever it took, but the council had tied his hands. They said they wanted him to succeed yet they wouldn't define success.

The image of Crescent Hill blazed through his mind. The dilapidated mansion. The beautiful girl. It wasn't too late for him to prove he could do this job as well as he'd done his last one. He'd go to Jenny's dinner tomorrow night, talk to Camden. Perhaps they could work out a deal, and he could present it to the council first thing Monday morning, before they swiped his job away from him.

Then he could begin to court a large business to put in the place of the mansion, something big and maybe even flashy. By fall, they would have something for the council—and the mayor—to tout on the campaign trail. And he would still have a job.

Louise slid the pen behind her ear. "I was able to get four more weeks for you."

"Four weeks for what?"

"To bring something new to Etherton. Something lucrative."

"I can have a solid proposal by then. Another direction."

"They're tired of the proposals, Alex. They want it signed, sealed, and delivered by June 4."

Twenty business days. Even if Camden agreed to sell the house tomorrow night, even if some business jumped on the idea of building in Etherton, there was no way they could have everything accomplished in a month. Before he could court a business, the town had to talk infrastructure—streets, parking, and utilities. Getting all the right people to return his calls and finish their plans would take much longer than four weeks.

"That's not enough time."

She slid her pen back over her ear and shook her head. "Unfortunately it's all the time you have."

Camden wandered through the guest rooms and the library and the formal dining room, on a quest for the handbag that carried her grandmother's letter. As she rummaged through dressers and shelves, she lost herself in her surroundings. An hour into her search, she dug out her camera and began snapping pictures of brass sconces, cracked leather books, beveled glass windows, blackened fireplaces, and cobwebs dangling like fine lace on top of the china to preserve her memories of this beautiful house.

She avoided the third floor, but she explored every inch of the first two. Except her grandmother's bedroom. Around noon, she climbed upstairs. It must have been agony for her grandmother to scale these steps in her later years, but there was comfort, she supposed, in the familiarity of spending your last days in your own bedroom.

As she approached the closed door at the end of the hallway, she lifted her hand. No one was inside to answer her, but she still had to knock, out of courtesy to her grandmother. So she thumped on the door and waited for a moment before she opened it.

The carved poster bed had been stripped, and an antiseptic smell lingered in the room. She rushed to one of the six windows, opening it wide. Fresh air flooded the space.

Everything else was exactly as she remembered it. Tan carpet. Dark antique furniture. Sage green walls. The only thing she didn't remember were the dozens of metal frames on the far side of the room, scattered randomly across the wall. She strolled across the carpet, and then stopped, blinking several times as her eyes scanned the gallery.

These weren't photographs. They were magazine clips, matted and framed—photos Camden had taken.

Her gaze roamed over the pictures. Orphans in Zimbabwe. The earthquake in Italy. The aftermath of a tsunami in Sri Lanka.

Her grandmother had kept her best work. The pictures she sweated and bled over in her attempt to capture tragedy and honor victims. Did her grandmother know how she'd poured herself into these photos? She must have. Not only had she kept them, she'd mounted them on her bedroom wall.

During her last years, her grandmother could look up and see what Camden had seen around the world. She'd scrutinized the devastation, the hurting faces, and perhaps within them, she somehow saw into Camden—the place she could reveal only through her camera lens.

Rosalie understood.

Sitting on her grandmother's nightstand was a much smaller picture, a three-by-five. The colors had faded, but the faces were clear. It was a picture of her along with Rosalie, upstairs by the fireplace in the theater, candles glowing inside instead of wood. Her grandmother wore a pale green sweater, pearls around her neck, and white slacks. The color of her long hair matched her slacks, and her blue eyes seemed to glimmer alongside the light.

Camden's blond pigtails stuck out at different angles on each side of her head. Her nose was sunburned, but she was grinning. Happy.

Maybe that last summer on Crescent Hill was one of her grandmother's happiest as well.

Her eyes watering, she dusted off the top of the frame with her hands and set the picture back on the nightstand.

It was time to visit her grandmother.

Jake threw a rock at a bluebird and clipped its wing. Squawking, the bird flew into the sky, and Jake flipped another stone in his hand before shoving it into the air. The bird fell to the ground, and Jake rolled his shoulders back. The stupid creature wouldn't bug him again.

He hated being outside. On afternoons like this, he was usually planted in front of his computer, conquering the dark Orcs and Night Elves in World of Warcraft. But Edward opted not to cruise around town today, and he was driving Jake crazy. Edward lit his cigar an hour ago, right when Jake was about to take out his opponent's expansion, and all Edward could talk about was the treasure, like it had been waiting around for almost two centuries just for Edward Paxton to stumble upon it.

What his grandfather didn't seem to realize was that without Jake's help, he would never even get close to finding this treasure. There was no way the old man could climb through that tunnel, up the stairs, and then spend a night searching the house. He may have more stamina than some people his age, but he still couldn't stay up past eleven.

When he got back to the house, Jake wanted more proof that this treasure existed. Something more than Edward's word, which he'd learned long ago wasn't worth the shirt on his back. If the treasure was a lie—and it probably was—he wanted Edward out of his life, mummifying down at the retirement home with his cousin Dotty. And he wanted Mariah back.

Picking up another rock, he hurled it at a tree and watched it bounce off into the water.

Mariah had been gone for too long, and the separation wasn't good for either of them. They were supposed to be together. Two hearts beating as one. He needed her almost as much as she needed him. And she needed him much more than she needed a little brat running around, distracting her attention.

When Mariah returned, he'd remind her why she shouldn't leave him again.

He walked a few steps and then stopped when he saw gravestones. Somehow, he'd lost track of where he was and wandered right into the Bristow family cemetery.

He backed away, toward the river. The ghosts of the past were probably lingering around the gravestones today—he'd heard they came to life while the living were away. If Rosalie saw him . . .

He shuddered. She'd probably take revenge for all those times he'd ruined her flower beds and egged her windows.

A noise startled him, but instead of running, he froze. Something moved through the trees, and he stumbled backward, into the water's edge, before he hid behind a tree. Peeking out, he thought for a moment he saw an apparition walking toward the cemetery, but it wasn't a ghost at all. It was a woman—the woman he'd watched sleeping in bed.

He licked the corner of his lips. He may have a healthy fear of the supernatural, but he wasn't the least bit afraid of Camden Bristow.

CHAPTER FIFTEEN

The musky scent of phlox sweetened the spring air. The sky was covered with gray, the breeze chilly, but Camden didn't mind. In her arms were hyacinth and daffodils and tulips, and this morning she would adorn her grandmother's grave with color and beauty.

She breathed in the soothing aromas of the forest as she walked down the path of white and yellow trout lilies that sprouted in the grass. Beside her the Ashter River bumped gently across smooth river stones and drifted back into the forest.

In the blurry memories of her childhood, she remembered the Bristow family cemetery hidden in the trees, at the base of the hill. She'd come down here often as a child, playing hide-and-seek and wading in the river with Jenny or other friends. Sometimes she came alone to visit the Bristow family graves.

Brushing past pine and oak branches, the trees opened into a small clearing. A chipmunk scampered by, and she watched it disappear into the undergrowth. Then she saw a bluebird lying on the pathway, eyes wide open.

She lifted a furry pine branch off the ground and covered the bird's fragile body. No creature, big or small, should be left so exposed. Slipping one of the daffodils out of her arms, she tucked it under the pine branch. It was what her grandmother would have done.

When she stepped forward again, she saw tombstones in front of her. Branches hung over the graying sandstone and slate slabs and hid many of the names etched long ago.

On the side of the small plot was a brick mausoleum, built in 1858 to commemorate the death of Joseph Bristow's oldest son, Matthew. The first person buried in the cemetery. A tall gate blocked the entrance to the mausoleum, and through the iron slats she could see the floor shrouded with dirt, leaves, and cobwebs. She'd never been able to read the epitaph on his crypt.

Something splashed in the river beside her, and she turned, scanning the trees and then the riverfront. She scolded herself for being so skittish. The gray day—and the mausoleum—played with her imagination. Next thing she knew, she would think she saw a ghost.

Hundreds of flowers decorated the freshly turned dirt of her grandmother's grave, like a garden had sprung up in the forest. It was the perfect tribute for a woman who adored gardens. Camden imagined the crowds tramping down here just days ago, reverently placing armfuls of flowers on the grave and saying their goodbyes.

She laid her own bouquet on top of the other flowers and sat down in the mud and grass beside the grave. Reaching forward, she rubbed her hands over Rosalie's name on the stone. Her birth date was there, but the date of her death hadn't been inscribed yet. Rosalie probably ordered the stone before she died—the simple epitaph made it seem like nothing had ever happened in the seventy-five years of her grandma's life. So many wonderful words could describe her.

How would people, generations from now, know about Rosalie's love and kindness and beauty?

She'd spent the past nine years living on her own, trying to forget most of her past, but she never wanted to forget her grandmother. She should have said no to at least one assignment and come to Ohio instead. It wasn't like her clients wouldn't hire her again because she'd gone home for Christmas or Easter. And even if they wouldn't have called her again, it shouldn't have mattered so much. She should have made the trip to Etherton.

"I'm sorry," she whispered to the mound of flowers. There was so much more she wanted to say, most of all a thank-you for the time her grandma had taken her into her home and loved her.

My prayer for you is that you embrace the future and the purpose that God has planted in your heart.

Her grandmother's words stirred in her, but she didn't know anything about her future or the purpose God had planted in her heart.

She wrung her hands together, wishing she could make that precious letter from her grandma reappear. What else had Rosalie written? Perhaps she'd told her what she wanted Camden to do with the house.

Standing, she wiped some of the mud off the back of her jeans. Her gaze topped the trees, but she couldn't see the house on the hill above them. She didn't want to sell the house or the property. Not because of all the Bristows who'd lived here in the past, but because this house was the only place she had ever called home.

There was permanence here. Stability. No one in the Bristow family ever packed a suitcase and left the house in the middle of the night, never to return again. They grew up here and either stayed or returned through the years to visit their family.

They knew where to find the people they loved.

She knew little about juggling investments, but it wasn't hard to figure out that even if she decided to sell every item in the house, she'd never have enough to keep up the place. The money might be enough to hold the house together for a year or two, but the house would eventually unravel despite the quick fix.

"What am I supposed to do?" she whispered, like Rosalie could hear her. Jenny may think Rosalie wanted her to keep the property, and maybe the missing letter from her grandma explained how she could keep it, but the letter was gone, and she needed to make a decision soon.

Her phone rang in her pocket, and she jumped. Stepping away from the grave, she pulled out her phone and answered it.

The woman introduced herself as Sasha Webb, the director of the Mansfield Home Agency, and then told her how sorry she was about her grandmother's death. Camden murmured something gracious in reply.

"I got your message about the items in the room." Sasha blazed through her words so fast that Camden barely understood her. "We had a team of personal care assistants attending to Rosalie around the clock so I called each of them, but they didn't leave anything at the house."

Goosebumps prickled Camden's arms. "But there were clothes and books . . . and a pair of shoes."

"Our people didn't leave them," Sasha replied briskly. "An overnight bag is all our assistants bring anyway, and they take their bag home with them."

"Maybe someone from hospice spent the night . . ."

"Oh, no," Sasha interrupted. "They visit the house to help manage pain, but they never stay the night."

Camden pinched the bridge of her nose with her fingers. She didn't want to talk about Rosalie being in pain. She only wanted to know who had been staying at the house.

"What did you do with the key?" she asked.

The lady paused. "We sent that back to a . . . Mrs. Eloise Bristow."

"My stepmother," Camden mumbled.

"She was the one who hired us."

Camden thanked the woman and then stuffed the phone back into her pocket.

If the clothes didn't belong to one of the caregivers, who else had been staying with her grandma? Maybe someone had arrived right before Rosalie passed away. As she stepped away from the cemetery, she thought about the Bible and the pregnancy book. Whoever had been staying in the room couldn't be very threatening. Still, it was creepy to think that someone she didn't know had been staying at the house.

And then another thought hit her. Her half-sister had the key to her house. Had Liza come inside the house while she was sleeping? Taken her bag? Though it seemed silly, the thought stuck with her.

Did Liza want her letter?

A drip of water hit her nose, and then another one slid down her ear. Pulling her hood over her head, she turned and ran back up the hill.

CHAPTER SIXTEEN

Alex flung his fleece jacket over his shoulders and hustled down the front steps of the town hall. The rain had stopped for the afternoon though it was supposed to return in the morning.

An Amish buggy ambled down the street beside him, and he slowed his pace. Jenny wouldn't care if he were late to dinner, only that he was coming. On his way to the Sprague's house, he could take a few moments to enjoy a respite from the rain.

When he took the job in Etherton, he'd hoped for unhurried times like this, walking and thinking and wondering about the future, and he'd envisioned putting down roots in this community for years to come, maybe even the rest of his life.

If the councilors fired him, where was he supposed to go from here? He'd been at the top of his game at Manz Marketing, and now he was about to be jobless. Going on unemployment was the ultimate slap in the face. Failure. He could almost hear the crowds from the opposing team shouting, "Loser. Loser."

From the top of his game to the bottom. In less than a year.

Yesterday he'd talked to Louise about his idea to acquire Crescent Hill, and then he'd formulated a plan to convince Camden to sell. If he pushed too hard, she might turn and run without even considering it. He had to let her know how important her property was for their town. This entire deal hinged on her, and if she were willing, he would do everything he could to get the property ready for a new business. Once he secured the acreage, the council would have to give him a few more weeks to complete his plan.

Turning onto Vine Street, he glanced up at the large Victorian home on the corner. The house was divided into four apartments, and his home was on the second floor. When he moved into the apartment last September, he hadn't planned to stay but a few months, but it was near the heart of the small downtown, and that's where he wanted to be—close to work and church and the friends he'd made during the past year.

He walked quickly past his apartment and a row of houses built from the same mold in the forties—small white boxes with shutters cut and colored like a deck of cards. Red hearts, black spades, red queens, and black diamonds.

He didn't want to say goodbye to Etherton. He didn't want to fail at this job. And he didn't want to watch this town collapse. If he succeeded, the entire town of Etherton would succeed, and that's what he wanted—for himself and for the people who were struggling to work and live in the community where they'd been raised.

At the end of Vine Street was the Spragues' stone home. Opening the gate, he kicked a skateboard out of his way. Life at Dan and Jenny's was never dull, and often he stopped by their home simply to pump life into his scheduled world. Sometimes he left their house with a headache, but he never left without a smile.

The door flew open before he could ring the bell. Hailey wrapped her arms around his knees, and then two-year-old Kyle piled on top of her. Alex braced himself against the doorpost as they both clutched his leg and begged for a piggyback ride.

He tried to step inside the house. "Don't you know you're never supposed to answer the door without an adult?"

Hailey grinned up at him and whinnied.

"What if it were a stranger?" he asked.

"You're not a stranger, Uncle Alex," she said, pawing at his arm.

"But you didn't know it was going to be me."

"Sure, we did." She pointed to the window. "We were watchin' for you."

Jenny came around the corner, drying her hands on a dishtowel. When Hailey saw her mother, she whinnied again and galloped away without her piggyback ride.

"Don't trample on the clean clothes," Jenny yelled toward the hallway.

Scooping Kyle up in his arms, Alex closed the door behind him. "I'm guessing she's a horse today . . ."

"Believe me," Jenny said as she threw the towel over her shoulder, "it's much better than the snake that slithered through my house this morning."

"A poisonous snake?"

"No idea, but Kyle's sporting bite marks on his legs, and Hailey's got a sore behind."

"So you're grateful for horses."

She nodded. "Very."

Kyle squirmed out of Alex's arms and ran off toward his sister.

"Dan's in the living room," Jenny said as she stepped back toward the kitchen. "Camden should be here any minute."

He'd taken only a few steps toward the living room on his left when the doorbell rang.

"Can you get it?" Jenny called to him and then she yelled. "Only one carrot, Hailey, and wash it!"

Turning back toward the door, an unfamiliar feeling clutched his gut. Nervousness. He shook his head slightly. Why should he be nervous about seeing Camden? Neither of them could really think this was a viable date. It was a business meeting for him, at a friend's house. He couldn't help it if the friend was trying to marry him off.

But he wouldn't think about that tonight. Business meetings were safe, productive. Guarded. And he was determined to stay on his guard.

The grin on Jenny's face was so large when Camden walked into the dining room alongside Alex that she almost turned and ran. Dan nodded at her, and Alex Yates wore a smile as well, but his wasn't nearly as welcoming nor was it as mischievous. The confidence she'd seen at the café a couple days ago had dropped a notch or two.

Jenny may think she was playing matchmaker, but Camden was only here to talk to Alex about Crescent Hill.

"So glad to see you," Jenny said, kissing Kyle and nudging him toward the archway that divided the dining room from the kitchen.

Jenny's sister peeked into the room, the baby in her arms. "There are four of them, right?"

Jenny sighed. "Last I counted."

"Then I've got them all. What time do you want them back?"

"Tomorrow morning."

Her sister caught Kyle's shoulder as he roared by her. "We'll be back in two hours."

"Good enough."

Seconds later, the front door opened, closed, and a strange silence enveloped the room.

Jenny didn't relish the silence. Instead she stepped toward Camden and hugged her. "Did you sleep at the inn last night?"

She braced herself. "Why would I sleep there when I have five perfectly good beds on Crescent Hill?"

And no money to pay for a hotel.

Jenny let go of her shoulders, her grin sliding to a frown. "It isn't safe to sleep there by yourself."

"No one bothered me."

Alex pulled out a chair for her, but Camden kept her eyes on Jenny. She probably shouldn't stay at the house again, not until she figured out who else had been staying there before her, but she couldn't tell Jenny she was broke. Her friend would insist she stay here, and she wouldn't get a moment of sleep.

Jenny stepped toward the kitchen. "It's not *people* I'm worried about."

"Oh, please," she laughed, but shot a warning look at her friend.

The last thing she wanted was the rumor getting around town that someone had seen something supernatural at her house. Ghost hunters would be knocking down her door.

A timer beeped in the next room, and Jenny flicked her husband's shoulder. "Can you help me get the salad?"

"That must be some heavy lettuce," Alex quipped. He didn't crack a smile, but Camden couldn't stop the laugh that escaped her lips. At least neither of them was thrilled about a dinner date.

As Dan and Jenny flew out of the room to rescue the salad, Camden plucked up the napkin from her place setting and smoothed it across her lap. Alex's eyes caught hers from across the table. "Jenny likes to think she's helping people by setting them up."

One of her eyebrows slid up. "You didn't put her up to this?"

"Of course not," he retorted. "I mean, it's not that I didn't want to have dinner with you, but I . . ."

She waved her hand. "You don't have to explain it to me."

"I didn't ask her to do this." He glanced back toward the kitchen. "But I did want to talk to you."

"About the house?"

He nodded. "Are you planning to stay in Etherton?"

She shook her head. "There's no way I can stay here."

He folded both of his hands on the table. "What if the town offered to buy the property from you?"

"Do they want it?"

He nodded again. "We've been looking to acquire some new property and develop it."

Hope rose slowly within her as she mulled over his words. The house would make the perfect museum or bed-and-breakfast or even a retirement home. If the city bought it, they could restore it, and she could come back and visit the legacy of the Bristow family.

It could be the perfect solution to her problem. They would get a deal on the property. She would be able to pay off her debt. And her grandmother's home would be preserved.

She steadied her voice. "I'd be interested in talking about it."

A slow smile spread across his face. "I'm glad to hear that," he said as Dan and Jenny escorted the salad into the room.

Tires screeching, Jake roared his truck out of the driveway and up the hill. He was done waiting around for Mariah. Done waiting, period. He was going to find his girlfriend and bring her home tonight, where she belonged.

She couldn't hide from him, not for long. He would find her, and he'd make sure she wouldn't leave him again.

He raced his truck past the Bristow dump and glowered at the place that was quickly becoming a pain in his backside. Camden was becoming quite the pain as well.

She'd spent the night again last night, but this time she'd locked her door. If he wanted, he could have picked the lock, but he didn't even try. He left her alone to sleep, just like he'd left her alone yesterday when she'd visited her grandmother's grave. He'd resisted the temptation to get close to Camden again. Even though Mariah didn't deserve it, he was faithful to her. . . and he expected Mariah to be faithful to him.

Camden's door was locked last night, and there was one other door on the third floor that he hadn't been able to open yet either—another storage room, probably. He tried to pick the storage room lock, but it seemed to be deadbolted from the other side.

An idea began forming in his mind. Perhaps he could give Camden a little incentive to give him a tour of the house and unlock the door to the storage room for him. She'd open the door, he'd take a quick look around, and then he'd tell Edward there was no sign of treasure in the entire house.

He'd pay Camden a visit—tomorrow. Tonight he needed to find Mariah.

He cruised through town, searching for Mariah's shiny black hair. At eighteen, her body was remarkably close to the chicks he liked online. All it would take was a little more effort on Mariah's part, a couple more hours of working out each week, and she would achieve perfection. But she was so young, so sensitive about stuff like her weight. He was only trying to help her get into shape. For both of them.

Other men stared when Mariah walked by, wanting what he had. They were jealous of Jake Paxton and his gorgeous piece of a girlfriend. They should be jealous—no one could have Mariah except him, and he was done waiting around for her to wander home.

Cruising down Main Street, he scanned the side streets and alleyways before he took a left by the drugstore. Slowly, he drove by the tiny building that housed the local Crisis Pregnancy Center, the place he'd caught her going into three weeks ago when she was supposed to be getting an abortion. He wasn't stupid—no one got an abortion at this place. They were all about tricking women into staying pregnant even when they had no one to take care of their kid. Some women weren't supposed to have children, and Mariah was one of them.

Turning onto Park Street, he saw a woman saunter down the steps of the Zandorf Inn. Liza Bristow had cropped blond hair and she was hot in a buttoned-up sort of way. Parking his truck a few feet from Liza, he hopped out onto the pavement.

"Liza?" he called, and she turned.

When she saw him, she pursed her lips together and then forced a smile. "Hello, Jake."

"I thought I'd be seeing more of you after the funeral." He zipped up his bomber jacket. "And I thought you'd have a For Sale sign on the old house by now."

Her eyes narrowed. "Rosalie didn't leave the house to me."

His eyebrows shot up, pretending he didn't have a clue. "What?"

"Someone messed with the will."

"I'm sorry to hear that."

She shook her head. "It's not over yet."

"I figured."

She stared at him, like she was trying to determine why he was being nice to her, but she didn't have to be afraid of him. He'd only tricked her once, more of a practical joke really, and it was to get back at her grandmother. Even after that little incident, she'd agreed to go out with him when she'd turned sixteen, probably to snub her grandmother as well.

He'd known she hated visiting Etherton, hated the "simple life" as she said in a way that was less than complimentary. Jake saw right through her from the beginning—she was all about getting more money and that was fine with him. He had an appreciation for money as well.

Money had to be the reason she stayed another night in Etherton. If it weren't to dispute the inheritance, she would have gone back to Columbus the moment they'd planted Rosalie in the mud.

He wasn't ready to play all his cards just yet, but it wouldn't hurt to have Liza on his team . . . just in case Camden wouldn't play. Mariah would have to wait a couple more hours for him to rescue her.

"You want to get some coffee?" he asked.

She tilted her head. "Why?"

"I know a few people in town who might be able to help you."

She checked her watch. "I've got twenty minutes."

"You'll give me an hour when you hear what I have to say."

CHAPTER SEVENTEEN

Fortunately, Rosalie left enough food in the pantry to last a month, including forty-one Ball jars filled with fruit and tomatoes, along with peanut butter, crackers, and a partial loaf of bread. The freezer was filled with meat although some of it was two years old. Camden figured the meat was still edible, and that was all she needed right now. Edible.

. . . *Thirty-four, thirty-five, thirty-six*. She recounted the jars in the pantry. There were five missing since she'd counted them on Thursday. She'd eaten two jars of canned fruit, but she'd been conserving so the food would last.

Sighing, she grabbed the jar of peanut butter from the bottom shelf. Was it possible she'd miscounted? Lately it seemed she was going crazy.

Twisting the lid off the peanut butter, she plunged her spoon into it and took a large bite—licking the peanut butter off the front and back. The crepes Jenny served last night were good, but she'd only managed to eat a few bites while responding to Jenny's inquisition about her travels. The questioning was purely for Alex's sake, and they all knew it. She'd tried to eat as she told them stories about her work, but before she was done, Jenny had swooped the plate off the table and run to the kitchen, leaving her and Alex alone again.

Jenny may have hoped they would talk about themselves, but Alex didn't volunteer any information about his life, past or present. He wouldn't even tell her about his family when she asked. Instead he'd thrown out a number, a price he thought the city council would be willing to pay for Crescent Hill. A number that was at least ten times more money than she'd ever had in her bank account.

He conceded that the offer wasn't as high as the property was worth, but with the down market, she figured that buyers wouldn't be knocking down her front door right now anyway. Alex planned to write up a letter of intent over the weekend, and they'd talk more specifics on Monday.

The doorbell rang, startling her, and she dropped the spoon onto the counter.

Did Alex write up the letter already? Everything was happening so fast, yet she didn't mind if they rushed the agreement. If she was careful, she could survive for a month on the food left in the pantry, but it would probably take at least a month to close on the house. The sooner she had extra cash, the better.

As she hurried out the kitchen and crossed the entryway, she pulled her hair back to the nape of her neck and tied it. She'd never tell Jenny, but she was excited about seeing Alex again, on several levels. Last night, he'd made it very clear he wasn't interested in a relationship, and she wasn't interested in Jenny's matchmaking attempts either. But that didn't mean she wouldn't enjoy sitting down for coffee with him, having a real conversation.

The bell rang again as she reached the door. Glancing out the window, disappointment washed over her. The man outside was definitely not Alex.

It was silly to be disappointed. She'd seen Alex last night, and she would see him on Monday morning. Besides the man only wanted to talk to her about the house, nothing else . . . perhaps that was why she was disappointed.

When she opened the door, the smell of stale cigar smoke seeped into the house. The man slid off dark aviator shades and grinned at her with a lazy confidence that said he expected her to admire him, but she didn't smile back. His tight T-shirt was gray with a gaming logo of some sort blazed across the chest, and he wore a faded pair of jeans and flip-flops. It was like he didn't even realize his clothes stunk.

She refused to admire him, but she had no problem doing a quick appraisal to see if the guy before her was friend or foe.

"Are you Camden?" he asked, the smile still plastered across his face. She squinted slightly, trying to place his grown-up face with the faces of the many kids she'd played with years ago on Crescent Hill.

"Do I know you?"

"I'm Jake Paxton." He thumbed toward the forest. "My grandfather and I live halfway down the hill, in the white and green house."

She knew the house, but she didn't remember him.

"Someone told me you just moved in, and I wanted to welcome you to the neighborhood."

"Thanks." The detail that she was only passing through Etherton wasn't any of his business.

"My grandfather is Edward Paxton," he said like the name should mean something to her. When she didn't respond, he continued talking. "He buys and sells antiques downtown, and if you're interested in selling any of the antiques in the house, he wanted me to tell you that he'd give you a good deal."

She blinked. All she had to do was hang on for a few more weeks, sell the house to the town for restoration, and she would have more than enough money to pay her bills. "I'm not interested in selling anything right now."

"I told him you wouldn't be interested, but he wanted to offer his help anyway."

"Okay . . ." She started to shut the door. "Thanks."

"One more thing I wanted to talk to you about." He brushed his hands together. "I'm planning to get married next month."

She managed a smile. At least he wasn't propositioning her. "Congratulations."

"My fiancée and I have dreamed about living in an old house just like this since we started dating." He nodded toward the picture window. "I completely understand why you wouldn't want to sell your family's things, but I wondered if you'd consider selling the house."

Her spine stiffened. Although Alex had talked to her about buying the house, the same offer seemed crass coming from this man. He'd yet to tell her he was sorry for her loss, or make any acknowledgement of the years her grandmother lived on this hill. She thought she would want someone knocking on her door, asking to buy the place, but coming from this guy, it just seemed wrong.

"I'm sorry, Jake, but you're a little late. Someone from the city has been talking to me about buying the place."

A frown replaced the easy smile on his face. "You're not thinking about selling it to them, are you?"

"I was considering it."

"Who gave you this offer?"

"It wasn't an offer, exactly . . ." Her feet shifted. "Alex Yates and I are discussing it."

"Did Alex tell you what they wanted to do with the property?"

"I was hoping they'd turn the house into a museum or a bed-and-breakfast."

He snorted, and she took a step back. What was this man thinking, knocking on her door, interrupting her morning . . . and then mocking her. She had plenty of other things to do, starting with the jar of peanut butter in the kitchen.

"You think it's funny?"

"It's not that." He licked the front of his teeth. "Do you really think the city is going to put a museum up here?"

She shrugged.

"Let me clear it up for you," he said. "The city wants the property, not the house."

"They can still use the house."

"They'll tear it down, Camden. Replace it with something newer and much cheaper to maintain."

"They won't tear it down," she insisted, but his words lingered in her mind.

"Is that what Alex told you?"

Alex never responded to her thoughts about restoring the place, but she thought he understood. She couldn't imagine someone knocking down her grandmother's home with a wrecking ball or plowing over it with a bulldozer. The house needed some work, but it was a landmark in Etherton. It was insane to think that the town might come in and demolish the place. And if they did rip it down, what exactly would they put on the hill to replace it? She was envisioning a park, but what if the city was thinking a parking lot instead?

Jake seemed to read her mind. "They'll tear it down and slap up some sort of factory or maybe a warehouse."

She tugged on the sleeves of her shirt, noticing for the first time a chill in the morning air. Her grandmother had left the house in her care; she couldn't sell it to someone to tear down. Even if she desperately needed the money, she couldn't do it.

"Are you saying that you and your fiancée would restore it?"

His hand went to his chest. "It would be an honor for us to restore a place as beautiful as this."

"I would need an offer."

"I'm ready to make one." The number he blurted out was twice what the city was willing to pay. Enough for her to be secure for years without work.

"I'll consider it."

"Please don't take too long," he said with another smile. "We're hoping to move in a couple weeks."

How long had he and his fiancée been waiting for Rosalie to pass away?

Kudzu swathed the trees along the border of the old plantation in front of Stephanie like a blanket draped over a corpse. Most everything under the dark green blanket had decomposed long ago. The house burned to the ground during the Civil War. The barns and kitchen had crumbled, probably under the weight of the kudzu, and from the desolate road, there weren't even any remnants of the cabins that housed hundreds of slaves who worked the land.

Suburbia had yet to reach this deserted area about fifteen miles outside Columbia. Even the wildlife seemed to have fled . . . or maybe they had traveled north to avoid the heat. The air was still and so heavy with humidity that every breath Stephanie took through her open car window felt like it had been filtered through wet coals.

She hadn't planned on traveling to Columbia today, hadn't planned on coming for another two weeks, but she couldn't seem to help herself. Her mother drove her past the plantation many years ago, long before she cared what her ancestors had done or where they lived. Long before she had read about Miriam and Rachel.

Her mother liked to talk about their family's roots, but Aunt Debra had immersed herself in them, especially after Trent went to prison. When the hope was stripped away from Debra's future, she seemed to cling to the past where there were few surprises and where the people you met on paper had already made their mistakes. It was much easier to relate to a deceased relative than to a living and breathing one who made a mess out of their lives . . . and yours.

Opening the car door, Stephanie dangled her foot outside, but quickly pulled it back into the safety of the car. She may not see much wildlife from this lonely road, but there would be plenty of snakes slithering through the kudzu, probably hundreds of them, and she didn't do snakes.

Besides, even if she got out of the car and walked along the dirt road, there was nothing left for her to discover. It wasn't like her family buried the missing jewelry under the house a hundred-plus years ago and walked away. Someone would have remembered and gone back for it. And if the jewelry had been hidden in the house, it was probably gone by now too. Mystery solved.

Still she wished she could see the sprawling plantation house where her ancestors enjoyed their parties and all the finery shipped from London and the cabin where Rachel and William raised their two children. Would the Ellison family have done anything differently if they realized the Civil War was shadowing them, ready to disrupt everything they took for granted?

Miriam never mentioned the jewelry in her journal nor did she mention the resources of their family. It was apparent they were wealthy by their lifestyle, but she seemed to take all their money for granted.

Glancing around the desolate property, Stephanie couldn't help but think how sad it all was. Once this land had been bustling with people and work and animals, but there was nothing left. So much had been lost, and not just material things. Lives and dreams and relationships between husbands and wives, children and parents.

She pulled out of the long driveway, steering her car toward her aunt's house in Columbia. Suddenly, she didn't care so much about the missing jewelry, or even solving her family's mystery. The question pressing her on was no longer about her family's missing treasure. The most important question was—

Where did William go . . . and what happened to his wife?

CHAPTER EIGHTEEN

When his telephone vibrated, Alex glanced at Liza Bristow's number and silenced her call. Apparently she thought he was the key to the sale of the Bristow property—property she didn't own—and he had no interest in helping her find an attorney or contest Rosalie's will.

She could play the sympathy card all she wanted; he could do nothing for her. It was in his best interest, anyway, for the city to buy the property from its new owner. When he'd mentioned last night what the town could potentially afford to pay, Camden hadn't turned ugly, like Liza had done.

He slid his phone into his jacket pocket and zipped it so it wouldn't fall out of his pocket during his bike ride.

Next time Liza called, he would tell her Dan Sprague was one of his best friends, and he stood behind Dan's work, including what he'd done with Rosalie's will. He wouldn't tell Liza the city planned to purchase the property, not until it was a done deal.

Topping off the air in his bicycle's back tire, he tucked the air pump back into his car. He didn't want to think about Liza today, or even Crescent Hill. Camden had expressed interest in selling the property, but he'd learned that a deal wasn't done until the final paperwork was signed.

He slipped one foot into a bicycle pedal and set his watch. Last time he'd made it up to Mansfield and back in four hours, along the bike trail that used to be a railroad bed. Today he planned to do the trip in three hours, forty-five minutes.

A car drove up in the parking lot behind him, gravel crackling under its tires. He prepared to push off on his bike, but before he started pedaling, a woman called his name.

His heart sank. How had Liza found him?

He almost didn't look back. He could pretend he didn't hear her, ride all the way to Mansfield and back in peace, but when the car door slammed behind him, he dropped his foot back to the ground. Might as well get it over with now.

Turning his head, he braced himself to confront Liza, but instead of Liza, Camden Bristow marched toward him, her blond hair pulled back and a baggy sweater covering her slender frame. He got off the bike, much relieved. At least he could avoid a battle this morning.

With a quick click, he removed his helmet and draped it over the handles. "Are you following me?"

She crossed her arms, not even cracking a smile. "Jenny told me where you were."

"That woman seems to know everything." He propped his bike against the car, wondering if he had done something to offend her. "You like to bike?"

One of her hands went to her hip. "I want to talk to you about Crescent Hill."

He'd planned to knock on her door first thing on Monday with the letter of intent in hand, but if she wanted to talk now, he was more than willing. "Do you want to grab coffee?"

She ignored his invitation. "When we chatted last night, you didn't mention you were planning to demolish Crescent Hill."

He took off his gloves and tossed them onto the hood of the car. This was the make it or break it moment for him. If he couldn't convince her that he would be responsible with her family's home, then she would go running in fear, taking with her the last hope of saving his job along with helping to save this town.

He stepped toward her. "Why do you think the town would tear it down?"

"Jake Paxton clued me in."

Jake Paxton. How did he find out Alex was talking to Camden about the property? Someone must have told Edward, and he sent in his grandson for reconnaissance. "I never said I was going to tear it down."

"But you would consider it?"

So much for avoiding a battle today. "I want what's best for both your property and for the entire town of Etherton."

"The best thing is to preserve the house for the future."

He leaned back against his car. Some people might lie at this moment, say he would never consider tearing down the house, but lying wasn't an option for him. Unfortunately he couldn't think of a good way to sugarcoat the news. "The house is about to collapse, Camden, and we can't expect taxpayers to front money for repairs unless the structure is going to provide income for the town."

She sighed. "It always comes back to money, doesn't it?"

"It does right now."

"But the house . . ." Her voice sounded small. "You would be destroying an important piece of the town's history."

"I don't want to destroy it," he said with a sigh. "It's just that every old house in Etherton is an important piece of the town's history, and we can't restore them all."

"That's not what I mean . . ." She paused. "Joseph Bristow was one of the founders of this town. He fought for slaves' rights long before the Civil War, and he died for this town and for freedom."

Thousands of people in their state had fought against slavery, but that wasn't a conversation he wanted to have. How could he go up against a man—and a family—that had sacrificed so much for their country? Even with Joseph Bristow's sacrifice, the town couldn't afford to preserve a house because of what happened so long ago. They were more concerned about today . . . and tomorrow.

"Maybe we can compromise," he said. "I will try to keep the house intact, but if we have to take it down because of structural issues, I'm certain the council would be willing to erect a monument on the hill, in memory of all that your family has done."

Her hands balled up, but her voice remained steady. "I don't want a monument."

Yes, you do, he almost said, but resisted. "You said you weren't planning to live in Etherton."

"It doesn't matter . . ."

"If you don't stay, who is going to care for your house?"

"Jake said he wanted to purchase the house and restore it."

Her words stunned him. It would take at least a million bucks to get the house into decent shape—he hadn't thought anyone else would be interested in investing that kind of cash right now, especially not someone like Jake.

Once again Edward Paxton was trying to destroy his plans. If a private buyer gave her a decent offer and would restore the house, there was no way he could convince her to sell it to him to use for a business, especially if it meant tearing down the house.

"Maybe we can look at some other options," he said. "A way where we could utilize at least part of the house."

"What type of options?"

"Depending on the foundation of the house, we could propose using a portion of the first floor for a restaurant or some sort of gallery."

She paused, the anger in her blue eyes softening for a moment. "It's not the same."

Of course it wasn't the same, but he was trying to accommodate her. He was good at the idea part of his job along with creating proposals to get things done. But mediation wasn't his gift, and after the Wal-Mart fiasco, he realized he wasn't good at reading people's minds either.

He hesitated. "Perhaps we can look at including the house in some type of retail center."

"A mall?"

"It's an idea," he said, although he'd yet to find anyone looking to build a shopping center in a dying town like Etherton. "Perhaps we can offer you more money than we originally discussed."

The instant the words came out of his mouth, he knew he'd said the wrong thing. She didn't seem like she was interested in making a fortune from this house.

Anger blazed across her face, and she stepped away from him. "I just wanted you to know I'm considering Jake's offer."

He couldn't lose this deal. "Can you give me a couple days, Camden? To look at some different options."

"I need to sell the house soon."

"I'll get back to you by Tuesday afternoon."

She hesitated "I want to trust you, Alex."

He would do everything he could to earn her trust. "I'll tell you the truth."

She nodded before she turned back to the car.

Edward paced like a snail in front of the fireplace, muttering to himself as he trampled the carpet. Jake gulped down a Red Bull and waited for his grandfather to say something audible. Edward had been back and forth across the floor at least ten times without saying a single word. If he was ticked, he should say something and get it over with so Jake could get back to playing Warcraft.

He didn't know why his grandfather was so angry anyway. He'd done exactly what Edward asked—visited Camden and explained that Edward wanted to buy her stuff. She hadn't been the least bit interested in the offer to sell the antiques, but she perked right up when he told her the city planned to tear down her house.

In a day or two she'd get off her high horse and climb down the hill to talk to him. He hated being around people who thought they were better than everyone else, and Camden Bristow was a classic snob. He'd like to drag her uppity attitude down a couple of notches, and he could do it. Easily.

Edward finally stopped walking. "You were only supposed to ask about the antiques."

"She doesn't want to sell her junk."

Edward sat down on the recliner. He may act like it was Jake's fault, but Jake knew he was mad because appraising the antiques was the excuse he needed to snoop around the house on his own. He would have firsthand info instead of having to rely on Jake to search for him.

Right now Jake held all the cards in his hand, and he wouldn't give away a single one of them until he was good and ready.

"We don't want to seem too interested in the house," Edward said. "Now you're on her radar."

"You bet I am."

"And what if she sees you inside the house? She'll nail you."

He finished the drink. "She's not going to see me."

"Ha! Like you have the money to buy a dump like that."

He hated Edward's stupid laugh. Hadn't the old man learned yet that he had plenty of smarts? He was the one who'd gotten them into the house, stolen Camden's purse. And it was his buddy down at the pool hall—the one who worked for the honorable Louise Danner— who'd heard the town wanted to tear the house down.

Even now, Edward didn't get his plan.

"I'm only giving her an offer." Jake crushed the aluminum can in his hands. "It doesn't mean I have to buy it." If he wanted to buy it badly enough, he could scrape together the cash, but he didn't want the dump. All he wanted was a tour of the third floor, a chance to get into the one room he couldn't unlock.

Edward slid a cigar out of his pocket and chewed on the end. "She really thought you were interested?"

"Me and my fiancée."

Edward's eyes narrowed. "She'll want to meet your fiancée."

"Mariah will be back before then."

Another barking laugh. "I don't think she's coming back."

"She's only been gone a couple days."

"Yesterday made three weeks." Edward laughed. "You've got to get better control of your women, Jakey."

"She won't leave me again." He rolled up his sleeves and stepped toward the stairs. Even with the Red Bull, he was exhausted. He'd spent too many nights inside the house, along with too many sleepless days.

Edward shook his finger. "You're going back in tonight."

CHAPTER NINETEEN

The creaking noise sounded like a door opening and closing in the balcony above her, but Camden chalked it up to the aches and pains of an old house. She'd groan as well if she'd passed her hundred-and-fifty-year birthday. There was no one in her house. No ghosts floating around, stealing things like purses and canned fruit.

Her hands swept over the mound of books on the library desk, and she inhaled the scents of leather and old paper. Heavy burgundy curtains hid the lofty windows, and she turned around, opening the drapes wide to let the daylight flood the darkness.

Jake Paxton. She rolled his name around in her head, trying to remember why the name sounded so familiar. Each summer there had been new kids to play with while other kids moved on. Jenny was the only one there every summer without fail. All the other faces were a blur.

Bathing in the richness of this room, she wondered about Jake and his fiancée. If she sold it to them, would they take good care of her family's home?

They'd change everything, of course. Redecorate and hopefully repair the walls along with the wiring and pipes that needed to be replaced. It would be strange to strip these old walls bare and haul everything of her family's out the door, but Jake and his fiancée could be the right people to care for the place. It certainly would be better than allowing the city to tear it down.

This part of her life would end, a distinct conclusion to the wonderful memories of her childhood. Then she would go back to New York. And then . . . she supposed she would live on the proceeds from the house while she waited for more work.

And she hated waiting.

Collapsing into an oversized chair, Camden pulled her legs close. What was she supposed to do until she started working again?

An ache ripped through her chest and loneliness settled over her. It wasn't like she had anyone in New York who missed her. Not a single friend had called to check up on her since she'd left town. Either they figured she was traveling in some other country, taking pictures, or they just weren't interested.

Would they ever realize she'd left the city or would they simply forget about her?

In that quiet moment, jealousy warred inside her. She wasn't jealous of the friends who worked for ad agencies and magazines and law offices across New York—they were putting in the long hours and weekends because there was no one to go home to at night. She was jealous of women like Jenny Sprague and even of the unfettered chaos in her friend's home.

If Jenny went away, a whole troop of people young and old would miss her. Dan would call up the National Guard. The FBI. Anyone who would get his wife back ASAP. Instead of traveling around the world, Jenny had chosen Etherton as her home. And she'd chosen commitment over a carefree life. Her four children and husband made sure her life was never lonely . . . or dull.

Constantly moving. Constantly traveling. Like a gypsy, movement was the only thing Camden had known since she was a child. Other kids took it for granted that they had a steady home, a place to go to school next year. Her mother never talked to her about next year, or even the next month, because her mother never knew what the future held.

But that was then—she no longer had to abide by her mother's rules. What if she stopped traveling for a season? Would she go crazy or would she enjoy the comfort of knowing where she would be sleeping tomorrow night? Maybe she could even make another friend or two who would know if she left town.

There was nothing left for her in the Big Apple, but where would her next home be?

On top of the stack of books was a worn King James Bible. She cracked open the cover, thumbed through the yellowing pages. Her grandmother used to read to her from the Bible every night before she went to bed. She'd tuck Camden under the covers, pray for the blessing of sweet dreams, and then pick up where they'd left off in one of the chapters with more red lettering than black.

Her eyes scanned the text through the book of Matthew, soaking in the words of Jesus. Words that her grandmother had read and followed.

At the end of the book, Camden stopped reading.

And, lo, I am with you always, even unto the end of the world.

She scanned the verse again and then again. Her gaze traveled from the Bible to the shafts of light filtering across the dusty shelves.

What would it be like to have someone with her always? She couldn't imagine. Once she believed Jesus would be with her always, back when she was wide-eyed with childish faith, but she'd never believed as an adult. Could Jesus be with her even now? It seemed too mystical that a man who lived two thousand years ago could be with her today. Her grandma had believed it, but Camden wasn't convinced. No one, not even a god, was that faithful.

She closed the Bible and twisted her chair toward the window, the light. If only she could have faith like her grandmother and return to what she had clung to as a child. If only she could ask Rosalie what it really meant to have Jesus with you, always.

Her eyes drooped, and she rested back against the suede chair. It felt good to rest her eyes, her body, and in the warmth of the light, she wasn't the least bit afraid.

The slam of a door woke her up . . . or did she dream the jarring sound? Groggy, she whipped around in the chair, rubbing her eyes, trying to remember where she was. The light in the room was much dimmer than it had been when she fell asleep, but she could still make out the shelves in front of her. The books.

Her ears were playing tricks on her again.

But then she saw something up in the balcony. A dark figure sweeping across the floor. She leapt out of her chair, the Bible on her lap crashing to the ground. Footsteps pounded above her, the shadow racing toward the other side.

"Hey!" she called out as the door to the third floor flew open. The shadow disappeared through the doorway.

Shaking, Camden pulled her cell out of her pocket and dialed the number

Bryce Kelley gave her. This time it wasn't her imagination. Someone was definitely inside her house.

Sergeant Kelley arrived at Crescent Hill minutes after Camden called. From the front step, she watched him park his patrol car and walk toward the house. There was no urgency this time. No flashing lights or sirens or a brigade of uniforms descending on her. Just one officer, in plain clothes.

She crossed her arms. "You have a gun under that jacket, right?"

He pulled up his jacket, showing off the holster underneath, but her hands still trembled. She wished a few other officers had joined him. There was safety in numbers.

Whoever was upstairs disappeared the last time the flashing lights and sirens had blazed up her drive. Bryce might be a big guy, but he was hardly as threatening by himself, dressed in jeans and a flannel work shirt.

She motioned him inside, but she didn't invite him into the parlor. Instead she led him to the breakfast table in the kitchen. The four walls felt like a fortress compared to the open dining room on the other side of the wall.

"What did you see?" he asked as he twisted around a chair and sat down.

She couldn't sit. Pacing the floor, she tried to explain the little she'd seen—at least she had seen something this time instead of just hearing a crash. Bryce wrote notes on a small pad as she talked, but she didn't have much to offer him.

"Was it a man or woman?" he asked.

"I'm not sure."

"For the moment, we'll say it was a man. Can you tell me what he was wearing?"

"A dark jacket, with a hood."

"How tall was he?"

She raked her fingers through her hair. Details were what he needed, and she didn't have any. She hadn't even caught a real glance of the person, male or female. Nothing substantial to help search for the perpetrator.

"I don't know," she blurted, tired and exasperated.

"Are you sure it was a person?"

"Of course it was a person." Frustration seeped out of her voice. Why were they sitting here, chatting, while there was an intruder in her home? Bryce Kelley wasn't helping her at all.

He scribbled another note, and she could only imagine what he'd written. *Doesn't know. Doesn't know. Doesn't have a clue.* The sergeant probably thought there was nothing but air between her ears.

He looked up from his pad. "I'm not doubting you, Miss Bristow."

"Yes, you are," she said, and he was making her doubt herself.

"Is anything missing?"

"A few nights ago . . . someone took my handbag."

"Did you report the theft?"

"No . . . I'm not sure someone stole it."

"Where was your bag?"

"I put it on my nightstand before I went to sleep, but in the morning it was gone."

He closed his notebook and slid it back in his pocket. "I'm going to take a look upstairs."

"I'm sure he's long gone by now."

He stood up. "I still want to check it out."

She followed him up the stairs to the top floor of the house. She didn't bother to ask about the strange protocol, letting her tag along while he searched for an intruder. It was a small town thing, she figured, and she wasn't about to dispute it because he might make her wait down at the kitchen table alone, two floors away from him and his concealed weapon.

At the top of the steps, she snapped on the lights and watched Bryce glance into the ballroom and then maneuver down the hall, toward the steps to the cupola. At the first doorway—a storage room—he flung open the door and she waited for him as he searched behind boxes and trunks. He did the same at the second and third doors. At the fourth doorway, the one at the base of the cupola, he tried to twist the knob, but it wouldn't turn.

"Do you have a key?" he asked.

She shook her head. "Dan only gave me one key to the house."

He turned the knob again, pushing with his shoulder. "It's not going to budge."

Her eyes flickered back and forth between him and the door. What if the intruder were inside the storage room, waiting for them? Bryce didn't seem nearly as concerned as she was, backing away from the door and moving toward the open steps of the cupola like there was nothing odd about a door locked from the inside.

Something wasn't right.

The thought hit her suddenly. She knew nothing about this man except he was a sergeant on Etherton's police force and said he attended her grandmother's church. That didn't make him a good guy. In her work, she'd seen plenty of "good guys" turn bad.

She didn't know Bryce Kelley's motives, but surely he should have brought a few other officers along with him tonight. He shouldn't let her search the house for a criminal alongside him, and he should be a bit more concerned about the possibility of an intruder hiding behind a locked door.

He stepped up toward the cupola. "Do you want to come up?"

She shook her head again. "I'll wait for you downstairs."

CHAPTER TWENTY

The elderly gentleman lived in Greenville, just thirty minutes up the road from Stephanie's apartment in Clemson. His dark forehead was etched with wrinkles, his body arched over a walker. He waved Stephanie into his trailer home, and she followed him into a shabby kitchen that smelled like raisin bread and bacon grease.

Aunt Debra told her that Howard Walters had been a machinist, working fifty-five years for the same company until his fingers refused to work any longer. Though her aunt wouldn't indulge her with any more information, this man also was supposed to know something about her family.

Howard motioned for her to sit and so she did, on a shredded vinyl chair.

"Debra said you go to Clemson."

"Yes, sir. I graduate this summer."

"My grandson, he went there too. Graduated top of his class back in the eighties." The man scooted into a chair. "He's over in Charlotte now, working for a bank."

"I'm hoping to go to work for a museum in the fall."

"An art museum?"

She shook her head. "History."

"When Debra called . . ." he started, but was stopped by a cough that erupted deep in his chest. "She didn't tell me what you wanted to talk about, but I figured it had something to do with your family."

She reached into her backpack and pulled out a plastic bag, double wrapped in a towel. Carefully, she folded back the towel and took out the worn journal that she had read through twice. His eyes followed her hands, as curious as she had been when her aunt first showed it to her.

"What is this?"

"It's the journal of one of my ancestors, Miriam Ellison."

He leaned back against his chair. "Is it, now . . ."

"Yes, sir."

"And what does Miss Miriam have to say?"

"She says a lot, sir. Mostly about her home and her family." She set the journal on the table in front of her. "She also talks quite a bit about one of her housekeepers. A woman named Rachel."

Another cough ripped through the kitchen, and he pounded his chest with his fist. When the cough faded, he answered. "I know a bit about Rachel."

She leaned toward him, hoping he could tell her about this woman. "What do you know?"

"Did your aunt tell you why you should come visit me?"

She shook her head. "She wouldn't say."

Her paper was due in three weeks, but instead of giving her the information she needed, Aunt Debra wanted to send her on a journey. She didn't mind coming here, talking to this man about Rachel, but she wished her aunt was more interested in putting together the puzzle than examining all the pieces.

"I've known Debra for a long time." He rapped his knuckle on the table. "Sorry to hear about her son."

Stephanie squirmed in her seat. Why did people want to apologize to her over something she hadn't done? She hated the apologies. And she hated listening to people talk about her cousin when they didn't know Trent was related to her.

Everyone in the state knew about the murder case. Strangers in coffee shops, in the student center, and at the park picked apart Trent's actions and his motivations, oblivious to the fact that Trent was her cousin. These days she only told people the second part of her last name. The innocuous Carter surname was much easier than the questions the name Ellison raised.

Was she sorry about Trent? Disappointed? It wouldn't do to tell this man she didn't have a bit of compassion for her cousin.

"I hadn't seen him in a while," she finally said.

"Strange thing about families, isn't it? No matter what happens, you're still tied together by blood."

Not in her mind. She wasn't tied to Trent at all. He'd made his choice to wreck his life when he ended the life of his girlfriend . . . and the life of their child.

Aunt Debra forgave her son for what he did, and if Trent asked, God would forgive him. Time, however, didn't forgive so easily. There was no second chance at a clean slate when you'd been convicted of murder.

"I'm tied to your Rachel by blood," Howard said.

"Really?" She blinked, focusing on the history of the Ellisons. "What did you know about her and William?"

"Your grandma mentioned William?"

She didn't really think of Miriam Ellison as her grandmother, but she played along. "She said he was trouble."

"Aah, that he was. For the Ellison family."

"Do you know what happened to him after he left the family?"

"I can't say that I do, but I know a little of what happened before he left."

She pulled out a binder and a pen and placed it on the stained table in front of her. She hadn't brought her laptop this time, afraid she would scare away this man.

"What happened to him, Mr. Walters?"

"Well, now . . ." The coughing erupted from his lungs again, and she waited as he beat it out. "It's a bit of a story."

"I don't have any place I need to be this morning."

"Good, good. You mind getting me a glass of water?"

She hopped up. Why hadn't she thought to ask? Obviously the man needed something to drink.

"You get yourself a can of something too," he said. "My daughter keeps the refrigerator all stocked up."

She grabbed a can of Coca Cola from the door and filled a glass with bottled water for him. "You need anything else?"

"Ain't you a sweet gal for askin'." He took a long sip of water. "I'm just fine though. Don't need much these days, you know."

He settled back into his seat. "So you want me to tell you about Rachel and William . . ."

She nodded her head, pen in hand.

"Did Miss Miriam tell you that they were slaves?"

"Yes, sir."

"Rachel died years before I was born, but I heard the stories from my grandmother. Rachel and William were her parents."

"Your grandmother . . ." She hesitated. "Was she born on the plantation?"

"That she was. Just a toddler during those years."

"She was the one . . ." Stephanie started to say, but couldn't finish her sentence. His grandmother must have been the one who had problems with her legs, the child Miriam Ellison threw out to the field because she wouldn't stop crying. How was she supposed to tell Mr. Walters that her ancestor had beaten his great-grandfather, mistreated his grandmother? She was the one who should be sorry.

"My grandmother Hannah was sick when she was a child," Howard said.

"Miriam mentioned it."

"If my eyes were better, I'd like to read that journal myself."

She could have volunteered to read it for him, but he'd probably heard plenty of heartbreaking stories passed down through the generations. There was no good reason to add another burden to his load.

Instead of asking her to read, he pushed a photo album to her, and she gently opened the brittle pages. Tiny triangles secured faded black and white photos to the album. On the second page, he pointed to the picture at the top. It was an elderly black woman sitting in a chair, dressed in her Sunday best with a light-colored hat angled on her head. Her arms were wrapped around the little boy in her lap, and the boy was grinning at the camera.

"That's me and my grandmama," Howard said proudly.

"Was she able to walk?"

"Not well," he said. "But she got around just fine."

Stephanie's gaze rested on the journal beside her. "At the end of the journal, Miriam said that William ran away."

He pushed back the water glass and rested his wrinkled hands in his lap. "William wasn't born on the Ellison plantation. They purchased him on the block."

"An auction?"

"That's right. His owner was from Kentucky, and even though William was young and able-bodied, his owner wanted to sell him because William had run away. When he was nineteen, he crossed the Ohio River and hopped onto the Underground Railroad.

"A slave hunter caught him up in Sandusky, Ohio, getting ready to sail over to Canada. His owner wanted nothing but the cash from his sale after that, and Arnold Ellison bought him, probably thinking that Columbia was too far south for any slave to consider runnin'."

She couldn't imagine journeying that far north on foot—being that close to freedom—and then being hauled back into slavery. It must have devastated the man.

"And yet he ran again . . ."

"Not right away. William stayed for five years with the Ellisons before he ran again."

"And he married your great-grandmother."

A smile spread across Howard's face. "That he did, and I thank the good Lord for it . . . even though slaves never really married, you know."

"But Miriam said they were married."

"In the sight of God, they married, but not in the sight of man. The marriage of slaves was never recognized by the law. It would have made it complicated when it was time to sell one of the spouses to another owner."

"But William and Rachel were committed to each other."

"That they were, and according to my grandmama, they loved each other dearly. Rachel was only twenty-five when William left the plantation, and she waited for him to return for the rest of her life."

"They had two children?"

He nodded. "But Rachel's son was killed in an accident on the plantation."

"Poor Rachel."

"Now, there." He reached out and patted her hand. "She was a strong woman. Lived on this earth until her ninetieth birthday."

"She never heard from William again?"

"When William left . . ." he paused, his eyes focusing back on her face. "Debra didn't tell you this?"

She shook her head.

"The plan was that William was going to send someone back to Columbia after he left, someone from up north to buy Rachel and then set her free."

"How was he going to buy her and their two children?"

Howard hesitated. "He took some jewelry when he left."

"The heirloom jewels?"

He nodded. "He was going to sell them . . ."

"And buy their freedom."

He drummed his palm on the table. "Rachel didn't know how he was going to get the money when he left. Didn't even know when he was going to leave. He was trying to protect her, you see, from getting flogged like he had when he ran the first time. If she had known what he was doing . . ."

"But Miriam loved Rachel," she interrupted. "She wouldn't have hurt her."

His eyes filled with pity. "Life was different back then."

Still, Stephanie didn't think Miriam would have beaten the woman. It wasn't like Rachel could have stopped her husband from running away, though she supposed Rachel could have told her owners that he was about to run. But what kind of woman would rat out her husband?

"So William stole the jewelry . . ."

When Howard coughed this time, she thought she would have to pick him off the floor. "It wouldn't have been hard for him to justify. He'd worked for years for the Ellisons without earning a cent."

"Debra said the jewels would be worth millions today."

"My grandmama said William wanted to have enough money to buy his wife and children and start a new life."

The telephone rang on the kitchen wall, but he didn't answer it. "The only problem was, they never caught William nor did he send someone down to buy his family . . . or if he did, Rachel never knew about it.

"The Civil War started a few years later, and when the fighting stopped, the slaves moved out on their own as free men and women. Rachel stayed as close as possible to the plantation in Columbia, waiting and listening as other runaways came back searching for relatives, but she never heard from William again."

Stephanie twisted the cold can in her hands, not wanting to imagine the worst, but unable to stop herself.

What if William ran all the way to Canada and then sold the jewels? As a wealthy man, it would have been easy for him to find a new wife, sire new children, and live a life of luxury. Maybe this man wasn't the hero his family envisioned . . . or maybe he was a hero and something bad happened to him.

There were three states between South Carolina and Ohio, and none of them would have been sympathetic toward slaves in the mid 1800s. Did

William even make it to Ohio? So many things could have gone wrong before he set his foot on free soil.

"He didn't even hint where he was going?" she asked.

"Rachel guessed he would go back up the same route in Ohio—it was the route he always talked about though he never gave specifics." Howard closed his eyes and then opened them again. "And then there was the poem."

She waited, listening.

"Supposedly, there was a station in Ohio, a day's walk south of Cleveland. Someone told William and others on the plantation that if they reached it, they would be guaranteed safe delivery to Canada."

She put the can on the table. "There were hundreds of Underground Railroad stations in Ohio."

"Yes," he said. "But only one was known as Crescent Hill."

As the band played, Camden scanned the small congregation of Community Bible from one of the back rows until she saw Bryce Kelley singing alongside his family toward the front. After he left last night, without finding an intruder, she knew she wouldn't be able to sleep on Crescent Hill. The wind hadn't smashed the glass on the third floor, and she had *not* misplaced her handbag. Someone was in her house, sneaking around even when she was home.

She slept a few hours at Dan and Jenny's house. Jenny had been up late with Kyle who couldn't seem to stop crying, and Hailey woke Camden up before dawn by hopping on her bed. Jenny stayed home this morning to take care of Kyle, but she insisted that Camden go to church with her family . . . even though they were a good twenty minutes late.

After so many years, it was strange to be back in the church that she'd visited many times with her grandma. Rosalie's presence seemed to be everywhere in this old building. In the stained glass windows and the baptistery and the silent organ tucked to the side of the drums.

The congregation sang out about a God who saved them, and as she followed the words on the screen, she realized that she was singing not only about a God who saved the people around her, but about a God who had saved *her*.

This was the place where she'd found Jesus as a child, but ever since she left Etherton, she hadn't given him much thought. What did it really mean to be in God's presence? Rosalie would be in God's presence right now, but if she died, would she join her grandma in heaven?

I am with you always . . .

If that were true, why did she feel so alone?

The worship leader sang out about God's presence—about fears being washed away—and the words filled her with hope. Maybe God's presence was around her. Maybe she just hadn't been looking for him.

Seeing the intruder in her home had shaken her up, but perhaps she didn't have to be afraid. Her grandmother embraced this hope. This peace. If God could wash away *all* fear, perhaps he could take away her fears about the house, about her intruder. Most of all, perhaps he could wash away the fears about her future.

As the people around her sang the beautiful words, she prayed softly, asking God to renew her sense of his presence . . . and take away her fears.

The worship leader finished the final stanza, but she didn't want the music to end. As the pastor prayed, she prayed along with him, asking God to be present in her life. Asking him for peace and wisdom.

When the pastor finished, she stood still for a moment as everyone around her began shaking hands and hugging each other. Someone tapped on her shoulder, and she turned to see a dainty woman dressed in a red and white hat that matched her blazer. The woman reached for her hand.

"Camden Bristow," Margaret Nixon said, shaking her hand. "The last time I saw you, you were sporting pigtails."

Jenny looked just like her mother, though it was clear that Jenny didn't inherit her mother's obsession for style. Even Margaret's shoes and lipstick matched her outfit.

Margaret leaned closer to her, whispering. "Jenny tells me there are some beautiful old quilts up on Crescent Hill."

She nodded though she wasn't sure she would call the worn quilts beautiful. "Several of my 'greats' liked to quilt."

"You know that Crescent Hill was once a station on the Underground Railroad."

"My grandmother used to tell me stories, but I was so young . . ."

"It's quite the heritage, to be a part of the Underground."

She sighed. Even with the heritage, there was nothing she could do to keep the house in her family.

Margaret continued. "Some people think they used quilts as maps along the Underground to direct slaves to the people who could help them and places they could hide."

"These quilts aren't maps, Margaret. They were probably used as comforters on the beds."

"Still . . . would you mind if I took a look at them?"

"Not at all."

Margaret clapped. "Oh, goodie."

"You can come tomorrow if you'd like."

"Tomorrow?" The congregation started sitting down around them, but instead of taking her seat, Margaret pulled out a BlackBerry and began clicking away. "Oh, no. I can't come for a visit quite yet. I've got a doctor's appointment tomorrow and then a baby shower and I'm going to the Parade of Homes in Columbus on Wednesday. How about . . . Thursday?"

Camden couldn't help but smile. It was like Margaret was doing her a favor. "Thursday's fine."

Margaret's voice lowered as she sat on the pew. "Jenny said there are pictures on the quilt blocks."

"I don't know about pictures . . . more like different shapes."

Margaret patted her shoulder. "Even if it doesn't have a map, every quilt has a story."

CHAPTER TWENTY-ONE

Alex unlocked his office door almost two hours before town hall officially opened. With a large coffee grasped in one hand, he propped his briefcase against his desk and marched down the hallway, toward Louise's office.

The mayor was pecking away at her keyboard like a hen deprived of food for the weekend, an opened can of Dr Pepper on each side of her desk. Even if the city council wasn't on his team, at least he had an ally in Louise. More than anyone else he'd met, she wanted Etherton to thrive, and revitalizing Crescent Hill was the exact shot they needed to their economy. He needed her to cheer on this idea, much more than she'd done for his last two proposals. The councilors respected her opinion, and this acquisition would be good for their town's future.

When she stopped typing, he laid out the plan he'd been formulating all weekend. A plan that should interest the councilors as well as Camden. As he explained, her smile turned into a frown. She had liked his initial idea of acquiring the property, but apparently she wasn't as interested in his idea of keeping the mansion intact.

"We can't," she said, her earrings batting against her cheeks as she shook her head. "That structure is violating more local codes than I can count."

He set his coffee on the desk. "Surely there is something we can do to help Camden . . . because of Rosalie."

"We've looked the other way for years on that house." Her fingers tapped the edge of the keyboard. "None of us wanted to put Rosalie out of her home, but I can't keep putting it off. Someone's going to get hurt up there."

"But if we condemn it . . ." his voice trailed off as the realization flashed into his mind. Unless she dumped a ton of money into the place, Camden wouldn't be able to keep it, and Jake Paxton wouldn't be able to purchase it until the repairs were made.

The city would own the Bristow property, without paying a cent.

"That's not right," he retorted.

Louise returned to her pecking. "It'll work out, Alex."

With his hand clenched around his coffee, he walked toward the door. Louise Danner wanted to play dirty, getting the house for the city without paying a dime.

His job may be on the line, but he was not going to steal the Bristow Mansion away from Camden.

Someone jumped on Camden's bed and flopped back and forth on the covers. A butterfly? No, that wasn't right. She rubbed her eyes, trying to wake up. A possum was her next guess until a gurgle bubbled out of Hailey's throat, arms flailing over her head. There was a fish in her bed, one, evidently, who was not happy about being out of the water.

The clock read 6:07—two hours before Camden usually greeted the morning with chai tea and a newspaper. Tugging her pillow over her head, she wished again for her bedroom up on the hill. But there was no deterring Hailey. Instead of swimming out of the room, the girl scooted next to her, sucking her lips together and squeaking.

If only she had a net and a line . . . or maybe a bigger fish would do.

Emerging from the pillow, Camden bore her teeth and made a chomping sound. Instead of running, Hailey giggled.

"You shouldn't laugh," she said with a yawn. "I'm a shark, and I'm hungry for breakfast."

Then she growled like she imagined a shark would do if he were awakened by a four-year-old bouncing on his bed. Hailey squealed and bounded out of her room.

Camden rolled over and squeezed her eyes shut, knowing it would only be minutes before Hailey returned as another critter. Her repertoire of both domestic and foreign animals seemed limitless. The child even revived a dinosaur from extinction, stomping around the dining room last night while the rest of the family attempted to eat.

None of the bedroom doors at the Spragues' house had locks, a precaution Jenny explained they'd taken after it took her twenty minutes to rescue her baby from a locked bedroom. She could guess which sibling put her baby sister in a cage.

When Camden awoke again, at the much more respectable hour of 7:00, someone was knocking.

"Good morning, sleepyhead," Jenny sang as she cracked open the door.

Camden threw a pillow at her friend, but it didn't deter her. Instead Jenny launched into a silly song about the sun tickling her sides, ready for her to play. It was a tune straight from Barney or one of those other annoying shows for kids under five, not their mothers.

Still Jenny kept singing it, over and over, until Camden managed a smile. "How's Kyle?"

"Running around like a crazy man."

"I better arm myself."

"Breakfast is in ten," Jenny said, leaving the door wide open for predators.

She almost fell back asleep, but minutes later, Hailey nudged her with her nose and roared. At least the girl was smart. A lioness was a good match for a shark.

By the time Camden wandered into the kitchen, the whole Sprague family was crammed around the breakfast table. Jenny handed her a mug of tea, but before she took a sip, a plateful of eggs and toast was pushed into her other hand. As she took the seat between Hailey and the baby, Dan asked how she slept. *Good, until about six.*

Breakfast raged through the kitchen like a tornado. Food was eaten, tossed, and smeared across the table . . . and then the family blew away. Dan retreated to his office, and the others carried themselves off to do damage someplace else in the house, leaving Jenny and her to pick up the pieces.

It was the first quiet moment she'd had with Jenny since she arrived, so she finally told her friend that the city might tear down the property. And she told Jenny about Jake's offer.

"Jake Paxton?" Jenny wrinkled her nose as she said his name.

"That's what he said."

"You may not like Alex's idea, but if you have to sell it to him, the property would be in much better hands."

"The property, maybe, but not the house."

"Still . . ." Jenny said.

"What's wrong with Jake?"

Jenny tossed a dish towel toward the sink, but it landed on the floor. "There's a whole list of things, actually."

"He said he and his fiancée want to restore the place."

Jenny stared at her. "Someone's going to marry him?"

"You can't possibly know everything, Jenny."

Her friend stuck out her tongue. "I know almost everything, and I've known Jake Paxton since I started kindergarten."

"He seems a little obsessed with himself."

"To put it mildly."

"You didn't go out with him or something, did you?"

"Well . . ."

She leaned back against the counter. "Jenny?"

"No, I didn't go out with him, but he asked me to prom when I was sixteen. I said yes at first. Out of shock, or something, I guess, because I really didn't want to go with him. My mother informed me that there was no way I was going to the prom with Jake Paxton so I called him back the next day and reneged."

"Was he ticked?"

"To say the least, but it was even worse when Dan called and asked me."

"You didn't . . ."

"I *really* wanted to go with him."

"Ouch."

"Jake's never forgiven me."

"But you have no regrets."

Jenny smiled. "None at all."

Camden swiped the dish towel off the floor and snapped it at her friend. "Seems like you're the one who's obsessed with herself."

"I would have gone with him if he was a good guy."

"Maybe he's changed after all these years."

Jenny snatched the towel from her and threw it onto the counter. "I don't think so."

"I don't have a good choice." Camden sighed. "Either I sell it to the city to be destroyed or I sell it to Jake to restore."

"I wouldn't trust Jake Paxton."

Her friend's words echoed in her ears.

Never trust a Paxton. Where had she heard that before?

She turned her head from Jenny to squeeze another cup into the dishwasher.

The words weren't Jenny's; they were her grandma's. Her grandma warned her about the Paxtons, after a little boy tricked her into following him into the woods and then scared her with a snake. It was probably a garter snake, but when you're six or seven and terrified of anything that slithers, it doesn't matter. She'd screamed and run back to the house where she'd sobbed in her grandma's arms.

Rosalie eventually coaxed her back out of the house, but her warning about the Paxtons stuck because never before had her grandmother told her not to trust someone. And she never told her again.

Had that boy been Jake? She didn't recall his name nor did she remember seeing him after the snake incident. Perhaps her grandma told him to stay away. Yet another question that would remain unanswered.

She crammed the last sippy cup into the dishwasher.

Even if Jake had set her up for the scare of her young life, it happened a long time ago. After twenty-plus years, did it really matter? She'd changed in that time, and surely he had too.

"I know you said you didn't want to sell the property for me," Camden began.

Jenny sighed. "You want me to put together the paperwork for Jake?"

"I think so . . ." she began as she closed the dishwasher, and then turned toward her friend. "I don't know what I want."

CHAPTER TWENTY-TWO

Not much shocked Camden these days, but as she stared at the phone in her hand, she was stunned. Zipping up her duffel bag, she hid it in the back of the closet in hopes that the Sprague kiddos would keep out of her things. Wishful thinking, she knew, but maybe hiding her bag would deter them.

Liza asked to meet her for lunch in twenty minutes. Camden suggested coffee instead, but Liza said if money was an issue, she'd pay for the food. Camden cringed at the barb. How was she supposed to admit to her half-sister that she was dirt poor?

Still she agreed to meet Liza at the Underground Cafe, more out of curiosity than anything else. Her sister had never contacted her before—not a phone call or a birthday card or any type of gesture to remind her they were part of the same family. Not that Camden had contacted her half-sister either. When she used to stay a night or two at her father's house as a child, Camden avoided Liza's nasty glares by sticking to her room.

She slipped out of the house and walked toward the café.

She couldn't blame her sister, not really. The animosity came top-down. Her stepmother hadn't wanted her in the house, or to have any part in their lives. Camden never once complained when her father drove her down to Etherton. She'd cherished those minutes in the car, the hour-long drive talking with her dad. He didn't laugh much at his house, but he always laughed in the car, with her. It made her happy to make him happy.

During the summer, her father would come occasionally to visit her and Rosalie on Crescent Hill. He should have come more often, but she stopped blaming him long ago. It was all in the past, and he was gone. Any hope of a renewed relationship ended the day that truck made an illegal U-turn in front of her father's Harley.

Camden sat down in a booth and thumbed through a magazine, waiting for Liza to show. Her half-sister said to meet her at 11:30, but the minutes passed with no arrival and no phone call apologizing because she was late.

A half hour later, Liza walked through the door, tall and sleek with her designer jeans and heels. Her blond hair curled back from her face in perfect waves, and her face was painted with such perfection that she looked like a celebrity. A quick glance around the café and she spotted Camden, but she didn't smile. Instead Liza sauntered over to the booth and slid her designer handbag across the tabletop.

"Did you order yet?" Her question sounded more like a demand.

"I have no idea what you like to eat, Liza."

"Just a salad for me." Liza lowered herself into the booth. "Think you can handle it?"

Camden scooted out of the booth and held out her hand, palm up. She didn't mind ordering, but she wasn't buying. Her half-sister could pay for lunch with their father's inheritance.

Liza begrudgingly handed over her credit card, and Camden turned toward the counter. Whatever this meeting was about, it certainly wasn't off to a good start. No hug or kiss on the cheek or anything to communicate that her younger sister was glad to see her. Liza had no reason to be jealous of her, but the hatred was still there, and it ran deep.

She ordered Liza's salad and a sandwich for herself. Even though she wondered why Liza was in Etherton—and why she wanted to meet—she wasn't anxious to return to the table. There was no feigning friendliness when Liza clearly didn't want to be friends.

With the food and two bottles of spring water balanced on a tray, she slid into the booth across from Liza. Her sister's nose wrinkled when she saw the salad. "There's iceberg lettuce in here."

Like Camden made the salad intentionally to spite her. "I ordered what you asked for."

"The menu said mixed greens."

She nodded toward the teenager working the counter. "Take it up with him."

It had been a joke, but Liza apparently didn't see the humor in it because she swept her plate off the table and marched back to the counter. Camden didn't wait. She took a bite of her chicken sandwich and relished the taste. At one time she might have complained about the food too, but not now. She was grateful for every slice of bread, meat, and cheese.

When Liza returned, her salad void of iceberg, Camden was almost done with her food.

"You are hungry, aren't you?"

Camden ignored her. "Why didn't you call me when you found out Grandma had cancer?"

Liza's eyebrow slid up. "Because I didn't think you cared."

"Of course I cared."

"Well, you have a lousy way of showing it, Camden."

She wiped her hands on a napkin. Liza was right, she did have a lousy way of showing it, but her sister didn't need to berate her. She could do that just fine on her own.

"You didn't even call after she died."

Liza twisted a piece of lettuce in the prongs of her fork and lifted it in the air like it was a flag. Unfortunately, there was no surrender in her voice. "We figured you were slumming around Italy or some other place. It wasn't like you called and said, 'Hey, I'm back in the States.'"

Camden glanced out the window, trying to stop the emotions lashing inside her. All they had to do was Google her name, and her Web site would have appeared, along with her contact information. A two-minute search was all it would have taken, and they could have tracked her down.

She pushed her plate back. If this wasn't going to be a friendly lunch between sisters, she wanted a few answers before she left. And the sooner this lunch ended, the better. "Did you leave some clothes at grandmother's?"

"What kind of clothes?"

"I found a sweatshirt, tennis shoes . . . and a Bible."

Liza snorted at the mention of a Bible. "Oh please . . ."

Camden swiped her keys off the table. That was all the information she had come for . . . that and the food.

Liza stopped her departure with her hand before she slid out of the booth. "I didn't leave anything, but I do want to talk to you about the house."

She slumped back against the seat. It seemed like everyone wanted to talk to her about the house these days. "What do you want?"

Liza tapped her nails on the table like it was a drum. "I want half of it."

"What?"

"When you sell the house, I want half the profit."

Camden punched her boots on the wood floor and launched out of her seat. Hadn't Liza received enough money when their father died? Now she wanted what Camden inherited as well. "It's not yours to ask for."

Liza swept a strand of hair out of her eyes. "Technically I should get the whole house."

Fury rose within her. "Not according to Grandma's will."

"If the attorney knew what I know, he never would have finalized it. Not with the state of Rosalie's mind."

"There was nothing wrong with her mind."

Liza's long lashes constricted. "How would you know?"

She almost blurted out because Dan and Jenny told her, but she opted to keep that information under wraps . . . at least until she figured out where Liza was going with this accusation.

Picking up her jacket, Camden pulled the sleeves over her arms. Perhaps she should feel selfish, keeping the house to herself, but she didn't. Instead, she felt vindicated. Except for the money that supported Rosalie, their father had left everything to his second family, and she guessed his nest egg had been in the millions, not to mention his life insurance policy.

Her inheritance of the house was unexpected, yet perhaps it was the right thing. Yin and yang. If nothing else, it righted a deep wrong, and for the first time in years, she felt like she was part of the Bristow family.

Zipping up her jacket, she looked back into Liza's cold face. "Dan said Grandma left you some art pieces."

"They're not worth crap."

"Some things are worth a lot more than money."

Liza's fork clanked when it hit the bowl. "I want half the proceeds from the house, Camden, or I'm contesting the will."

The warmth in her body clashed with the blast of cold. *Contest it?* Liza couldn't possibly have a case . . . could she?

She hadn't coerced their grandma into giving her the property, but what if Rosalie *had* been suffering with mental decline? Could Liza prove it? Camden didn't have the money to fight it out in court.

Words spurted out of her mouth. "You don't have a case."

"Oh, but I do . . ."

Camden shivered, wanting to get far, far away from this woman. "Grandma's will is straightforward."

Liza whispered. "But it doesn't mention the secrets."

"What secrets?"

Liza wound another piece of lettuce around her fork. "Something that will rock your world."

CHAPTER TWENTY-THREE

People are always trying to bum work off him," Jenny said with a laugh.

Camden's lips twisted into a smile, and she tried to laugh as well. Of course, Dan didn't work on credit. He had to make a living like everyone else.

Jenny stopped laughing. "Do you need something?"

"Maybe."

"I'm sure he'd do it for you at a fraction of what he usually bills."

She couldn't tell Jenny that she didn't have money for even a minimal fee, and there was no way she was going to try and get free legal advice from him because he was Jenny's husband. She would pay him like everyone else, and she would protect the house that had been left in her care.

As she walked back up to Crescent Hill, she hated placing the call, but she'd been left with no choice. She wouldn't hand over half the estate to Liza. Not without a fight. She had no doubt that Liza would contest the will, and she needed money to defend herself and the house Rosalie left in her care.

Camden shivered at the thought of Liza. Cynicism had filled her half-sister's laugh when Camden pressed her about the supposed secrets Liza lorded over her, and Camden left the café without answers. Liza enjoyed watching her squirm, and Camden wouldn't give her the pleasure of reveling in her angst.

If Liza was able to overturn the will, Camden had no doubt her half-sister would hand the place over to the town for a pile of cash. She probably wouldn't even return to watch the wrecking ball tear down a hundred and fifty years of memories.

Maybe that's why her grandmother left the house to her. Perhaps she knew that Camden would do everything she could to protect it. If only she could find the letter that had been taken from her, she felt certain her grandmother told her how to save the house. And maybe even why.

Without her grandmother's direction, she would do her best to preserve the memories, but she could sell a few pieces of furniture and art in the house without feeling like she'd pilfered the place. Perhaps she could even buy the pieces back after she had sold the house.

Edward Paxton appeared at her door fifteen minutes after she called, smelling very much like the cigar smoke that had clung to his grandson. His navy vest was buttoned to the top, and dark moles spotted his forehead. If he had ever been good-looking, the remnants of those looks had disappeared.

She invited him inside, and he hobbled into the entryway with his cane. Then she explained that she wanted to sell two or three antiques, to help with costs right now.

"I will do whatever you ask of me," he said with a combination of humility and flourish. "Your grandmother was a dear friend of mine."

Never trust a Paxton.

If he thought he and Rosalie were dear friends, he remembered wrong.

"The pieces I want to sell are upstairs, on the third floor."

His face lit up. "It will take me awhile to climb those old stairs, but I would be glad to appraise them for you."

She was hoping he would say "buy them from you," but she wouldn't push it. Not until she showed him what she had in storage.

With every step, Edward's cane tapped against the tile and then thudded on the carpet that lined the stairs. As she followed him slowly up the stairs, one step at a time, he chatted about the town where he had been born.

"My family's had an antique business in Etherton for seventy years," he said.

"How's the antique business these days?"

"Not so good here." He stopped for a breath. "Of course, I don't do much business in Etherton any more."

"Where do you—"

"I still acquire things here of course, but I sell almost everything online."

"Craig's List?"

He laughed. "Something a little more reputable."

Hopefully, the stuff she showed him upstairs would appeal to the "reputable" crowd.

It seemed like an hour passed by the time she and Edward reached the top floor. The man liked to wander, stopping and looking at books and furniture in the balcony around the library. When they got upstairs, he circled the theater, critiquing each piece of art.

She told him there was nothing she wanted to sell in either the balcony or theater, only in the storage room, but it didn't deter him. He wanted to stop and comment on the exquisiteness of these items, in case she would like an appraisal later.

Once they reached the first storage room, she turned on the light and pointed toward a double dresser with carved knobs, topped by an ornate mirror decorated with porcelain flowers. It was old and gaudy, and hopefully valuable to someone who had disposable money to spend on these sorts of things. Edward's fingers swept over the wood and mirror, and then he opened each drawer, examining them at the same slow pace it took them to climb the steps. Murmuring sounds trickled from his lips as he probed the dresser, like talking to himself would help him calculate its worth.

"It was built toward the end of the nineteenth century, probably in France," he said. "Impressive quality."

Impressive wasn't how she would describe it, but she didn't care as long as it was valuable. "What do you think it's worth?"

He pulled a small camera out of his pocket and snapped a couple shots of it. "I'll have to do my homework before I can give you a number."

Her heart sunk. How long would it take for him to do his homework?

"What else do you have?" he asked.

She showed him two pieces of artwork and a lamp she thought might be a Tiffany. He didn't seem as impressed with the lamp as she'd hoped, but he took pictures, and then stopped and leaned over a trunk that her grandmother once told her came over on the boat with the original Bristow family. She wasn't interested in selling that heirloom. Not yet.

Still he wanted to look and so she let him. No harm in having him appraise more items, she supposed, just in case she needed more cash before she could sell the house.

They approached the hallway, and Edward nodded toward the three doors at the far end of the hallway. "Would you mind if I looked in those as well?"

She must have looked as skeptical as she felt, because he continued. "Sometimes people have valuable items in storage, items they never would have guessed could bring them thousands or even hundreds of thousands of dollars."

"I don't think there's much . . ." she started, but he was already moving toward the next door. What was she going to do, kick his cane and wrestle him to the floor?

So she followed him to the next room. On the chance he would spot something valuable.

There was a cracked window in the third room, probably the room where the police had found the broken vase, but there wasn't much in the way of antiques in this room. Mainly boxes and boxes of papers and old clothing that she should pack up for Goodwill. Still, he peeked into boxes and sifted through bags. It was almost as if he were looking for something.

She didn't even attempt to stop him when he headed toward the last door in the hallway. His hands turned and twisted the knob repeatedly.

He took a three-point turn with his cane. "It's locked," he said like she was trying to hide something from him.

"I realize that."

"Do you have the key?"

She stiffened. It wasn't any of his business if she had the key nor was it his business what was inside that door. She'd shown him what she was interested in selling yet he didn't seem to be listening to her.

She pointed toward the far end of the hallway, away from the cupola. "Thank you for coming, Mr. Paxton."

"I'd just like to see inside that one last room, Miss Bristow. You never know . . ."

"I'm not ready to show or sell what is in that room."

His gaze lingered on the doorknob before he turned. He walked even slower down the stairs, in silence, almost as if he wanted to punish her for not letting him inside that final room. As she followed him down, she tried to erase that crazy thought. She'd shown him several good pieces to appraise, and she was sure he'd add a healthy commission for himself when he sold them so there was no reason for him to be angry. Yet his chattiness vanished as he focused on the balancing act between the banister and his cane.

She sighed. It was going to be a long trip back down.

Edward slammed the back door of the house and shuffled into the study. "There's a locked room!"

Jake paused his computer game and swiveled around in his chair. His grandfather never bothered to ask if he was in the middle of something important. He was trying to tech up his army, and two seconds was all it took to lose his momentum.

"Did you buy her antiques?"

"A locked door!" the man repeated like Jake was deaf.

"I heard what you said the first time."

"Why didn't you tell me there was a locked door?"

Jake shrugged. "I didn't think it was important."

"You didn't think! You didn't . . ." Edward snatched a mug off the table and threw it. Jake covered his head as the ceramic splintered against the wall, and coffee splattered across the white paint, raining down to the floor.

He turned and glared at the old man. "Cool it, Pops."

He didn't care why Edward was ticked—the old man did not want to start a fight with him. The losing side wouldn't wear well on his skin.

"I didn't ask you to think about this. Not once." Edward stepped forward, pointing his cane at Jake like it was a sword. "I asked you to go into that house and search every corner, knock on every wall. You said you did it. You said there was nothing else to find."

"There wasn't anything to find."

"There's a locked door, Jakey." The look in his eyes was pure disgust. "A locked door that *you* failed to mention."

Jake snorted. Like Edward was telling him everything *he* knew. There were plenty of things his grandfather failed to mention over the years, especially that nugget of info in Rosalie's letter.

It didn't matter that he and Edward were family. Family ties didn't keep the Paxtons from cheating on each other. Lying to each other. In fact, it seemed to be the Paxton way. Pretend you're helping your brother or sister or uncle by offering them a piece or two of the pie, and then, *wham*, once they help you, you take the whole pie and run. Everyone in their family was always looking around corners, waiting to see who would outsmart the other and win.

His mother won the grand prize. She'd escaped this miserable town for sunny California.

Edward was in his face, his breath reeking from his daily cigar. "You want me to pick up that phone right now and place a few calls? Don't think I couldn't have your butt hauled off to jail before dinnertime."

Jake waved away the smoke. "I wouldn't do that if I were you."

"Don't think for a second that I'm afraid of what you can do."

"You should be afraid of what I know."

Edward stared him down, and Jake stared back. Most people would back off, look away, but he'd show Edward who had the brains in this family. He was the one thinking ahead of his grandfather this time.

Edward blinked first. "Why didn't you tell me about the room?"

"I was waiting to get inside first."

"You don't have a clue what you're doing."

He rolled his fingers over the controller and squeezed instead of throwing the punch he ached to throw. "Before I put an offer on the house, Camden will have to give me a tour of the place," he stated, ice coating his words. "Show me every room, every closet, every square inch."

Edward studied his face as he talked. He was listening and watching to see if Jake was telling the truth. "Go on."

"I can't give her a written offer before I see that room on the top floor. Who knows what Rosalie could have hidden in there?"

His grandfather backed away a few steps, a new respect in his eyes. Another notch in the ladder. Just wait until Edward found out what he had uncovered. Once he decided to tell the man, Edward would never call him stupid again.

He set the controller on the desktop. "I didn't want to tell you about the room, because I didn't want you to stress about it. It's not good for your heart."

"My heart's stronger than yours."

Hardly. "I'm going to get in that room, Edward. It's only a matter of time."

"You'll go back in there tonight, pick the lock."

"I already tried, and it won't open," he said. "Once Camden unlocks it for me, I'll make sure it stays that way."

"Next time something like this happens, you better tell me about it."

With a smile, he faced the computer again. He didn't have to tell Edward a thing.

CHAPTER TWENTY-FOUR

Alex ducked under a low branch and turned toward town hall. Tuesday had come too soon. He was supposed to knock on Camden's door this afternoon, but without good news to deliver, he avoided the trek up Crescent Hill.

Louise was still intent on tearing the house down, and he couldn't blame Camden for wanting to save her family's home. But how much of her desire was about preserving the memory of the Bristow family, and how much of it was about something deeper, a desire to preserve her own memories? It was like the house was so much a part of her grandmother that she couldn't separate the place from the person.

The house was on the verge of collapse. Without a doubt, the town could condemn her property because the exterior damage violated at least a dozen city housing codes. The structure would jeopardize whoever lived in it—whether it was Camden or Jake.

Even if Jake Paxton swore before a judge that he'd fix it up and signed some sort of agreement to repair the house, he didn't know if Camden would really sell it. In fact, if they were placing bets, he'd go with the odds of Camden getting cold feet. She didn't want to sell the place nor did she want to move on.

A painful jolt surged through his chest, and he battled against his own memories. He hated the familiar scene that played across his mind without invitation. Hated that it seemed to haunt him wherever he went. Quietly, he began to pray, asking God to steer his mind away from the past.

Pain used to be his constant companion, but that was before he chose to lay down his bitterness and remorse and follow Christ in spite of his desire to cling to his anger. It had been a last-ditch effort to find peace and one last attempt to understand why God had taken his sister and nephew away. He didn't know why God had taken her, but daily he asked God to shield him from the pain.

God had been faithful, giving him an unexplained peace in spite of the circumstances. A peace his family still didn't understand. Even so, when he began to wonder about the hurt in other people's lives, the pain sometimes returned.

A block away from town hall, Alex passed the stone columns that outlined the entrance to the library. Camden hinted at the historical significance of Crescent Hill when he saw her on Saturday, but she didn't remember many of the specifics. What if he could find something that would make the place appealing to tourists? Something momentous that would force City Council to oppose its demolition.

He turned around and jogged up the cement steps to the double doors. He doubted the house had anything so significant about its past, but it wouldn't hurt to check.

At the center of the library was an enclosed area with a *Reference Desk* sign dangling over the front computer. On the other side of the desk was a woman in her early twenties who smiled demurely when he stepped up to the counter. Her brown glasses matched her short brown hair, and she wore a tight green sweater and plaid skirt.

Ever so slowly, the woman moved a stack of books to another counter and then looked back at him. "How can I help you?"

He cleared his throat. "I want to research a local house."

"You're in luck." She sat down at a computer, and her strong perfume accosted his nose. "Research happens to be my specialty. What are you looking for?"

"I want to read everything you have on Crescent Hill."

She glanced up at him, her brown eyes wide. "I love that old place!"

He rested his elbows on the counter. "What exactly do you love about it?"

"Maybe *love* is the wrong word." She folded her hands in her lap. "I'm more intrigued. Don't you think it's mysterious . . . maybe a little creepy?"

He shrugged. "I've never been inside."

"Me neither, but I know plenty of people who've seen ghosts up there."

He choked back a laugh. "I didn't think you could see ghosts."

"It's the lights they've seen, moving about on the top floor."

The shadowed face appeared in his mind, staring out the window at him when he went to visit Camden last week. He shook the thought away. "I don't believe in ghosts."

"That doesn't mean they don't exist." She turned her body back to the computer and started typing on her keyboard. "A little boy supposedly haunts the place. They say he's looking for something."

Alex grabbed the handle of his briefcase and swung it up onto the counter. "Maybe he'll find what he's looking for soon and stop bothering the Bristows."

"My name's Bethany," she said as she scribbled a call number on a card and slid it toward him. Her fingernails matched the sea green color of her sweater. "In the reference section, we have a paper someone wrote on the house in 1968."

He took the card from her hand. "Is that it?"

"That's the most current information." She stood up and smoothed her hands over her skirt. "But we also have the *Etherton News* on microfilm dating back to 1842 if you'd like to look at those."

"I would." He picked up his briefcase. Sitting in the library, browsing though old newspapers, didn't top his list of things he wanted to do today, but he was curious about Crescent Hill's past life. And he was curious about the Bristows.

Bethany scooted out of the reference area and directed him to the microfilm reader. As she stretched her arm over his shoulder, her hand brushed his back. He cringed and moved away.

As she demonstrated how to advance and rewind the film, she leaned even closer to him. "If you need anything else, please come get me."

"Thanks," he muttered, and then, thank God, she was gone.

Rolling the knob, he skipped past the clunky, black-and-white ads for boots, parlor stoves, and buggies. A quick perusal of the headlines showed the articles were about the rebellion in Rhode Island and the attempt to impeach President Tyler. Then he skimmed an announcement from 1846 that said Joseph Bristow, one of the town's founders and a businessman who made and supplied iron to Mansfield, recently married Camden Reese, the daughter of a reverend in Mansfield.

Quickly, he scanned the articles through the 1840s. There was an occasional mention of the Bristow family, business-related items. As he rolled into the 1850 papers, almost every edition of the weekly paper featured an article about a new law called the Fugitive Slave Act that penalized any individual in Ohio, or across the North, who aided in the escape of a slave and rewarded those who returned the runaways.

He couldn't imagine what a law like that did to neighbors and families. Any time you added money to the mix, it forced families to debate what was right and what was lucrative. Many a family collapsed under the weight of that dispute.

Turning the pages, he stopped when he saw the headline for August 1851.

Joseph Bristow Nears Completion of Mansion

A hand-drawn picture showed the partially built mansion on the hill, and it explained that after the birth of Joseph and Camden's first son in 1845, Joseph purchased a forty-five-acre parcel outside Etherton and named it after the peculiar shape of the hill. The article described how the interior of the house was crafted with the finest wood and many of the plush furnishings were imported from Europe.

Rubbing his eyes, Alex looked back at the picture. Camden may think preserving her family heritage was important, but he still didn't understand what made the Bristows any different than the typical wealthy family in the 1800s, or a family today, who spent their time and income collecting the best things money could buy. It didn't mean the Bristows were bad people. They just didn't seem remarkable—at least not as remarkable as they were in Camden's mind.

He turned the page to finish the article and read that the Bristows were planning to complete the project in the spring of 1852. Then they would move out of their house on Pleasant Street and into the new home.

In the following articles, there were frequent mentions of Joseph Bristow's business, but there wasn't another mention of the Bristow's house until the headline on July 3, 1858.

Bristow Son Disappears on Crescent Hill

The article explained that Joseph and Camden's thirteen-year-old son Matthew had disappeared. The Bristows thought their child had wandered off during the night, but no one could find him. Frantically, the family and neighbors searched the house and then the hillside, but he was gone.

Alex's pulse quickened as he raced to the next week's paper and discovered that the child had not yet been found. The newspaper reporter speculated that he had been kidnapped, yet there were no requests for ransom. The Bristows were frantic, begging for information to find their son.

Tears moistened Alex's eyes, the pain acute. The Bristows may have lost their child over a century ago, but it didn't matter when it happened, it hurt to lose someone you loved. No one should have to face death like that, not knowing what happened to your loved one.

He wiped the back of his hand over his eyes and flipped the pages until he found the next story on the Bristows, a short article reporting they found Matthew's body. No other details were given except the family was building a mausoleum at the base of Crescent Hill to honor the boy's life.

The lack of details disappointed Alex. He wanted to find out what happened to the Bristow's son.

He didn't hear Bethany slip up beside him, but when he turned his head, she was staring at him, perplexed. "Are you okay?"

"Sorry." He cleared his throat and shut off the machine. "My allergies have been bugging me this spring."

She reached out and squeezed his arm. "Allergies are the worst."

"Yeah, the worst." He jerked his arm away and reached under the table for his briefcase. "I've got to get back to work."

She held out a blue binder. "I found this for you."

The History of Crescent Hill.

He took the binder and opened it to see the neat, typed pages held together with a three-ringed prong. Scanning the table of contents, he made a quick assessment of what would be on the following pages. The history, like the title said, appeared to be covered in-depth. The book included a breakdown of the home's interior. And—he blinked—information about a tunnel.

There was a tunnel on Crescent Hill?

He scanned the first page of the report and silently applauded Mrs. Dorothy Sherman for her detailed writing. Maybe her work would answer a few of his questions. Any house that had an entire manuscript devoted to it must have some gem of significance hidden inside.

His phone vibrated on his belt, and he glanced at the number. It was Louise, and he knew exactly why she was calling. He was late for the budget meeting.

He pushed the binder back toward Bethany. "I'll have to come back to look at this."

"Tell you what." Instead of reaching for the book, she smiled at him again. "I'm working again on Thursday. Why don't you bring it back then?"

His eyebrow rose. "You're allowed to give me a reference book?"

She stepped toward him, her voice low. "You'd be surprised at what I can do."

He stuck the binder under his arm and fled the building.

CHAPTER TWENTY-FIVE

Camden ripped the paper off her front door.

CONDEMNATION NOTICE. In bright red letters—just in case she missed it.

The town could have sent someone by the house to explain the issues with her home, but no, they had to paste her problems across the front door where any visitor could read it. As bright as it was, anyone passing by on the street could probably read it as well.

With her fingernails, she scraped away the tape they'd used to secure every inch of the paper to her door. Like they didn't want her to take it down.

She didn't need another problem right now. Liza was contesting the will. The limit on her credit card inched closer each day. And now the city was condemning the house. She'd expected Alex to stop by with the letter of intent to buy the house, but he'd called instead to say he was still working on it. Now she knew why. The town wouldn't purchase a house they were about to condemn.

She hadn't been looking for drama. Didn't want it. All she had wanted was to see her grandmother and find a quiet, safe place to rest while she figured out what to do next. Instead, just by showing up in Etherton, she'd gotten herself in the midst of a mess.

Part of her wanted to turn around and run someplace where she didn't have to fight for a house she needed to sell, but she didn't want to run back to New York and certainly not back to France, or Italy, or wherever her mother was at the moment.

She opened the door to a pile of papers that someone had stuffed through the mail slot. She picked up one sheet and scanned it. The town was giving her thirty days to comply with the town's code or they were taking the house from her. She ripped the paper and let the pieces scatter onto the floor.

Fix the roof. Replace the glass. Repair the crumbling chimney. The town might as well have asked her to fly to the moon in her Miata. She didn't have the money to do any of it. Even if she sold every piece of furniture and artwork in the house, she doubted she would have the money to comply with their demands.

With a swift kick, Camden sent the papers swirling, and then she plucked her phone out of her pocket, dialing town hall. What they were doing couldn't be legal. This was her property now. Her home.

"Alex Yates, please," she said as she marched toward the kitchen.

"This is Alex," he answered like a professional.

Had he been the one sneaking up Crescent Hill, tacking the notice on her door? If so, she would never trust him again.

"You said the town was interested in buying the place."

He paused. "Camden?"

"You said you were going to give me an offer."

"I'm still working out a few details."

She threw her jacket onto the kitchen table. "This notice says that if I don't make a bajillion repairs in the next thirty days, the city is taking the property."

"What notice?"

"The condemnation notice you plastered on my door."

"I didn't plaster anything . . ."

"Well, someone from your office did."

"I didn't know anything about it."

Her phone sandwiched between her shoulder and ear, she stomped toward the library.

"There is no way I can comply in a month."

"I'll get you an extension."

An extension. What would it buy her? Sixty days? Ninety? The town could give her an entire year, and it wouldn't make a bit of difference.

It would cost her hundreds of thousands of dollars to fix this place. Maybe a cool million. Not even someone like Jake Paxton would buy a property that was about to be condemned. If he and his fiancée didn't comply, the city would take it from them too.

Her eyes caught the spiral staircase, and she decided to go up to the balcony where she could sit and think. It was three in the afternoon. No one would bother her in the light.

"Are you still there?" Alex asked.

"I'm thinking."

"I can come over right now," Alex said. "We can talk about it."

"I don't know . . ." She circled up the spiral staircase. Her head popped over the edge of the balcony . . . and she gasped.

Before her was a girl, sixteen or seventeen, with dark brown eyes widened in terror. Her hair was covered by the hood of a brown sweatshirt, but nothing could cover the bulge in her belly.

Camden dropped the phone to her side. "Who are you?"

Instead of answering, the girl turned and ran away.

"Hey!" Camden yelled as she hustled up the remaining steps.

The girl's footsteps pounded across the balcony and Camden followed, hoping to catch her before she reached the next door.

The flash of brown disappeared at the end of the balcony, up the next staircase. Camden stopped running. She was too far behind to stop the girl, but she wouldn't leave the only exit to the third floor unguarded again. This time her intruder wouldn't get away.

"Is everything okay?" Alex asked, and she jumped at the sound of his muffled voice. She lifted the phone back up to her ear.

"She wouldn't stop . . ." Camden began, but her words were cut off by her struggle to fill her lungs. The short sprint, and the shock, had stolen her breath away.

"Is someone at your house?" he demanded.

A young woman was in her attic, and she didn't know why or how she got inside the house. She didn't look dangerous, but looks could be deceiving. Maybe others were staying here. Maybe the girl was part of a gang.

"Are you there, Camden?"

"I have to go."

Stephanie spread a map of Ohio across her kitchen table and scrutinized the names of towns across the state, names of roads. She'd already tried to find Crescent Hill online with no luck—she couldn't find a single mention of a city, street, or even a landmark with the name. Crescent Hill may have been a popular station on the Underground Railroad, but the record of it had been lost to history. No one even mentioned it on a blog.

The hill might have met the same demise as her family's plantation, with the exception of the kudzu. If there was a house left on Crescent Hill—and it hadn't been demolished—it was probably stripped bare. Too much time may have passed for her to resolve this mystery.

Ohio was filled with small towns, hundreds and hundreds of them. Which were the towns—and the houses—that once stashed slaves in their attics or cellars? And which ones protected William on his run north?

Stephanie wanted to get in the car and drive up to Ohio tonight. She could imagine the route William took as she cruised through North Carolina and West Virginia's mountains. Maybe she would cross paths with the trails he walked. The places he hid.

With her thumb, she smoothed a long wrinkle in the map. Maybe she would see some of the same places William saw, but a drive in her air-conditioned car would be much, much different than his trip. He probably hid in humid swamps, in damp caves. His feet would have been bleeding, and he would have been terrified.

Had he made it all the way to Canada or had he been stopped along the way? If he made it, had he become drunk on his newfound freedom and wealth, forgetting those who he left behind? Or did something bad happen to him before he could buy his family's freedom?

She sat down in a chair. A drive to Ohio wouldn't help her experience William's journey, not really, but a long drive might help her clear her mind. And who knows what she might find? She could leave after her classes tomorrow and ask her history professor to vouch for her skipping the rest of her classes this week. Once she was on the road, she'd call her parents, say she was going on a research trip. Her mother would worry, but she'd understand.

This search was becoming more than a school project . . . it was becoming personal. And maybe that's what Aunt Debra wanted. Stephanie didn't know why she was driving herself so hard to find out what happened to William, but she felt like she needed to, for her own sake and for Rachel's family. And not just to write about the mystery either, but to uncover the truth about what happened to Howard's great-grandfather.

With a red pen, she circled the area around Cleveland, and then she made another circle, a littler larger. Howard said Crescent Hill was a day's walk from this city though she had no idea how far a runaway slave could walk in a day. Ten miles? Twenty? She skimmed the map again for towns named Crescent Hill, but no luck. There were lots of nearby places with "Hill" in the name—Highland Hills, Sagamore Hills, Seven Hills. Just no Crescent Hill.

In her research, she'd discovered the Underground had no established route through Ohio. Instead, it had been a tangled web of stations that began along the shores of the Ohio River and zigzagged all the way up to Cleveland. Some of the stations existed for weeks or months. Others harbored slaves for years. Even though she had no way of following William's exact route, she would arm herself with maps and the pages she'd printed of known Underground Railroad stations that led to Canada. And she would get as close as she could to following his trail.

Even if Crescent Hill had been renamed, perhaps someone at one of the former Underground homes would have more information.

Her roommate strolled into the kitchen and tugged open the refrigerator door, retrieving a strawberry yogurt. Spooning a huge bite into her mouth, Tricia pointed down at the map. "Are ya going on a trip?"

"I'm going to Ohio."

She took another bite. "What's in Ohio?"

Stephanie paused, glancing down at the map again. "Answers."

CHAPTER TWENTY-SIX

Alex followed a white truck up the driveway of Crescent Hill. Giant letters blazed across the truck's side. LOCKED OUT? CALL VERN.

Camden had hung up on him, right when he was trying to find out if she was okay. He'd expected her to call the cops if someone really was in her house, but instead, here was Vern.

Vern hopped out of the white truck and walked with Alex to the porch.

The two men entered through the unlocked door, found the library, and climbed the steps to the balcony. Camden was sitting on the balcony, her back against a door. She jumped up to greet them.

"What's going on?" he demanded.

She eyed him, and then looked over at Vern. "Do you take credit cards?"

"Yes, ma'am."

"Good, because I need your help."

Vern glanced behind her. "This the locked door?"

"No. It's up these stairs." She hesitated. "And I think someone might be inside."

Alex cocked his head. Was she starting to believe the ghost stories?

"What did you see, Camden?" he asked.

"It was a girl. A very pregnant girl."

He looked at Vern; the man's ruddy face had paled.

Camden didn't seem to notice the man's apprehension. "The hood on her sweatshirt covered most of her face."

Alex reached for the phone on his belt. "We should call the police."

"No," she insisted. "I don't want them involved."

"But what if this girl's dangerous?"

"She's not," Camden said though her voice wavered.

Alex wrung his hands together. There was no way for her—or any of them—to know if the intruder would pose a threat or not. "I really think . . ." he started.

"You don't have to stay, Alex."

"It's not safe."

She caught his eye. "I didn't ask you to come."

No, she hadn't, but he knew he was supposed to be here. Whether it was the prompting of the Holy Spirit that drove him or the urgency of her voice—or, perhaps, a combination of the two—he was supposed to be here. She didn't ask him to come, but she also didn't tell him to leave. He'd stay until they found out who was haunting her house . . . or until she kicked him out.

Vern looked at the door again. "Maybe you ought to pre-pay."

"No problem," Camden said, handing him her credit card.

Vern took a clipboard out of his backpack and made an imprint of the card with a pencil before she signed the form.

"This is crazy," Alex muttered as he followed Vern up the narrow staircase. The locksmith was the only one who acknowledged his words, noted by the nervous look in his eyes.

Alex may not agree with what Camden was doing, but he certainly wasn't going to let her go upstairs alone with this man. If something went wrong, he suspected Vern would be the first to run, and Alex wouldn't leave Camden unprotected, not if someone really was hiding in her house.

Two years ago, his sister told him to leave her alone, and he had listened. If he had done what he should have, protected Angela when she was the most vulnerable, she would still be here today. He'd known he should have stayed with her, gotten her help, but he didn't. And he lost his sister as a result.

Camden could protest all she wanted, but he wasn't going to lose her as well.

❧

As Vern worked to open the door, Camden's heart thumped so loudly that both men could probably hear it echoing off the walls. She tried to stop the anxiety that clamored through her like an alarm, warning her to get away. It was the same alarm that shrieked whenever she was in a situation beyond her control.

Except this time there was no reason for her to run. It was only a girl behind this door . . . and all Camden wanted were answers.

But what if the girl hadn't hidden herself behind this door? She would be embarrassed, she supposed, and maybe a bit relieved that someone wasn't hiding here, but that didn't explain whom she'd seen running across the balcony, twice now. And how the girl was getting in and out of her home.

Alex asked again about calling the police, but she ignored him. The dispatcher would probably send Bryce Kelley, and she didn't want the sergeant to do another worthless search of her house. All she wanted was an end to this so she could sleep in the house again, by herself.

Vern finished unlocking the door and then stepped aside to give her the honor of opening it. She took a deep breath as Alex joined her side. Her hand went to the door, and the echo of footsteps behind her signaled Vern's abrupt departure from the scene. She was almost glad he didn't stick around to see who was on the other side.

Camden pushed the door open, and then her hand crept along the wall beside the door until she found a switch. Light illuminated the small storage room, and Alex gasped behind her.

In the corner of the room, a teenaged girl sat on a cot. Her long dark hair was greasy; her pale lips chapped. On the floor beside the cot was a Bible and the pregnancy book Camden saw earlier in the nightstand. Stacked neatly beside the cot were shirts and jeans.

The girl pulled a blanket over her stomach, her eyes wide. "Are you calling the cops?"

Camden stepped inside the room and then glanced at Alex behind her. His phone was in-hand, but he wasn't dialing.

She'd been so certain before, calling the locksmith, leading the charge up the steps. Now she didn't know what to do. "Should I call the cops?" she asked quietly.

The girl shook her head.

"Good." She pushed the door wide open. "You want to come out here and talk?"

The girl reached for her brown sweatshirt and pulled it over her head.

The three of them walked in silence out the door, down to the balcony along the library. As they climbed down the steps, she looked over at Alex, and he winked at her.

They sat in leather chairs in an alcove, but when the girl looked at Alex, the fear in her eyes was unmistakable. Alex must have realized it as well because he hopped back up.

He caught Camden's eye. "I'll look around a bit."

She nodded at him and focused back on the woman in front of her. This girl looked more like a wounded cat than one ready to bare her claws.

Was it illegal to harbor a runaway? She had no clue what was right or wrong in this situation. Or who to ask about it.

"What's your name?" she asked as Alex walked toward the next alcove.

The girl's eyes shifted toward the window beside Camden, and then she looked at the chair beside her. "Mariah," she whispered.

Camden took a deep breath. "Where is your family, Mariah?"

The scared look in the girl's eyes hardened. "Mansfield."

End of discussion. Another question about her family, and Camden felt certain she would be chasing her up the stairs again.

"Okay." She wove her fingers together and wrapped them over her knee. "How did you get in my house?"

The girl dug a necklace out of the front of her sweatshirt and held out the key that dangled from the chain. "Rosalie gave it to me."

Camden collapsed against the chair. "I don't understand."

"So I could get inside . . ." The girl fidgeted with her shirt's long sleeves. "Are you Camden?"

Camden hesitated before nodding. Mariah knew Rosalie, and she knew Camden's name, but Camden didn't have a clue who Mariah was.

Anyone could have read about her grandmother's death in the paper. Camden's name should have been in her obituary as a survivor, or at least, she thought they would have listed it. Information was only as good as the distributor.

Still, even if her name was listed in the obituary, it didn't explain the key. "How did you know my grandmother?"

The girl tugged on her sweatshirt, forcing the material to cover her swollen midriff. "Rosalie let me stay here."

"Okay . . ." Camden's voice trailed off, not sure of what to say next. Did anyone else know about this girl staying here? Liza, or even Jenny? She glanced at Alex. He was engrossed with whatever he was reading, or at least he pretended to be. "How old are you?"

"Twenty-two."

Mariah's nose twitched when she said it. An obvious lie, but Camden opted not to call her on it. Not right now. She couldn't be older than seventeen, but age was the least of their concerns. The truth would have to come later. "When are you due, Mariah?"

The girl's eyes sank to the floor. "I don't know."

She wasn't an expert on pregnancy, but looking at the girl's belly, she guessed that the date was three or four months away. "Why were you staying here?"

Instead of answering the question, Mariah grasped her belly with both of her hands and closed her eyes. Camden leaned toward her, hoping dearly that she wasn't going into labor. "Are you okay?"

Mariah didn't answer right away, but she slowly opened her eyes and turned up the sleeve on her right arm. On her pale skin was a labyrinth of faded bruises. "My boyfriend . . ." she started.

Anger surged inside Camden, at the bruises and the force behind them. "He hit you?"

Her eyes were on the bruises. "He wants me to end my pregnancy."

"Is it his child?"

The girl nodded, her eyes sad. "But he doesn't want me to keep the baby."

Camden's stomach rolled. What kind of man forced his girlfriend into having an abortion—eliminating one person and wounding the woman who was trying to protect the baby's life?

"So Rosalie took you in?"

Mariah looked toward the window, her face basking in the sunshine. "She did."

"How long have you been living in that storage room?"

"A couple of days, I guess."

"And before that?"

"I was in your room."

Camden pulled her legs to her chest and crossed them. "The afternoon I walked upstairs, a vase was shattered on the floor in one of the storage rooms."

Mariah's gaze fell to her toes. "I was trying to get back up to the locked room without you hearing me, but you came into the hallway. I hid in one of the other rooms, waiting for you to leave."

"But then I shouted."

Mariah nodded. "And I knocked over the vase by mistake."

Camden clutched her hands together around her legs. Had Mariah snuck into her room when she was asleep that first night as well? Stolen her bag? Her shoulders stiffened. Just because she knew about the vase, it didn't mean her intentions were good.

"I have another important question to ask you."

Mariah met her eye with strength, like she was ready to meet any challenge Camden might throw at her. "Go for it."

"The first night I was staying here, someone came into my bedroom and stole my handbag. I'd like to know who took it." The ensuing silence hung like a curtain between them. Mariah didn't speak and neither did she.

"You think I took it?" Mariah asked in a wary voice.

"I want to know the truth."

Mariah glanced down at her stomach again. "I . . . I took some food to eat, but he told me I could take anything I needed after Rosalie passed away."

"Who told you that you could take food?"

Mariah shook her head, refusing to supply a name. Was she talking about her boyfriend? No, that didn't seem right. The boyfriend wouldn't know she was here. Maybe she was trying to distract her from the missing handbag. Camden watched her face closely, wondering if she was lying again.

"Rosalie helped me," Mariah persisted. "I would never steal anything from her or from you."

Camden studied her face. She was pretty although dark shadows bowed under each of her eyes. In her travels, she'd seen a number of desperate people do desperate things, like steal when they were hungry. "How did you find Rosalie?"

Mariah stared at her bare feet. "I really can't say."

"Where is your boyfriend?"

Mariah shook her head. "I can't say that either."

She took a breath, willing herself to be calm. She would sniff out the truth eventually. "Does he know where you are?"

"No."

"Are you sure?"

"Absolutely."

For that, she was relieved.

She stood up and caught Alex's worried glance. In his hands was an open book, but he wasn't reading. For the moment, she was grateful she wasn't alone.

She turned back toward the alcove. "I don't know what to do now."

"But Rosalie said . . ."

Camden met her eye. "What did my grandmother say?"

Mariah bit the side of her lip. "She said you would take care of me."

CHAPTER TWENTY-SEVEN

Alex stuffed his hands into his pockets and paced along the porch of Community Bible Church as the night air pressed down on him. Automatic lights popped on one by one around the church's portico, casting sheaves of bright light into the darkness. Even with the darkness, he didn't try to go inside the building.

The colder it got, the clearer he could think, and he wanted to embrace his thoughts tonight. He used to try and erase his memories with a pack or two of beer, but he'd learned the hard way that even when he tried to dull the pain, it always returned. Often worse than before.

Someone had hurt the girl hiding in Camden's house, just like Trent Ellison had hurt his sister. He'd seen the questioning in Camden's eyes, the wondering if this girl had stolen things from her. It didn't matter if she stole food or even a purse. The important thing was that she was safe . . . and that she was asking for help.

He blinked and for a moment he saw his sister, lying on the floor of her kitchen. Angela's forehead was cut, her arms marked black and blue. She was coherent, but the light had vanished from her eyes, beaten out of them. It was like she didn't care anymore.

In the other room, his nephew was whimpering in his crib. No telling how long he'd been crying by himself. Alex made a bottle, took Ethan from his crib, and fed and rocked the child until he fell asleep.

Then he made the biggest mistake of his life. He picked up his phone, started to call the police, but Angela stopped him, saying if Trent's buddies on the force found out what was happening, he would kill her. Alex agreed not to call on the condition that she let him take her away that night, hours before Trent came home from work. He'd done his homework and found a safe house over in Atlanta where Angela and Ethan could hide until she decided what she would do next.

That same night, he was scheduled to attend a client meeting about branding, like the brand of the client's paper towels really mattered. The towels wiped up spills—the same as every other paper towel on the crowded grocery store shelves—but his client wanted an entire campaign to demonstrate that their company's paper towel was superior to the competition's. The client wasn't at all happy with the slogan Alex's team created to brand their product, and so they called for a powwow over dinner.

At the time, he thought the client meeting was critical—critical enough to leave his sister and nephew for an hour so he could appease the paper towel guys. The dinner stretched to two and a half hours before he excused himself, knowing he had to get back to Angela before Trent did.

Alex fell back against the church's wood siding, his heart racing.

When he came back to the apartment, it was too late. Trent had already been there, and he—

The door opened, and Shawn Lambert stuck out his head. "You've got to be freezing, Alex."

He looked over at the pastor who'd befriended him days after he moved to Etherton and introduced him to the Savior. "I'm not cold," he said, his chattering teeth contradicting him.

"Come in, my friend."

Alex chattered again. "In just a minute."

After Shawn went back inside, he tucked his hands under his arms to warm them.

With Angela's death came a burden he'd never anticipated. A year before she died, his sister purchased a large life insurance policy and named him the beneficiary so he could support her son in the event of her death. When Ethan was killed as well, he became the sole benefactor of her estate.

The inheritance was blood money, and he couldn't bear to spend it or see it spent on frivolous things, so before he moved to Etherton, he put the money into a savings account and left it there. His family was angry that he'd been the one to receive the insurance money. Her murder, and then the subsequent inheritance, tore his family apart.

When Alex stepped into the church lounge, Shawn shoved a mug of hot coffee into his hands and turned up the heating unit on the floor to high. The cold that laced his skin began to subside, and with it, the piercing memories. Still, he couldn't shake them entirely. The guilt, Shawn once told him, would wash away with the blood of Christ, but it was almost like the devil enjoyed taunting him with it. He'd made the worst decision of his life, and Angela suffered the consequences.

Alex told Shawn what happened on Crescent Hill, without revealing Mariah's name.

"You need to call the police," Shawn said.

"Camden doesn't want them involved."

"Have you met Bryce Kelley?"

Alex nodded. He'd met the man at church and played against him a few times at basketball. Every time he lost.

Shawn picked up his phone and began to search for the number. "Why don't you call Bryce directly? Just to see what he thinks about the situation."

"I can trust him?"

Shawn stopped dialing and looked over at him, confident in his words. "Absolutely."

"Camden won't be happy," he said, but even as the words came out of his mouth, he realized he didn't care if Camden was happy. He only cared that she and Mariah were safe.

~

The doorbell chimed through the house, and Camden rose to her feet. Mariah had locked herself in the bathroom over an hour ago—apparently it had been a week since she'd taken a shower. Camden tapped on the bathroom door, and Mariah cracked it open.

"Someone's here," Camden told her. "Can you stay in this room?"

"I won't leave the bathroom."

"You can come out here," she started, but Mariah already closed the door and locked it again.

Camden sighed as she walked out of the bedroom, toward the main stairs. Vern would probably get another call or two from her before this was all over—if he would come back to her house. She might have to try another locksmith next time, one who wasn't afraid of locked doors.

The doorbell chimed again.

"I'm coming," she yelled, though she doubted the person on the other side of the door could hear her.

So much had happened in the past four hours that her mind was still reeling from it all. Alex insisted that Mariah stay with her for the night. Camden wouldn't have kicked her out, even without Alex's pleas, but she might have called social services or somebody for help until she could sort everything out.

Even now, she was having doubts about letting her stay. Tomorrow they would figure out where Mariah would go next, far away from the boyfriend.

If her grandmother wanted her to care for this girl, surely she would have mentioned it in the letter. But now she could only speculate as to what her grandmother wanted her to do. Maybe this was why Rosalie left Crescent Hill to her. Maybe she expected her to care for Mariah.

But that still didn't make sense. Her grandmother must have known Camden could never afford to keep the house.

Camden crossed the entryway to the door, and this time when she peeked out the side window, she didn't see a stranger. She saw Bryce Kelley.

There was no way she would let that man back into her house. He'd yet to help her out, which was what a police officer was supposed to do—help and protect and enforce the laws of their land, which included stopping intruders from invading private homes. Bryce Kelley was a sham, and she should have spotted it the first time he came to her house.

She started to climb back up the stairs when her phone rang. Reaching down, she slipped it out of her pocket and looked at the number. Bryce Kelley was calling her.

She ignored the call. There was no law that said she had to open her door to him without a warrant—or at least, she didn't think there was one. The ringing stopped, and then, after she took a few more steps, it started again.

She could find out what he wanted, she supposed, without letting him through the front door.

"Hello?" she answered like she didn't have a clue who was on the line.

"It's Bryce Kelley," he said. "Could you please open your door?"

She hesitated.

"I saw you through the window, Camden. I know you're inside."

She stopped walking up the steps. "What do you need, Sergeant Kelley?"

"I need to talk to you about Mariah."

Her mouth dried up. Could Bryce be the boyfriend? She'd read about cops who beat their girlfriends, yet she'd seen a wedding band on Bryce's left hand. A ring didn't mean much today, she realized, but how else could Bryce know about Mariah?

Turning around, she glanced down at the door. "Who?"

He sighed. "The girl who's staying with you, Camden."

"How do you know—?"

"I was the one who brought her here."

"You brought her here?"

"So Rosalie could protect her."

His words crumbled the armor around her. If Bryce knew that Mariah was at her house . . . that would explain a few things, like why he seemed to resist searching for her intruder.

She slowly closed her telephone, and then she opened up the door.

Jake curled his fingers into a tight ball. "You can't buy Camden's junk. Not yet."

Edward didn't look the least bit phased by his outburst or his fist. "I can do whatever I darn well like."

"If you give her cash, she won't agree to sell the house to me."

Edward rolled his eyes. "I'm not going to give her that much cash."

"Wait a day or two," he told the old man. "Just until she gets back to me on my offer, so I can persuade her to let me look around."

"She's not going to sell the place, Jakey."

"Of course, she is."

"I think our little Bristow girl wants to keep the property for herself."

He squeezed his fist even tighter. "You don't know that."

"She may give up a few antiques, but not the house," he paused. "Not without some incentive."

"I'll give her incentive."

"No, you won't."

"You're not helping me!" Jake spat.

Edward flashed him a look of disdain. "Why am I supposed to help you?"

"We're supposed to work together to find this money."

The wrinkles around Edward's mouth turned into an eerie smile. "Who said anything about money?"

Jake stared at his grandfather. Was he going nutty? They were searching for some sort of stockpile. Cash or gold or something like it.

"I said 'treasure,' Jakey." Edward's voice turned to a whisper. "Not money."

Jake stumbled back into the wall and slammed his fist against it. "I've been looking for cash."

"You've been looking for hiding places."

He shook his head. "You're crazy."

Edward thumped his finger on the side of his head. "I'm the one playing it smart."

"I want to know exactly what I'm looking for."

Edward glanced back down at the *Reader's Digest* on the table. "When it's time, Jakey, you'll know, and you'll be glad you waited for it."

His fingers cramped, and Jake slowly uncurled his fist.

He wouldn't be happy until Edward Paxton was in the grave.

CHAPTER TWENTY-EIGHT

Alex took another sip of decaf coffee and flipped the binder open. The coffee shop was crowded for a Tuesday night, but the buzz of voices calmed his racing mind. It was good to have people around. Noise. He glanced out the window and watched a stream of headlights circling the town square.

Bryce said he needed to talk to Camden alone—and his pastor told him to trust Bryce—but everything inside him wanted to get in the car and dash up the hill. It was a curse and a blessing, wanting to protect the women in his life. Not that Camden was in his life. Or Mariah. But it was almost like God planted both of them in his path.

If he was supposed to help them, though, he wasn't sure exactly how to do it. All he could do right now was wait, and it was better to wait in a busy coffee shop, with something to read, than drive himself crazy in his apartment.

Sipping his coffee, he skimmed the first page of Crescent Hill's history and then turned to the next page. Before Joseph and Camden Bristow built their mansion, Dorothy Sherman wrote, the family lived in a much smaller house at 246 Pleasant Street. When their first son was born, Joseph Bristow purchased property near Pleasant Street that included most of the hill, trees, river access, and farmland.

Like the newspaper article said, the house had been completed in 1852, built in the popular Victorian style of an Italian villa. Six years after they moved into their new home, the Bristows lost their son Matthew, and the family crypt was built at the bottom of Crescent Hill to commemorate his life.

The writer took a break from the story of the Bristow family and began to describe the detailed construction of the house. Wide eaves. Bay windows. A cupola. Then she said the inside of the house was as grand as the outside with the ornate ceilings, carved fireplaces, and marble floors. On the next pages were black and white photos of each elaborately decorated room, and Alex examined each one. Years ago, the Bristows must have been quite wealthy, and he wondered for a moment what happened to their money.

It was a tragedy to tear down this beautiful home that Joseph and Camden Bristow built. It was too bad that someone in the family couldn't restore it.

Turning the page, he expected to find another picture, but instead there was a hand-drawn map with double lines that connected the Bristow Mansion with their first house on Pleasant Street. Mrs. Sherman talked about a legend of a secret passage built to connect the two houses, a tunnel to hide runaway slaves and help them escape from the slave hunters who searched for them.

Joseph Bristow never revealed the entrance to this tunnel, but rumor has it . . .

Alex turned quickly to the next page to see what rumor had, but the next page was about the elaborate parties held in the house after the Civil War. He glanced up at the page number, 32, and then turned back to the last page, 27.

He flipped through the remaining pages, but there was no 28, 29, 30, or 31. Four pages were missing from the book.

He leaned back against the booth. Had someone taken the pages out of the binder? It was odd that only the pages to the tunnel were missing.

Was the tunnel still there? If so, who was trying to keep the rumor about it under wraps?

"Come on." Camden waved Bryce Kelley toward the kitchen, and they sat around the kitchen table, just like they'd done when he was here to investigate the shadows she'd seen on the balcony. He'd known it wasn't the wind that had broken the glass, and he knew exactly who was living in her attic.

"Why did you bring Mariah here . . ." her words trailed off as she tried to make sense of what had happened.

He brushed his hands over his uniform pants. "Because I knew she would be safe."

"Safe," she repeated the word slowly. "Aren't there shelters around here for battered women?"

"Not in Etherton," he said. "There are shelters in Columbus and several over in Mansfield, but when they're full, I need to take women to a temporary place."

"So you brought them to Rosalie."

He nodded.

"How many women?"

He glanced down, his lips murmuring like he was praying. A minute passed and then two as she waited for him to speak again. "I've brought about two hundred women and children to Rosalie, from across the county. She never turned away anyone in need."

The thought emerged slowly, sending a chill through her skin. "Two hundred people?"

"Approximately."

"And now my grandmother wants me to take over . . ."

He shook his head. "She would never want you to be a part of this unless God puts the desire in your heart."

"Even when my grandmother was so sick, you brought Mariah here."

"Mariah needed a safe place to sleep, and I knew she would find it here. Rosalie would have been furious with me if I'd left her on the streets."

"Who else knows Mariah is here?"

"The last caregiver knew someone was staying with Rosalie, but not the details. Your grandmother had been helping women for a long time."

She leaned forward, craving information. "How long?"

Bryce settled back in his chair. "In 1998 a friend came to Rosalie and asked if she could care for her daughter and granddaughter until she could get her relocated to another city. The daughter's boyfriend was abusive, and the friend was afraid for her life."

"Rosalie took her in?"

"She did, and after she helped the girl move away from Etherton, she cornered me at church one Sunday and said she'd be willing to help other women and kids who needed a safe haven. I secretly began bringing people to her until we could relocate them."

"Surely some of the women told their abusers about Crescent Hill."

"Rosalie knew using her home for a shelter was dangerous work, yet she chose to do it," he said. "As far as I know—by God's grace—it's still a secret."

"The abusers could have hurt you too."

Bryce placed both of his large hands on the table. "I have three daughters, Camden, and if one of them were being hurt, I would want someone to help them."

Camden's gaze traveled over the white sink and the cracked countertops. Many years ago people escaped to this house in their run toward freedom from slavery. Now Bryce was telling her that her grandma used the house to help women and their children escape today, this time for freedom from husbands or boyfriends or fathers who were hurting them. It was almost like the house had been built to be a safe house.

"Why didn't you tell me about Mariah when I first came to town?"

He twisted his hands on the tabletop. "I didn't know if I could trust you."

"So you let her trespass."

"I would have taken her away if I could."

She massaged the knot at the bottom of her neck. "And now you trust me?"

He looked away. "I don't have a choice."

At least he was finally being honest.

"You're willing to sacrifice your career over this?"

He paused. "I am."

"You're a good man, Bryce Kelley."

He shook his head slightly, standing up. "Can she stay with you for now? Just until I can get her into the shelter in Columbus . . ."

She squeezed her eyes closed. She wanted to be able to help women like Mariah yet she wasn't sure if Mariah could be trusted. What if she stole from her? Or brought her boyfriend with her? Or something else?

"She can stay tonight."

"And after that?"

She rubbed her neck again. "I don't know."

Another cop car sat outside the house on the hill. It was like Camden had made best friends with the entire force and kept inviting them over for beers or something. Or maybe one of them had the hots for her and kept stopping by to check up.

Or perhaps someone else had broken into her house.

Jake twisted his hands, the thought gnawing at him. His grandfather couldn't be the only one who knew about this treasure—whatever the treasure was. Maybe someone else had gone inside looking for it too. He hadn't been in the house since last week so they weren't looking for him unless they'd found some sort of clue that might lead back to him.

Had he left a glove in the house? Torn his jacket? It wasn't like they would be combing the floor for a piece of hair or skin or something. No one had been murdered or even hurt. Still, there'd been an awful lot of interest from the cops since he'd first gone inside.

He backed away from the trees and followed the well-worn path back down the hill. Edward was no place to be found on the first floor of their house; he was probably up in his room putting together an appraisal list for Camden's stuff. The man said he wanted whatever it was that was in Camden's house, yet he wasn't helping a bit with Jake's plan to move ahead with an offer on the house.

He settled into his chair to play Warcraft when he looked over at a pile of stuff beside the couch. On top of it was Camden's purse, the red straps as bright as licorice. He reached over and picked it up. Not that any cop was going to search his house, but it was stupid to keep something like this around. He started to walk toward the back door to toss it in the garbage can.

Then he stopped.

It might be fun to play a little trick on Camden, make her doubt that someone had been in her house. Make her think she was going crazy.

He smiled as he opened the door to the closet. Ducking down under the low ceiling, he reached for the metal loop on the carpet and pulled up the door.

Tonight he'd visit her house again, but he wouldn't search for treasure. Tonight he'd mess with her mind.

CHAPTER TWENTY-NINE

Wipers smeared rain across Alex's windshield in a steady rhythm that almost soothed him to sleep. He grabbed the metal coffee mug in the holder and took a long swig as he drove down Pleasant Street. Maybe he should have spent the night in his car, with his wipers on, instead of going back to his apartment. The rhythmic noise would have put him to sleep before four o'clock. His mind had raced for much of the night.

Memories of his sister flooded his mind, and then he thought about Camden and Mariah, wondering if they were safe for the night. When he still couldn't sleep, he wondered why no one had mentioned to him the legend about the tunnel under Crescent Hill.

Maybe Louise didn't think the legend was important to the acquisition. Or perhaps the rumor had been proven false a long time ago. Even so, the feeling gnawed at him. What if someone didn't want him to know?

In the dim morning light, Alex drove up and down Pleasant Street, but the 249 address mentioned in the binder didn't exist. In the three-block span near Crescent Hill, the numbers started at 554 and went up to 672.

He sighed as he turned the car around. Even if he found the house, it was hard to imagine that someone could have built such a long tunnel between houses back in the mid 1800s. Though it didn't seem possible, he'd read about the legendary tunnels in Europe—secret passages linking castles and churches and houses hundreds of years before the Bristow tunnel would have been built. Perhaps the Bristows had replicated a ley tunnel in the States. Perhaps . . .

If Joseph Bristow had traveled to Europe, he'd probably heard of the ley tunnels, but how could the Bristows have built that extensive of a tunnel without the town knowing about it?

Or was he the only one in Etherton who hadn't heard of the tunnel?

Alex turned and drove down the street one last time, but all the numbers were in the five and six hundreds. The two hundreds didn't even exist. He wondered if the author of Crescent Hill's history was writing fact or if she sprinkled a little fiction in with her research. And then he wondered if Dorothy Sherman were still alive.

The library didn't open for a couple hours but he gambled and dialed the phone number to see if someone was there early. A man answered, and Alex explained that he was trying to locate the woman who had researched the Bristow family in the 1960s. The man paused, asking why he needed that information.

Alex told him his name, that he worked for the town, and after a few seconds of small talk, the librarian explained that Dorothy Sherman was still very much alive, living at Beaverdale, the assisted living facility on the edge of Etherton.

As he thanked the librarian, Alex swung the car around to head east, toward the other side of town. He'd seen the Beaverdale sign from the street, but he'd never actually been on the property. If he could find Dorothy Sherman, maybe she would be interested in talking to him about the Bristow mansion.

Trees blocked the view of the facility from the main road, but after driving through the forest for a couple minutes, Alex parked near a rambling set of buildings woven into the green. A fountain marked the entrance, and he stepped into the lobby through sliding glass doors.

When the receptionist asked if Mrs. Sherman was expecting his visit, he explained that he had read something she'd written and wanted to ask a few questions.

It took another ten minutes for Mrs. Sherman to approve his visit, and the receptionist pointed him to a side door and told him to keep walking past the cafeteria until he reached a lobby; Mrs. Sherman would be waiting for him.

Before he turned down the corridor, Alex silently prayed that this woman would be willing to talk to him about the Bristow family. He wanted to find out the whole story of Crescent Hill, not just the few bits and pieces fed to him by people like Louise and Camden.

He found her in a small lobby, sitting in a wheelchair. Her thin wisps of hair had been curled and sprayed, and she wore a peach-colored suit with pearl buttons. Patches on her ivory-toned face were mottled with black and blue yet even with the bent of her shoulders, it was clear that she had been a member of the politer society.

He extended his hand. "Mrs. Sherman?"

She sat up in her wheelchair, the wrinkles around her eyes crinkling as she inspected him. "My friends call me Dotty." She leaned toward him. "But I'm not sure if you're a friend."

He chuckled, but she didn't laugh with him. Her eyes were focused on his face, studying him.

"I'm certainly not an enemy," he said as he sat down on a stiff-backed chair beside her and introduced himself.

"Are you Lucy Maddock's boy?"

"No, ma'am. My name is Alex Yates."

"Well, you look just like Lucy." She inched even closer to him. "I know just about everyone in Etherton, but I never laid eyes on you."

"I'm new in town."

"And you decided to come visit an old lady in a retirement home?"

"I read a paper you wrote and wondered if you would be willing to answer a few questions about it."

She cocked her head. "I've only written one paper worth anything."

"*The History of Crescent Hill*?"

She paused, her gaze falling to the worn hands in her lap. "It's my little contribution to Etherton's past."

"Did you spend a lot of time on Crescent Hill?"

A smile edged up her face. "They used to have the grandest parties on the hill when I was a child."

He leaned back in his chair. Even though he wanted to start by asking her about the missing pages, he suspected Dotty Sherman moved at her own pace. "What were the parties like?"

"They were glorious." She closed her eyes for a moment and then reopened them. "The adults would dance in the theater upstairs under the most beautiful sparkling lights. Sometimes I would dance, but often I would wander around the house and explore the wonderful corners. One time, Philip Bristow found me sneaking into the library, and he gave me a grand tour."

"Who was Philip Bristow?"

She paused. "Where did you say you were from?"

"South Carolina."

"Oh . . ."

He struggled to regain her trust. "But Etherton is my home now."

"I was born in Etherton," she began and then started talking again, like she'd decided to trust him in spite of his unfortunate birthplace. "I used to write articles for the local paper about the town's history. Silly little snippets, really, but the people around here liked them.

"I wrote a couple articles on Crescent Hill, and then my friend called from the library and asked if I could do a full history on the place for their archives. I got excited, called Philip, and he agreed to let me take pictures."

"The detail in your writing is impeccable."

"Flattery will get you nowhere, Mr. Yates." Her wrinkled cheeks turned into a grin. "But it doesn't mean it's not appreciated."

He couldn't help but smile back. Dotty Sherman must have charmed a few men in her day. He imagined she got pretty much what she wanted when she was young, and probably still did.

"You wrote about a tunnel under the house."

"Pish, posh," she replied with a wave of her hand. "It's just an old rumor."

Alex watched her carefully. "But you think there's a tunnel."

"I've never seen it."

"But you've heard about it."

She shrugged, and he realized he wasn't going to get any more information with direct questions.

"You talked about a house on Pleasant Street," he said.

"I vaguely remember . . ."

He'd bet good money that she had a stellar memory. "So I went to find the house that connected to Crescent Hill, but there was no 249."

"Of course not," she started, but as her gaze traveled over his shoulder, she whispered. "Hush . . ."

Someone approached his side, and when he turned, he saw Edward Paxton beside him. The man's navy vest hung like a loose blanket over his chest, and in his left hand, he clutched the crook of his cane.

"Hello, Edward." The politeness in her voice soured. "I was just speaking to a friend of my granddaughter's. Alex, this is my cousin, Edward."

Edward ignored the introduction and turned his hard eyes on Alex. "Alex Yates. How do you know Natalie?"

"Old friends."

"So you met her at Ohio University?"

He almost started to nod when Dotty reached for his arm. "Edward, you know good and well that Natalie went to OSU."

"Just trying to keep my facts straight." Edward glanced at him. "Why don't you join us for breakfast?"

"I wish I could, but I've got to get to work." He stood up and winked at her. "It's a pleasure to see you, Dotty."

She smiled at him. "Please come back again soon."

He reached down and shook her frail hand. "I definitely will."

The wind startled Camden awake, rattling her windows. Then her phone rang. Swiping it off the bedside table, she stared at the screen until the number came into focus. A New York area code.

She scooted herself up in bed and answered the call with as much professionalism as she could muster.

"Hey, Camden, it's Grant Haussen."

She couldn't stop the gasp that escaped her lips.

"I know. I know. It's been a long time. After the fiasco over at *Fount*, I haven't been up to talking to anyone."

"Sorry to hear about the magazine," she said, though all she wanted to do was ask him what happened to the money they were supposed to pay her.

"Did I wake you?"

She looked over at the clock as the numbers rolled past 9:30. "I was just getting started for the day."

"Good. Good. I waited as long as I could but I was positively busting at the seams to talk to you. Couldn't wait a moment longer."

She couldn't wait a moment longer either. "When are you going to pay me for the Indonesia gig?"

"Oh, that," he said, his voice resigned. "I wish I could pay you, Camden, but that money is long gone. Not that it helps, but those jerks never gave me my last paycheck either."

"It doesn't really help," she muttered, reminding herself that Grant had gone to bat for her numerous times at the magazine.

"I've got something that should put a smile on that pretty face of yours."

"I need a good smile."

"I've got a freelance thing going over at another magazine for the month, and we're doing a four-page spread next issue on the wildfires in California."

Wildfires? She hadn't even checked the news in a week.

"They want the best photography for this story," he said. "I told them I knew just who to call."

A photography assignment? She was ready to get back to work. "When do you need me to go?"

"Yesterday," he said. "But I could settle for this afternoon."

She glanced out the rain-soaked window at the foot of the bed, the branches outside batting the wind. How could she leave today? She needed to deal with the town. Talk to Dan about the will. Take care of Mariah.

Her life was suddenly full of commitments.

"So, can you go to Cali for me?"

She slid out of bed and walked toward the rain-streaked window. "I don't know, Grant."

He paused, probably shocked. She'd never turned him down before. "If it's a money thing, I'll have my assistant line up everything for you," he said. "Airfare. Hotel. Car. They'll bill the magazine so you don't have to spend a cent out-of-pocket."

Then he told her how much they'd pay her for her jaunt west, and she almost gasped again. It would give her enough to hire Dan Sprague and chop a nice chunk off the top of her credit card.

"How long do you need me?"

"Three or four days. Maybe longer if the fires keep burning."

She turned away from the window. "Can I get back to you on this?"

Silence met her answer, and she started pacing the floor. Never before had she asked for extra time with Grant's requests, but she figured an hour or two was a reasonable amount of time to return his call, especially since it had taken him two months to return hers.

"I need to hear back in an hour, Cam, or I've got to hire someone else."

She paced as Grant awaited her reply.

Maybe she should just tell him yes right now. No one was stopping her from jumping on a plane and flying to California. Etherton could have the property. Bryce could take Mariah to another safe house. With Grant's new gig, she might have more opportunities to work. This afternoon, she could go to California and then back to New York to resume her life. No strings attached.

She reached the far wall and turned back toward her bed. Then she stopped. Blinked. The red handle of a handbag stuck out from under the bed frame. She reached down and pulled out the handbag. Her bag.

She opened up the bag, but everything inside was gone.

"Do you need more time?" Grant asked.

"Give me two hours," she said as she unlocked her bedroom door.

CHAPTER THIRTY

"Where's the letter?" Camden demanded, waving the empty handbag in front of Mariah's face.

She was trying to calm herself, but anger and frustration boiled to the surface. Even though she'd tried to trust this girl, given her a chance, Mariah had stolen from her. How could she trust her if she wouldn't tell her the truth?

She repeated the question, but Mariah didn't say anything.

"I don't care if you took it," Camden said, trying to steady her voice. "I just want my letter back."

"I don't know what you're talking about." Mariah's lower lip quivered, probably angry that she'd been caught.

She never received justice for her stolen things in Indonesia, but Mariah was right here, as a guest in her home, and Mariah owed her an answer.

Camden tossed the bag onto the bed where Mariah had spent the night. "I don't need the other stuff in my purse, but I would really like the letter my grandma left for me."

Mariah backed toward the doorway. "I didn't take it."

Camden sighed, collapsing onto the messy bed. She wanted to believe her, but she didn't. No one else had been in the house the night the handbag disappeared except her and Mariah . . . and Mariah had been hiding upstairs.

She'd probably been looking for money in Camden's room, and Camden couldn't blame her. Still, the letter wasn't worth anything to her. All Mariah needed to do was tell the truth and give back the letter. Then they could figure out what to do next.

"Please, Mariah," she begged. "I'm not going to kick you out of the house. I just want my letter back."

A tear slid down the side of the girl's face, but she didn't offer up the letter. Or even confess to what she had done.

Camden stood and opened a dresser drawer beside the bed, frustration rattling inside her like the wind against the windows.

How did Bryce know Mariah was really who she said she was? How was Camden supposed to know the truth? The tears might be a front. An act. She'd seen it plenty of times around the world. The threadbare "orphan" begging for money for his parents. The girl who faked being pregnant so she could be first in line to eat. In their desperation, people pretended to be something they weren't.

Rosalie was an elderly woman with a houseful of valuable books and antiques—a mother lode for a crook. Mariah wouldn't even have to know the house was used to help battered women. She could just have been playing on Rosalie's sympathies before she robbed her.

Camden turned back to her, her gaze traveling down to the sweatshirt sleeves that covered Mariah's arms. The bruises seemed real, but she could have hurt herself another way, not necessarily from a boyfriend who hit her.

Maybe her name wasn't even Mariah.

She opened the next drawer and rummaged through the shirts and underwear.

"What are you doing?" Mariah's voice sounded small.

"Looking for my letter."

"I swear, I don't know where it is."

Camden turned. "I really want to believe you, Mariah, but that doesn't explain who stole the stuff out of my handbag and then hid it under my bed."

"It wasn't me."

She shook her head. "I don't believe you."

Mariah opened her mouth again, and then she clenched it shut. Turning on her heels, she bolted for the door.

The tab on the beer can broke off in his hands, and Jake swore. He was thirsty and wanted a drink. Now. Grabbing a fork out of the sink, he stabbed the top of the can with the handle. Fizz squirted out, soaking his face and hands.

He swore again, mopping up his face with a towel. Anxiety wouldn't get the best of him. He would be calm. Settled. And he would move ahead with his new plan.

There was no treasure. He'd realized it as he was stumbling back through the tunnel a few hours ago. Edward had some sort of ulterior motive for getting into the house though Jake had yet to figure out what it was.

It didn't matter. As he picked the lock on Camden's room last night, another idea began to form in his mind. He'd pretend to continue chasing Edward's imaginary treasure, but he was really flying solo now.

He checked his pockets one more time. Both books were still there. Books that would probably bring a couple hundred bucks online.

And these books were only the beginning.

His hands shook as he rinsed out the towel. Then he began sopping up the liquid on the floor.

He could do this on his own. No problemo. As long as he only took a few things from the house at a time, the possibilities were limitless. He could make enough money to get his own place. No more living with Edward. When he found Mariah, they would move someplace far from here, buy a place of their own. A place where the cops wouldn't find him if Edward decided to turn him in.

The front door opened, and he heard his grandfather limp into the house.

Edward didn't bother with pleasantries. "What are you doing?"

Jake kept wiping up the mess. "Getting a beer."

"Looks like you're taking a shower."

Jake spun around. "What do you want?"

"I want to know where you went last night."

He slammed the can on the counter. "Since when do I have to answer to you?"

"Your truck was in the driveway so I know you didn't drive."

"Maybe I walked."

"The door to the closet was open."

"So . . ."

"Don't mess with me, Jakey. I know you went back in the house."

"Who cares if I did?"

"The treasure is mine to find, not yours." Edward aimed his cane at him. "You don't go into that house without telling me why."

Jake didn't bother to acknowledge the cane pointing toward his face. With one heave over his knee, he could snap it in two. "I wasn't going into the house to search for your stupid treasure."

Edward lowered the cane a few inches. "It's not stupid."

"You don't have a single bit of proof that there's even a treasure."

"I do have proof."

His eyebrow shot up. "I don't believe it."

"I do, but I'm not going to show it to you." Edward's eyes narrowed again. "What did you find last night?"

"Absolutely nothing." Jake knocked the cane away and leaned toward Edward. "But I found something very interesting when I was in the house last week."

The cane shook. "You've been hiding more stuff from me?"

"You bet I have." Jake laughed. "Same as you're hiding stuff from me."

"I'm hiding it for your own good."

"And I'm hiding what I found for my own good too."

Red washed over Edward's face. "What did you find?"

"A letter," Jake said, relishing the old man's angst. He liked being the holder of the secrets. "From Rosalie Bristow."

"What did she say?"

"All sorts of things. Call me crazy, but I thought the most interesting part was about the birth of her son."

"What did she say?" Edward demanded again.

"Seems like she was trying to clear her mind. Get some stuff off her chest. It was a real sweet letter, her wanting her granddaughter to know the truth."

A light tap on the door behind them stopped the conversation. It sounded more like a scratch than a knock.

Edward nodded at him, and Jake opened the curtain at the top to look out. Rage and relief shot through him, both vying for control. After all this waiting, Mariah had finally come home.

He reached for the handle, and then waited a beat. God knew, he wanted her back, but he couldn't let her know. For the past five months, she'd taken him for granted, and she must learn to appreciate what she had.

He opened the door slowly, staring at the wet hair that stuck to her head and face. Her clothes were drenched, her face gaunt, and her belly bulged like the gut of a pig, even bigger than when she ran away three weeks ago. It would be easy to get rid of the gut, but hopefully, she could clean up her face too.

He held out one of his hands to direct her inside, but she cowered back.

Edward laughed, and Jake almost struck her across the face to remind her that she was his, but Edward didn't like him to be physical with her. People could see bruises, Edward told him, especially on the face. They would ask questions, and Edward hated questions. He preferred much more subtle methods of coercion.

Even so, Mariah would tell him later where she'd been.

After all he'd given her, he had asked for one simple thing. Just one. Abortion was an easy procedure—done in an hour. Thousands of women did it every day, and she had refused him. And then she'd run.

It wasn't like she could care for a baby, and he wasn't about to raise her kid. This pregnancy was messing with her mind—that, and the fact that she started going to church a month or so ago. Those church people were probably messing with her mind too, making her think she would be a murderer or something by doing the right thing. None of them cared a bit about her well-being.

Let them judge all they wanted. He knew what was best for both of them.

He put his hand on her stomach. "We'll get this taken care of right away, and then we'll start over."

Her eyes narrowed. "I'm not getting an abortion."

He shoved her away. "Yes, you are."

"Whoa," Edward said, nudging Jake with his cane. "Where have you been, Mariah?"

She shrugged. "Wandering."

"Wandering, where?"

Before she responded, the front doorbell rang, and Jake glanced into the living room. He couldn't see who was at the door, but he could see the cop car parked outside the front window. Had she gotten herself into trouble?

He smiled. If she was in trouble, she'd come to the right place. He would help her, and then she could pay him back.

He escorted her through the living room, into the study's closet, before he opened the door to Bryce Kelley.

"What's wrong?" he asked, glancing up and down the street.

Bryce didn't mince his words. "Is she here?"

"Who are you talking about?"

The sergeant stared at him, hard, and he had to stifle the urge to laugh at the man.

"Did Mariah come back here?"

"I've been looking all over for her," Jake said, his tone bathed in concern. "Do you know where she is?"

Bryce's voice rose, like he knew Mariah was here. "There's been a misunderstanding."

Jake closed the door and stepped outside with him. "What kind of misunderstanding?"

"I want to know if you've seen her."

He shook his head. "Not for weeks."

"If you hurt her—"

He stepped back. "I would never hurt her."

"Some people in this town might be scared of you and your family, Jake, but you don't intimidate me."

A smile slid up his lips. "Then maybe you aren't as smart as you seem."

Jake stood on the porch and waved as Bryce drove away. Mariah came back on her own—the police could do nothing even if they did find her in his house.

Still, it was none of Bryce Kelley's business if Mariah was here. She was his girlfriend, after all.

CHAPTER THIRTY-ONE

The cushions along the cupola's window seats were soaked with rainwater, but the clouds had started to dissipate and warm light poured over the dampness. The light was what Camden always loved about the cupola when she was younger. Sitting here with her easel, she used to fill page after page with light and color.

Life had seemed so simple back then. The choices so much easier.

Tree limbs bounced outside the window, and the breeze whipped through the broken glass. She rubbed the chill out of her arms.

She'd searched everywhere for Mariah, but the girl was gone. The front door was unlocked, and she assumed Mariah had fled outside, into the rain. She'd looked in the garage, but Mariah wasn't there.

When she called Bryce, trying to explain why Mariah ran away, Bryce promised that he would search for her. She told him that she found the missing handbag under her bed. He doubted Mariah took it, and she understood—she didn't want to believe Mariah stole her purse or the letter either. Yet there was no other explanation. Things didn't disappear on their own.

Trust was a fragile thing. Even her grandma recognized the importance of trust, and she'd guarded it. Only Bryce knew the secret of her house, along with the women who stayed with Rosalie over the years.

Would her grandma have trusted Mariah? Even if she was certain Mariah had stolen from her? Rosalie's loving arms encompassed almost anyone in need, yet she had a keen sense of what was right and what was wrong. What Mariah did was clearly wrong.

Camden squirmed where she was standing. What would she do if she didn't have a penny left on her credit cards or anywhere to stay? If she were really honest with herself . . . she might steal something too.

She looked out the window as a shock of blue emerged from behind the clouds.

She could understand the stealing, but what she didn't understand was the lying, especially when Camden gave her the opportunity to tell the truth.

How was she supposed to balance the truth with compassion? How could she love Mariah while keeping her accountable for lying? She didn't want to enable her bad choices, but she also didn't want to send someone back to an abuser if they really wanted to change.

What would Rosalie have done?

In an instant, she knew exactly what her grandma would have done. Not about Mariah, necessarily, but in any situation, Rosalie would ask God for wisdom.

Camden bowed her head and prayed quietly. *Please help me know what to do about Mariah and the photo assignment and this house.*

She wasn't Grandma Rosalie, and she never would be. Yet this was her time to decide if she was going to forgive and protect this girl like her grandma would have done. She'd never risked her life for anyone before. She'd been in plenty of frightening situations, but she'd never thrown herself into a situation to protect someone else.

Maybe it was time for her to stop taking pictures of hurting people for a season and start helping them instead.

The words from her grandmother's letter came back to her. "Protect them. Love them. Fight for them. And give them back to God."

She opened her phone and called Bryce's number again. "Please bring Mariah back here," she said.

He hesitated. "I couldn't find her, Camden."

"But her boyfriend . . ."

"I paid him a visit, but he said he hasn't seen her."

Camden sighed. "She wouldn't tell me her boyfriend's name."

"You don't want to know."

She did want to know, but perhaps she was safer without that knowledge. "Is the boyfriend lying?"

"Probably."

"Can't you lock him away or something until he tells you the truth?"

"Not if she doesn't press charges."

She squeezed her eyes shut. "So all we can do is wait . . ."

"I'll keep looking for her."

~

The Wednesday morning staff meeting was supposed to start three minutes ago, but they were still waiting for the arrival of the mayor. As Alex sat down at the conference table, he greeted the eight other employees who made Etherton run.

"I heard the Truman farm proposal was tossed out," one of the women whispered to him.

"They didn't even consider it."

"Too bad," she said as she tapped the keys on her BlackBerry. "We needed the revenue."

"I know . . ." he muttered. He'd failed her and everyone else in this room. If the Crescent Hill deal didn't come through, most of the staff would be looking for a new job soon.

Opening his laptop, he set it on the table and listened to the chatter around him about where they would pull money to meet payroll next week. Instead of adding to the worry, he took Dotty Sherman's binder out of his briefcase and began to skim through it one more time. He could almost see this woman as a child, marveling as she explored the many rooms in the mansion. Her imagination running wild.

"*Guten Morgen*," Louise spouted as she breezed into the room and rounded the table toward him. She plucked the binder out of his hands. "What is this you have, Alex?"

His stomach sank. He shouldn't have brought Dotty's info to the meeting. "It's the history of Crescent Hill."

"Really?" Louise flipped through the pages. "Suddenly you're fascinated with history."

"I've always been fascinated with history," he said. "But this is homework."

She sat down beside him, scanning the photographs, and he felt all the eyes at the table on Louise and him. "And what have you learned about Crescent Hill?"

"The report is mainly about the Bristow family." He stopped and decided to take a gamble. "But there's a whole section about a tunnel under the house."

Her shoulders jerked back ever so slightly. "A tunnel. Really?"

"Someone removed all the pages about the tunnel, but I figured you would know about it."

She slammed the book shut. "No one has ever found a tunnel."

"But if they did—"

"People talk about a tunnel the same way they talk about a ghost haunting the third floor." She smoothed her fingers over her necklace. "Do you believe in ghosts?"

"Of course not."

She pushed the binder toward him and stood up. "There's no tunnel under Crescent Hill, but you can go check for yourself when we acquire the property."

"Camden is going to fight the town on this."

"She can fight all she wants, but until the house is fixed, there's nothing she can do."

"And if she decides to fix up the property?"

Louise glanced around at her staff. "Then we'll celebrate the restoration of one of the town's finest homes."

Alex's stomach churned at her lie. The mayor could pretend all she wanted that she would celebrate if Camden complied with the town's requests to fix the house, but he knew the truth.

Louise took her place at the front of the room and whipped a four-color postcard out of a folder. She held it up so everyone could see her smiling face above her new slogan, "Preserving our Past. Fighting for our Future."

"What do you all think?"

"It's catchy," Becky said, but her voice was strained. She probably wondered, like Alex did, where Louise was getting the money to mail out five thousand postcards along with the billboards that were springing up around town. The mayor was good at raising cash when she needed it, but few people in Etherton had the money right now to dump into a campaign. They all knew Louise cared about the preservation and future of their town, but the question appearing in the editorials was if she should continue leading it.

As Louise moved from the direct mail pieces to the budget, Alex's phone vibrated on his hip. He picked it up and read the text from Camden.

M. missing

He stuck his phone back into the holder, tapping his fingers on the desk.

"We need to hire four more policemen," Becky said.

Louise pointed to a report in her hands. "We don't have the money."

"If there was a major incident . . ."

"This is Etherton," Louise said with a slight roll of her eyes. "We need cops to babysit the middle schoolers and write tickets for the older kids who cruise Main on Friday nights."

Alex tried to listen to the discussion about the police force, but he couldn't concentrate.

His phone vibrated again.

Help, please

Alex closed his laptop and put it back in his case. "I'm sorry," he said as he pushed back his chair. "It's an emergency."

"I didn't mean to scare her off," Camden tried to explain as she and Alex hiked down the back side of Crescent Hill, searching the trees for Mariah. He was obviously ticked at her for accusing Mariah of stealing the letter.

"Why did you have to blame her for it?"

"Because she did it!"

"Seriously, Camden." He stopped walking and turned toward her, his eyes searching her face. "Why would she want your grandmother's letter?"

She looked away from his gaze. "I don't think she wanted the letter. I think she was looking for money."

Alex shouted Mariah's name into the trees as they continued walking, searching. "What makes you so sure she wanted cash?"

"It just makes sense."

"It doesn't make sense to me," he said. "And if she did take it, why wouldn't she have put the letter back in your room along with your purse?"

"I don't know." She shrugged. "Maybe she felt bad."

"Or she never took it."

"But there was no one else in the house!"

"Things aren't always as they seem, Camden."

She squinted into the forest. If Bryce couldn't find Mariah, then they probably wouldn't be able to either. It wasn't like the girl would run out into the trees and wait for them to find her. She was probably long gone by now. At the boyfriend's house, like Bryce suspected, or back with her family in Mansfield.

She checked her watch. She'd told Grant she would call him back in two hours, and her time was up fifteen minutes from now. He wouldn't wait another moment to call a different freelancer, and he may never call her again if she turned down this gig.

"Someplace you need to be?"

She lifted her eyes, meeting Alex's gaze.

"I'm supposed to leave for California this afternoon."

He stopped walking. "Vacation?"

"No . . . it's for work."

"You can't leave until we find Mariah."

She fidgeted with her watchband. Why did she need to wait until they found Mariah? She needed to work, and she needed the money from this assignment even more. Mariah had been her grandmother's responsibility, not hers. And she was the one who'd run away when Camden asked her about the letter.

"Mariah already chose what she wants to do."

"She's hurting, Camden. She doesn't know what she wants."

She hated it when men purported to know what a woman wanted. "How would you know?"

"I don't know exactly what she was thinking."

She sniffed. "Of course not."

"But I know much more than I'd like."

Camden started to walk around a large rock, but she stopped. "What do you mean?"

He leaned back against a tree, his eyes focused on the forest in front of them. "My sister was a lot like Mariah."

"Your sister?"

"Her name was Angela, and she was the kind of kid whom everyone loved because she loved everyone." He pushed away from the tree and stood beside her. "I protected her the best I could when we were young, but it was a hard job. Her heart was tender, and she would do anything she could to help someone in need, giving away dozens of hugs along with all the money in her piggy bank."

"And now?" she asked.

"Now . . ." he started, but his voice trailed off. "She met a young cop when she was in nursing school, said she fell in love. He was good to her one moment, but then the next he . . . he wasn't so good. She thought she could tame his anger with her love."

"A recipe for disaster."

"It was a disaster. Trent got angry and beat her to death . . . along with their son."

Camden sucked in a mouthful of air, sinking down onto the rock. How was she supposed to respond to that? No wonder he freaked out when he learned Mariah was gone. He'd lost his sister to a man just like Mariah's boyfriend.

"The cop?" she asked.

"Life in prison without parole."

"So you do know what Mariah's thinking . . ."

"Angela kept telling me that nothing was wrong. She didn't need my help. Girls like Mariah have taken a huge step just asking someone for help."

She felt sick to her stomach. "And I scared her away."

"It probably doesn't take much to scare her right now."

She placed both hands on the cold rock and stood up. Alex was right. She shouldn't have gotten angry at Mariah, not like that. Treading softly would have been a much better idea. Instead she struck out, and the girl hid.

"I need to find her."

Alex fell into step beside her. "I'll help you look."

CHAPTER THIRTY-TWO

Camden turned on the lamp on the nightstand and peeled back the bed's freshly washed covers. The window was dark, but the lamplight cast a warm glow across the room, illuminating the quilts at the foot of her bed.

Part of her wished she were sleeping in a tent on a California hillside, even with the smoke settling around her. She would be near the perimeter tonight, hundreds of people surrounding her in base camp and firefighters battling the blaze. But she'd made the choice to stay on Crescent Hill instead of flying to California. And she was alone.

She punched her pillow, trying to get comfortable in the bed.

Today was one of the worst days of her life. Grant freaked out when she turned down the assignment—the only work she'd been offered in almost two months. She and Alex never found Mariah, and after what Alex said about his sister, she didn't want to think about Mariah going back to the man who'd hurt her.

The floor creaked above her, and she froze under the covers before she forced herself to breathe again. Now that she knew who'd been sneaking through her house, there was nothing to fear. Her grandmother slept in this house, alone, for decades, and Camden had spent entire summers in this bed and no ghosts had bothered her. In the past seven years, she'd slept in much more threatening places, like war zones in the Middle East and the camps near a forest fire.

Turning over on the pillow, she faced the locked bedroom door.

The house was almost *too* quiet, but at least it was calmer than Dan and Jenny's house. And much cheaper than a hotel. She'd just pretend she was ten years old again, staying with her grandmother who was sleeping right down the hall.

The ceiling groaned again, and she sat up, opening her nightstand to retrieve the Bible she'd found in the library. The one her grandmother would read to soothe her to sleep. Not that she was afraid tonight, but maybe the same words would help her sleep again.

The pages crinkled under her fingers as she turned to the heart of the Bible.

The Lord is my light and my salvation; whom shall I fear? The Lord is the strength of my life; of whom shall I be afraid?

Camden looked up at the quilts. She'd always been independent. Strong. She didn't need anyone else to take care of her like her mother did.

But if she were honest, tonight, in her soul, she was scared. Maybe not of the creaks in the house as much as she was afraid of losing her independence. And of being alone.

They'd sang at church about being in God's presence, about their fears being washed away. If only she could feel this light so she wouldn't be afraid.

Please help me feel your light.

She squinted at the quilt in front of the bed, made by an ancestor who took pride in her work and in her family. The shapes on one of the blocks looked like small stones in the shadows, and the blue ribboned block looked like a river.

She wanted to cling to this house. To her family's heritage. There was security in the foundations of a strong family. Even though she had spent most of her childhood days with her mother, she knew all about the Bristow family, and their legacy of strength and compassion had secured her feet through the shakiness of her life. The legacy had been her foundation. The one certain thing in the midst of all the uncertainty.

She didn't want to sell the house, but if the town was going to tear it down, she had no choice. Jake Paxton seemed to appreciate the mansion. Maybe he really would restore the rooms and share their beauty with his family.

Someday she could bring her own kids back to Crescent Hill and show them the lovely mansion where their ancestors lived. If she sold it to Jake, the house would still be here, returned to its former glory, which was so much better than bringing her children to some industrial site and trying to explain the heritage that once rested on the hill.

She would be the last of the Bristow family to own the house, but at least she would be responsible with it. She could pass it on to a family who would cherish it and create their own memories within its walls.

Heaviness weighted her eyelids as she began to fall asleep, the triangles and circles and squares on the wall swirling in her mind.

The mountain dropped down into an abyss of darkness, and Stephanie's car hugged the white line away from the cliffs. The night sky glowed with thousands of stars, all of them twinkling like white Christmas lights on an evergreen, but she focused on the pool of light created by her headlamps. Only a few cars passed her along the Blue Ridge Parkway. Mostly it was just her and the darkness and the trees that clung to the mountainside.

She couldn't imagine being a runaway slave, alone in the mountains like this. When the nights weren't cloudy, they could see enough to travel through the forest by starlight, but they must have been scared of the mountain lions and bears and snakes in the wilderness. Or maybe they were more afraid of the slave hunters pursuing them and taking them back to bondage.

The techno ringtone on her phone startled her out of her quiet revelry, and she linked her headset over her ear. She might be by herself out in these mountains, but she was far from being alone. And she was grateful for it.

"Your mother tells me you're on your way to Ohio," Aunt Debra said when Camden answered.

"Much to her chagrin."

Her aunt laughed. "She's proud of you, Steph. Worried but very proud."

"She shouldn't worry."

"That's what parents do."

She rounded another sharp curve. "I just want to find out the truth."

"You're awfully dedicated to this term paper."

"It's more than a paper, and you know it."

"I was hoping it would be."

The road straightened for a moment between a line of trees, and she relaxed her grasp on the steering wheel. "Don't you ever wonder what happened to William Ellison?"

"I do, but I was never able to find him."

"Did you go to Ohio?"

"No, but I searched through a number of newspapers from Cleveland and Canada West in the 1850s and 60s, hoping to find a mention of him. If he sold our family's jewelry, he would have been quite a prestigious black man."

"Howard Walters told me about a place where he thought William may have gone."

"Did he now—"

"Said it was called Crescent Hill."

"Crescent Hill?" Aunt Debra paused. "Hold on a second."

Over the top of the mountain, Stephanie could see the lights of a small town below. Maybe she could find a hotel where she could sleep for the night.

"I just read an article about Crescent Hill."

Stephanie swallowed hard. "Where?"

"In a small paper, the *Etherton Daily News*."

The newspaper she'd turned into a fan. "Why were you reading that paper?"

"I like to keep up with . . ." Debra hesitated.

"With what?"

"After the . . ." She stopped talking again, and Stephanie realized she was crying. "After the incident, Angela's brother went to live in Etherton."

"You're keeping tabs on Alex Yates?"

"He took a job with the town last year, and I just wanted to know . . ."

"It's okay, Aunt Debra." If reading the *Etherton Daily News* helped her aunt heal, she could subscribe for the rest of her life.

"I pray for Alex every day," Debra said. "By God's mercy, I pray he'll be okay."

CHAPTER THIRTY-THREE

Haze settled over the house, and Camden stumbled forward on her hands and knees, searching for the door of the mansion, someplace in the fog. In front of her was wood, splintered pieces that peeled back with her touch so she could see inside.

The inside of the house was warm and smelled like roasted turkey and cranberry sauce. Music rang from the walls, a symphony with trumpets and flutes and a tambourine.

And there were children. Dozens of them. Riding down the wide banister and playing leapfrog and hiding in the front closet.

It was a dream—even in her sleep she knew it—but maybe it was a vision of things to come. Perhaps a few of them were her children, singing and playing together. The thought made her smile.

Then one of the kids turned toward her, and her stomach sank. She didn't know the boy. Glancing around the room, she realized that she didn't know any of the kids. They were strangers. Or maybe she was the stranger—a stranger in her family's home.

In the corner of her eye, she saw a ball. A shiny, silver toy the boy was bouncing. Up and down. Up and down. As he bounced, the ball began to grow, swelling until it turned into a massive wrecking ball. The wrecking ball swung through her mind, and she screamed as her home crumbled to the ground.

Camden's eyes shot open, her heart racing. She reached for a pillow and hugged it to her chest. There were no children. No wrecking ball. It had only been a dream.

The sunlight of a new day warmed her face and slowly restored reality.

She couldn't remember the faces in her dream, but the feelings were potent. She had been lonely. Sad. She wanted what those people had—a family to love and celebrate. People who loved her back.

The wrecking ball left behind a crater on Crescent Hill. And a giant hole in her heart.

At that moment she knew. She couldn't sell the house. Not to the town and not even to someone like Jake Paxton who promised to restore it.

Family relationships had been fleeting in her life. Even when her father was alive, he'd been too distracted to spend much time with her. Her mother was still alive, but she was too busy trying to hold together the pieces of her own broken life to be interested in Camden's.

Grandma Rosalie had been her only real family. This mansion had been Camden's home. Not only had her grandma welcomed her, but her grandma turned the rooms into a welcoming place for so many more as well. Hundreds had come here for safety. For love.

She pushed her feet over the bed. She had no money to restore the place, but she would fight for it. Alex was on her team and so were the Spragues. She would try and keep it as long as she was able or until, she shuddered, the city brought a wrecking ball up here and knocked it down.

~

When Alex woke on Thursday morning, he eyed the blue sky through his window and wished he could spend his day on his bicycle instead of at the office. His bike was calling for him to cruise up the path to Mansfield this morning . . . but the call to go back to Beaverdale and visit Dotty was even stronger. He may not really know Dotty's granddaughter, but at least he got an invitation to visit again. Today he would find out about the house on Pleasant Street and ask Dotty if she thought the tunnel ever existed. And if it was still there.

When he asked for Mrs. Sherman at the reception desk of the retirement center, the woman gave him directions through the maze of hallways and courtyards, to Dotty's apartment.

"Aah, Natalie's best friend," Dotty said when she answered and motioned him inside.

The apartment was larger than he expected. A full kitchen looked out onto a living room and patio with a view of trees and a trio of cherubs spurting water. Dotty pointed the remote at the television in the corner of the room and muted Dr. Phil.

"People around here have been talking about my handsome visitor yesterday."

"I hope you don't mind."

"Of course not. You just have to be more careful about what you say out there. Ears everywhere, you know."

"Does your cousin come visit you often?" he asked.

"I'm Edward's legal caretaker if something ever happens to him." She laughed. "As if I could take care of him."

"So he comes to check in on you?"

She nodded. "He wants to make sure I'll be nice to him later in life."

He leaned toward her. "What happened when he came yesterday?"

"I didn't want Edward to know you were asking about the house."

"Why not?"

She paused. "Where did you say you were from again?"

"Columbia, South Carolina."

She shifted the afghan on her lap. "The nice thing about big cities is that only a few people know your business. In a small town, your business is everybody's business."

"So I've discovered."

She glanced around her apartment. "But most people forget about you once you move into a place like this."

"Did you want to move here?"

"My son took a job in Japan a few years ago, and my daughter is in Florida." She shook her head sadly. "I didn't have a choice."

Alex stopped worrying about the stack of paperwork on his desk and about trying to convince Camden to sell her property. Sitting in front of him was a woman hungry for a taste of the outside.

He stood up. "Would you like to take a drive with me this morning?"

Her face lit up. "We can talk without all the ears."

"You bet." He pulled his keys out of his pocket, but hesitated before he stepped toward the door. "Are you allowed to go outside?"

She put both of her bony hands on her hips and tsked. "This isn't prison."

He laughed. With her spunk, he would probably enjoy the ride even more than she did. "I don't know how it works."

So she explained exactly how they could break out.

He pushed her to the elevator, signed out at the front desk, and helped Mrs. Dotty Sherman into his car. As they pulled out of the property, she giggled like a schoolgirl.

They drove through the town, and she pointed out where she had gone to school when she was a child even though the building had been replaced with a supermarket. A gas station and strip mall sat on the farmland where she used to pick strawberries and buy fresh eggs, and the corner store had been demolished two decades ago, she said, to make way for a parking lot.

"It's too bad they keep tearing down all the old buildings." She sighed. "It's like they're not important anymore."

"Most people have an appreciation for the past."

She laughed, but there was no joy in her laughter. "They only appreciate it if it's worth money."

He glanced over, and she was gazing out the window. She probably saw things in her mind's eye that he couldn't see. Places long gone. "What's valuable to you?"

"My faith in God and my family." Her eyes teared. "And my friends, of course, though most of them aren't around anymore."

"I'm sorry."

She tapped her fingers on the ceiling of his car. "They're waiting for me up there."

They drove up the brick street, toward Crescent Hill, and when she saw the Bristow mansion, Dotty asked him to stop.

"Did you know Rosalie?" he asked, his eyes resting on the house.

She nodded. "We were the best of friends when we were children."

"And as adults?"

She shook her head. "We both wanted to marry the same man."

"Philip Bristow?"

Dotty stroked the side of the window, lost in the past. "Philip was wealthy and handsome, and best of all, he didn't seem to care about either of those things. He would have been successful in business or politics but all he wanted to be was a doctor."

"And Rosalie?"

"She was an artist who loved people with all the passion in her heart."

"How many children did they have?"

Dotty fidgeted with her hands. "That's a tricky question."

"At least one . . ." he prompted.

When she didn't respond, he did a quick double take, thinking Dotty's mind might be slipping away. "Camden Bristow's father . . ." he coaxed.

She shook her head. "Rosalie was dating someone else before she married Philip. A man who deceived her."

He suddenly felt like he was trespassing. This was a discussion for Camden, not him. "Were you and Rosalie ever friends again?"

"Of course." Dotty snapped back to the present. "I met and married my Charles, and we had three children. Rosalie was the one who suffered."

"And yet you were the one to write the history of Crescent Hill?"

"Philip and Rosalie gave me piles of information about the place though neither of them were as interested in the history of the house as I was." She laughed. "I would have married Philip just to live on the hill."

A comfortable quiet settled over the truck as it crawled slowly down the hill, past the grove of trees. He stopped at the intersection of Pleasant and Bristow Avenue.

"Pleasant Street was expanded in the 1970s and the street numbers were changed," she said.

He glanced over, but didn't try to rush her.

She pointed at the tall, green-trimmed house across the street from them. Edward Paxton's home. "In the golden days, that was 249 Pleasant Street."

Camden showered quickly and dressed before she began the walk down the hill. To Jake Paxton's house. He seemed so intent on buying the house, but if he knew the place was about to be condemned, he probably wouldn't be as excited.

The house was a terrible investment, but it was the perfect place to help protect those who needed a shelter. No wonder her grandmother kept the house for so long. No one seemed to suspect that she'd been stowing people away.

A couple kids rode by the Paxton house on their bicycles, laughing as they pulled their hands off the handlebars and tried to ride hands-free. She waved at them before opening the white gate and strolling into Jake's small yard and up the stairs to the cement porch.

She had no idea where she would get the money to fix up the house, but she didn't want to leave Crescent Hill.

If she could sell the valuables inside the house, she could make some of the repairs and set up a small studio to take pictures of families and babies and maybe even help a few hurting women and children like Rosalie had done. It would be a small legacy, but one she could carry on for the Bristow family. While she was here, she'd talk to Edward about his appraisal.

Jake opened the door before she knocked, and joined her on the porch, quickly shutting the door behind him.

"Hi, Camden." He pointed to one of the patio chairs, and then sat down beside her. "I'm hoping you're here to talk about my offer."

"The city is getting ready to condemn the house."

His eye twitched. "They can't do that."

"I'm going to fight it, but I don't think it's a good time for me to sell the place."

"It is a good time," he said, with an easy smile. "I can fix it up."

"There's probably a million dollars of repairs needed to get it up to code."

"Perhaps I could lower my original offer to help with some of the expenses."

"I'm sorry," she said. "But I've decided not to sell it right now."

The smile vanished from his face. "Why not?"

"It may sound sort of silly . . ."

He leaned toward her. "Try me."

"I'm . . . I guess I'm sort of discovering myself here in Etherton, and this house is a part of who I am."

"As part of the Bristow family?"

"I've always wanted to be part of a . . ." she started, but stopped. She wasn't going to share her heart with him.

"Your grandfather was the end of the Bristow line."

"No, my father . . ."

He stood up. "I'll be right back."

As he went inside the house, she tried to settle back in her chair, but something felt very wrong. She could understand if he was disappointed about her not selling the house, even a little upset at the turn of events, but his reaction was a bit weird. Maybe she should leave while he was inside . . .

She started to stand, but Jake was back at the door and this time he was carrying a piece of paper. He held it out to her.

She scanned the type—it was a birth certificate for Timothy Lawrence Paxton.

"Where did you . . ." she started to say, but her words trailed off as she read the last name of her father again.

Paxton.

The birth certificate said her father was the son of Edward Paxton and Rosalie Stull . . . but that wasn't right. Her father had been born to Philip and Rosalie Bristow.

Rosalie Stull?

Her fingers froze on the paper as she read Rosalie's maiden name again. The date was correct. March 8, 1957. But the name. The name wasn't right at all.

"You may want to be a Bristow," Jake whispered. "But your father wasn't a Bristow and neither are you."

"Yes, I am," she said, but her voice wavered. All her life she'd been a Bristow. It was the one thing she'd been sure of. "But my father . . ."

He finished her sentence. "Your father was adopted by Philip."

"Adopted?" she whispered. It was all too much, too fast. She was a Bristow. Her father was a Bristow.

Jake was lying.

"My father would have told me—"

Jake flashed her a funny look. "Really?"

Her mind swam. It wasn't like she and her father talked much, certainly not about their family's history. Maybe he decided not to tell her. Or maybe he didn't know.

"The whole town would have known the truth."

"No one knew who Rosalie was sleeping with." Jake laughed. "They just knew she was pregnant."

Her body stiffened. How dare he condemn the woman who had shown God's love to so many people?

"Apparently, she got married soon after your dad was born," he said. "She just didn't marry Timothy's father."

"But . . ."

"Rosalie was too embarrassed to tell people about your dad's history. She wanted to keep it a secret."

"Then why are you telling me?"

"Your name is really Camden Paxton instead of Bristow."

Her stomach rolled as he leaned toward her. "But if you sell me the property," he whispered, "I'll promise to protect the Bristow house and the Bristow name."

CHAPTER THIRTY-FOUR

Jake hadn't even shut the door completely when Edward snatched the birth certificate out of his hand. "Where did you get this?"

Jake bolted the lock and stood tall, relishing the power he had over his grandfather. "I found it."

Edward dropped the certificate and slapped Jake across the cheek.

His hand flew to his face, anger flaming inside him. "Don't touch me again."

"Did you show her?"

He rolled back his shoulders. "It was a little insurance."

His grandfather lifted his hand again, but Jake caught his fingers in the air. "I said, *Don't*."

Edward lowered his hand. "You dimwit," he muttered. "You've shown her all our cards."

Edward poked his cane into Jake's leg, and Jake swiped it out of his hands. His grandfather stumbled back onto the couch. "I'm only giving her a little incentive," Jake said.

"Did it work?"

He twirled the cane. "She'll sell the house."

"Give me the cane, Jake."

Jake took his time considering Edward's request.

Edward pushed himself to the edge of the couch. "You're an idiot."

"I am *not* an idiot," he said, throwing the cane at Edward. "Why didn't you tell me you were her grandfather?"

"It's obvious, isn't it? Because you couldn't handle the information."

"But her father was your son."

"No, he wasn't." Edward emphasized each word with a stab of his cane on the hardwood floor.

"But the certificate—"

"I told Rosalie if she wanted to keep that baby, she was on her own."

"So Philip Bristow adopted him."

"Rosalie was supposed to destroy that certificate so no one would find out."

Jake straightened his shoulders. "I waited until the right moment to tell Camden the news."

"This was not the right moment." Edward glared at him. "Who else have you told about the certificate?"

"Only someone on our side."

"No one else is on our side."

"Liza Bristow is."

Edward jabbed the cane toward Jake. "What did you tell her?"

Jake walked slowly into the den, Edward following at his heels. He pounded on the wall of the closet where Mariah had hidden when Camden knocked on the door, and he waited until she crept out and sat down in the chair behind him. His grandfather might call him an idiot, but he was one gigantic step ahead of him. As the victor, he wanted his woman enjoying this moment of glory with him.

He straightened his shoulders. "I told Liza that Camden wasn't really a Bristow."

Seconds passed as Edward digested the information. "Why did you tell her that?"

"So she can contest the will." When Edward's mouth dropped open, Jake proceeded. "If Camden isn't really a Bristow by blood, then maybe Liza can get Crescent Hill."

Edward's face turned red. "And why do you want her to inherit Crescent Hill?"

This was it. His moment of brilliance to prove that he was as smart, as conniving, as any other member of the Paxton family. "It's all about the timing, Pops."

"Liza is going to sell it to the city."

"Not if I give her a higher offer."

Edward was seething now. "I don't get it."

"I'm buying more time for us to search for your treasure." And to steal more items so he could sell them online.

"In the midst of your brilliant planning," Edward said, "did it ever occur to you that Liza isn't really a Bristow either?"

Jake started to protest, but stopped. Edward liked to confuse him, and he wasn't going to play along. "You don't know what you're talking about."

"Who was Camden's father?"

"Timothy Bristow."

"And who was Liza's father?"

"It makes no difference to me."

"It was Timothy Bristow, genius."

He blinked. "But Liza lives in Columbus."

"They're half-sisters, you idiot!"

He slumped back, his great plan slowly crumbling into pieces. He'd thought it out so clearly. If Camden wasn't related by blood, Liza could contest the will. Liza would offer to sell him the house, and he would look around the place, decide what he wanted to take, maybe even find the treasure. Then he would cart out as many valuable things as he could through the tunnel. With the money, he wouldn't buy Crescent Hill, but he could buy a little house for Mariah and him. Far away from Edward Paxton and Etherton's law enforcement.

He'd never shown Liza the birth certificate, but she'd been so receptive to what he said. So excited. The plan had seemed foolproof.

Mariah was first to break the silence. "Who are you talking about?"

"Shut up," Jake growled.

His phone rang, and he looked down to see Liza's number on his screen. She wanted proof that Camden wasn't related by blood to take to her new attorney. If Edward was right, she wasn't related to the Bristows either. He'd promised her ammunition, and now he had squat to offer her.

"Hey," he said as he turned toward the back door, and then he laughed into the phone. "I've got something kinda funny to tell you."

He glanced over his shoulder, laughing again, but neither Edward nor Mariah were laughing with him.

Camden flung her clothes into her bag and rushed out of the house.

She didn't belong here, in Etherton. Everything had been a lie. She'd spent her childhood steeping in the Bristow heritage and history, and the truth was that she wasn't even really a Bristow.

She was a Paxton. Camden Adelle Paxton. She shivered. Her parents had named her after an ancestor that wasn't really hers. The Paxtons couldn't be trusted, and here she was, the granddaughter of one.

She hopped into the car and drove it down the hill, around the square. How could her grandma deceive her like this? All this time, Rosalie knew the truth, along with Jake Paxton's family.

No wonder why her father rarely came back to Etherton. Maybe he knew the truth too.

A red light stopped her, and she picked up her phone and called Grant Haussen's number. If he still needed her, she would fly to California this morning and take pictures of the fire.

"It's Grant."

"Hey," she said, trying to sound casual. "I wondered if you still needed someone in California."

"Camden?"

"That's me."

"Sorry, but . . ." She heard voices in the background. "I've got to go, Cam."

The sinking feeling returned. Where was she supposed to go now? "When you need me, I'm ready for another job."

She waited for his response, but he was already gone.

Fingering the phone in her hand, she thought about calling Jenny, but Jenny had a houseful of kids with plenty of injuries. She didn't need Camden crying on her shoulder as well.

Tears poured down her cheeks. Tears of sorrow and anger and grief.

Jake could tell the whole world she wasn't a Bristow. She didn't care anymore.

Alex never imagined he'd be sneaking something out of a retirement center, but under his coat was a copy of the original *History of Crescent Hill*, all pages intact. Dotty had handed him the binder she kept hidden under the bed, and he copied her entire manuscript at Beaverdale and bound it together with a rubber band.

Now he needed to figure out what to do with it. He would go to Louise, eventually, and ask her to wait before the town condemned the house. First, though, he wanted to corroborate Dotty's work. The author was clearly biased toward Philip and Rosalie, but that didn't mean her facts were wrong. He just needed to prove her story right before he talked to the mayor.

He braked at a stop sign and started to go again when he looked left and saw a blue Miata barreling down the hill at him. He slammed on his brakes and the crumb of a car flew through the intersection, not even hesitating at the stop sign.

He caught a glimpse of Camden talking on her phone, oblivious to the fact that he'd almost broadsided her.

A BMW flew down the road behind Camden. Liza Bristow caught his eye, but she didn't wave. Nor did she smile. Instead she turned her head and turned left onto the road leading back to Columbus. Maybe she was finally going home.

He didn't care where Liza was going, but something was wrong with Camden. He turned to follow her car up a hill, heading north of town, and watched her race around a curve and bump over the train tracks. When she slowed down, he honked and waved out of his window, and she pulled into a lot beside a barn.

Slamming his door shut, he rushed across the gravel to her car and tapped on her window. She rolled the window down, but she didn't turn to face him.

"You almost ran me down back there."

She leaned her head against the seat. "I don't have the energy to fight, Alex."

Of all the things she might say, he never expected defeat. "I, uh, I wasn't trying to pick a fight. I was only trying to . . ."

"I mean the house," she said, her voice monotone. "You can have it."

"What?"

"You and Louise can build your hospital on Crescent Hill. Or a car lot. Or garbage dump if you want."

"Wait a second." He thought about Dotty's papers back in his car, along with the secrets they held. He wasn't ready for Camden to give up yet.

"I want to go home, Alex."

"New York?"

Tears welled in her eyes. "I don't know."

She focused on the steering wheel, her arms limp beside her. He much preferred irritated Camden to the woman surrendering before him. He had to shake her from this defeated state. He needed her help to figure out the truth.

He glanced to his side and saw a small pond beside the barn, and then he opened her door. "Let's go talk."

She followed him under the wooden fence and they sat at a bench beside the still water.

"What's wrong?" he asked.

She groaned in response. "Everything."

He leaned over and picked up a rock, tossing it into the water. The ripples slowly spread across the surface. Louise might have his job if he shared this information with Camden, but Crescent Hill was still her house. She deserved to know the whole truth.

"Do you want to tell me what happened?" he asked.

When she shook her head, he didn't press her.

"There's a woman up at Beaverdale who wrote a history on the Bristows and Crescent Hill," he said.

She groaned again. "I don't want to talk about Crescent Hill."

He paused and then nodded toward his car. "I'm pretty sure I can change your mind."

The barista wiped the counters at the Underground, but other than her and Alex, the coffee shop was empty. She hadn't wanted to return to Etherton, but there was no place else for her to go. Even if she drove back to New York or all the way to California, what would she do when she got there? She had two hundred dollars left to spend before she maxed her credit card, and she'd just turned down the only assignment she'd received in months. She had no work. No backup plan. Only a house that didn't really belong to her.

"What happened?" Alex asked again. This time his voice was much quieter, as if he was scared she would run away like Mariah had done.

"I'm not really a Bristow."

His voice grew louder. "Who told you that?"

"Jake Paxton." She folded her hands on her lap. "He showed me my father's birth certificate."

"And how did he get that?"

"I'm not sure . . . it must have passed down in his family."

"It's an awfully convenient time for it to appear."

"He was probably waiting until I wouldn't sell him the house."

"Nice guy," he quipped. "So you decided to run away?"

She shrugged. "I didn't know what else to do."

The look in his eyes was compassionate. Intense. "Running won't help."

She propped her elbows on the table, resting her chin on her hands. She'd gotten angry at her mother for running whenever life got tough, and yet here she was, doing the same thing.

Staying in one place, facing her problems—it wasn't in her blood. And she wasn't sure she wanted to learn how to face them either. It was so much easier to leave, start fresh again someplace where people didn't know her or her family's history.

"It doesn't matter about a birth certificate," Alex said. "Some ties are stronger than blood."

"I don't know . . ."

"You're still Rosalie Bristow's granddaughter, and the Bristow family is your heritage. You're the only one left to fight for the house."

"Since when do you want me to fight for Crescent Hill?"

He hesitated. "I want you to do the right thing."

She didn't know what was right at the moment. This town felt comfortable to her, a place to be at home. Still, it didn't mean she was supposed to stay.

"I don't think Jake wants your house," Alex said.

"Yes, he does."

"He may say he wants to buy your house, but I think what he really wants is the tunnel."

She sighed. "What tunnel?"

He set a stack of papers on the table, held together by a rubber band, and pushed them toward her. "This is a complete history on your house."

She pinched the top sheet and lifted it to glance underneath. She'd heard plenty of stories, but she'd never seen anything written about Crescent Hill's past. "Where did you get this?"

"It was put together by Dotty Sherman, a friend of your grandparents." He reached over and shuffled through the pages. "According to her research, your house had a tunnel and the tunnel provided a refuge for runaway slaves."

"That story's been around forever, Alex. No one believes it."

It was like he didn't hear her.

"The tunnel wasn't just used as a station on the Underground Railroad though." He pushed a page toward her, and she saw a pencil sketch of a tunnel. "It was a meeting place for stationmasters across Central Ohio. They would sneak in through several different entrances and meet under the house."

"Under the house?"

He nodded. "These stationmasters would plan different routes to guide runaway slaves through Northern Ohio and across the tightly guarded border around Lake Erie."

She rubbed her temples. She'd heard the stories about the house being on the Underground Railroad before, dozens of times. From her grandmother and from the kids in the neighborhood who made up all sorts of stories about a tunnel and lost treasure.

But she didn't know what this had to do with her today. Or Crescent Hill. Even if there was a tunnel—and Jake wanted it—why should she care?

"I'm glad the Bristow family helped runaway slaves, but that doesn't help me now."

"It might," he said, leaning forward. "Dotty said the tunnel connects to the Paxton house."

Her heart started to race. "Jake Paxton?"

"Exactly. Jake and Edward's house. The other entrances to the tunnel have never been found."

Did Jake Paxton have access to her house? The thought made her stomach roll.

"So you want to find this tunnel?" she asked.

"If we discovered it, Etherton would never let the council tear the house down."

She shook her head. "I've explored the house from top to bottom, and I haven't found an entrance to a tunnel."

"Dotty said there's supposed to be an entrance on the top floor of the house."

"There isn't."

"Dotty's grandfather used to talk about it, but she was too young to remember details." He brushed his hands over the papers. "He also said there was a map to a third entrance. It was supposed to be a way for the owners of the house to direct slaves so they didn't have to knock on the door."

"I don't know, Alex."

He leaned closer, whispering. "Legend has it that the map was stitched into a quilt."

She looked down at the paperwork in his hands, Margaret Nixon's words ringing in her ears. *Every quilt has a story.*

Could it be possible? She didn't remember Rosalie talking about the quilts, but perhaps her grandma didn't know.

What if they did find the entrance to the tunnel? What if they could save the house?

She may not be a Bristow by blood, but Alex was right. She was the only one left to battle for the Bristow house . . . and the Bristow legacy.

CHAPTER THIRTY-FIVE

He'd only gone down to the pool hall for a beer or two—it never occurred to him to take his jacket. But when he walked back in the door—after five or six beers—and saw the books in Edward's hands . . .

He never should have left his stupid coat behind.

He thought Edward was going to throw the books at him, but his grandfather, even in all his anger, couldn't bear to throw anything that valuable. Instead, with shaky hands, he set the books on the coffee table.

Jake stepped forward. "Where's Mariah?"

"Upstairs. Locked in her room."

Jake nodded at the books. "You catching up on your reading?"

Edward glared at him. "Are you trying to go back to jail?"

"Of course not. I just thought I'd get a little treasure for myself while I was searching for your pot of gold."

Edward pointed his cane at him. "You're willing to risk it all for a couple hundred dollars?"

"A couple hundred bucks is sounding real good right about now."

"You have no idea . . ." Edward said as he hobbled over to the bookshelf.

"I'm playin' it smart, Pops. I'm only taking a few things at a time, from different rooms. Camden will never know she's missing a thing."

"They'll catch you."

"Not a chance," he slurred. "I'll make a boatload more than a couple hundred bucks from books like these when I'm done. And I'll make much, much more than you'll ever get from your *treasure*."

Edward slipped a photo album off a shelf and opened it. "Let me show you something."

On the first page was a black and white picture of a man with a bushy mustache and curly hair that sprung out of his head. No sign of a smile on his lips or in his eyes.

The picture made Jake laugh. "A grumpy old man."

Edward didn't share his laughter. "He was my great-grandfather. Arthur Paxton."

"So that would make him my great . . ." He didn't have a clue how many "greats" it would be.

"Don't strain yourself," Edward said as he reached behind the plastic covering.

"So what does this great-grandpop of yours know about the treasure?"

"A lot." Edward pulled out a paper from behind the photo. "He passed down the information to his son who passed it down to me."

Jake looked at the paper, curious now. What if there really was a treasure? It probably would be worth more than the entire stock of books and art in the house. And, if they found it, it would take a heck of a lot less work to carry one treasure out through the tunnel than the rest of the stuff.

"How did Arthur know about it?"

Edward hesitated. "Let's just say he saw it with his own eyes."

His grandfather handed him the letter, and he opened it. The words were written in a smooth cursive, the words faded but still legible. It looked like some sort of list. Necklaces. Bracelets. Rings.

"The treasure is jewelry . . ." he started.

Edward smiled. "Very expensive jewelry, and I have a couple buyers lined up to take it off our hands."

"Does this Arthur fellow know where the jewelry went?"

"It's in the house, Jake. He just didn't know where."

"I've looked all over the house."

"Not everywhere."

He hesitated. "You think it's in that storage room?"

"It's the only room that's locked."

Jake picked up the books from the coffee table and tucked them under his arm. "You're a chip off the old block, Pops."

"What makes you say that?"

"Your great-grandpop stole some jewelry and now you're about to steal it again."

"I didn't say he stole it . . ."

Jake stepped back. "How did you find out about the tunnel?"

"My father told me about it." He smiled again. "But I was the one who found it."

"When was the last time you were down there?"

Edward sat down on the couch beside the bookcase. "Twenty years ago. I had to dig a hole through the bricks."

"I thought the roof collapsed."

"Oh no, it didn't collapse. The Bristows blocked it."

"Why would they block it?"

Edward lowered his voice. "Because they didn't want Arthur in their house."

Alex opened the door for Camden, and they both walked out of the café. Beneath her astonishment, he could glimpse a hint of excitement over what they might find, and he was glad to see spirit returning after the bomb Jake dropped.

Jake's timing was impeccable, delivering the news about Camden's father days after Rosalie was gone. The man was after something in, or perhaps under, the house, and Alex intended to find out what was going on. If they found evidence of a tunnel, he would talk Louise into issuing a stay on the condemnation. The town couldn't tear the house down until they discovered the truth of what was underneath.

"Hello, you two." Alex turned and saw his boss walking toward them, waving and smiling. He introduced Louise to Camden.

"Glad to see you're talking again," Louise said.

Alex nodded at Camden. "We're trying to work together."

"Now that's the best news I've heard all day." Louise rubbed her hands together. "We're all on the same team."

He took a deep breath. "We think we're on to something."

"Really?" She lowered her voice. "What are you talking about?"

He motioned her away from the café door, and the three of them huddled together in an empty parking space. "We think we might be able to find the tunnel under the Bristows' house."

The mayor shook her head, but he didn't stop. "If we find it, we could open a museum, and I could talk to some people about building a boutique hotel and a new restaurant or two to accommodate the influx of tourists."

"It wouldn't be enough," Louise replied.

"Yes, it would," he insisted. "People would come from all over to see tunnels like these."

"A museum wouldn't bring in nearly as much revenue as a shopping space."

"But it would keep with the heritage and feel of the town, and all the revenue would go directly to the town."

"But only if you and Camden find this tunnel . . ."

"Did you know my grandmother?" Camden asked.

"Oh, yes, my dear. She was a close friend."

"Did she ever talk to you about a tunnel?"

Before Louise answered her question, Camden's phone rang, and she took a step back and excused herself to take the call.

Alex watched Camden stroll over to a bench. She'd been through so much the past week, and yet she still moved with beauty. Grace. For a moment, he wished Jenny had set them up before all of the mess with the house. Maybe something could have happened . . .

"You're smitten," Louise said.

He jerked his head back toward his boss. There was no smile on her face. "That's ridiculous."

"A shopping center will bring in more revenue for the city than a museum."

"Not necessarily . . ."

"Your job's on the line here, Alex."

"My job is to improve the economy of the town, and that's exactly what I'm trying to do."

Louise glanced over at the bench. "I think Rosalie's granddaughter may be a little smitten herself."

His face grew warm. "This isn't about Camden and me."

"I'm not changing my mind about the condemnation notice."

"We only want a little more time."

"You've got three weeks left, Alex," she said before she walked away.

He glanced over at Camden and then back at the mayor as she rounded the corner. Louise was usually the first one to fight for preservation for this town, and he had just presented her with the perfect plan to preserve this historic property and generate revenue.

Something else was going on.

CHAPTER THIRTY-SIX

This is a basic Nine Patch pattern, but the stitching around the calico blocks is impeccable," Margaret mused. "Not one stitch is uneven."

"But what about the shapes on the blocks?" Jenny asked her mother.

"I'm getting to that."

Camden glanced over at Alex, and he winked at her. She'd invited him along for this consultation with Jenny's mother, and he took her up on the offer before she'd finished her invitation. So far, Margaret hadn't said much of anything useful though she muttered a lot, saying over and over that the quilt was a fine piece of work. Camden didn't doubt its quality, but even with Dotty Sherman's legend ringing in her ears, she doubted the blocks contained some sort of map or message.

Even if they didn't find the map, she felt better this afternoon than she had in days. Dan Sprague had interrupted her conversation with Louise today, but she was glad she took Dan's call. Apparently, Liza's attorney had contacted him this morning about contesting the will, and Dan informed him there was a provision in the will that stated anyone who contested it—and won—would be required to wait five years to sell the house.

An hour later Liza dropped her suit.

Jenny pointed toward the first block on the quilt. "This looks like a green hill, with flowers."

Margaret brushed Jenny's hand away from the quilt. "Don't rush me, Sweetie."

Jenny stepped back from the wall and folded her arms across her chest. "She's still bossy," she mumbled, and Camden bit back her laugh.

Margaret made tsking sounds as she continued to examine each block.

Camden sat down on the bed and waited. She wanted to be as intrigued as the others instead of exhausted by it all, but at this moment, she didn't really care if a tunnel existed under the house or if this quilt was some sort of pre–Civil War map. Or even if the house had really been used to hide runaway slaves. Right now, she was trying to sort out what she should do about the house and how she could find Mariah.

Margaret clapped her hands. "I've got the first six blocks."

Reluctantly Camden got up and hovered around the quilt with the others as Margaret tapped on the first block. "This green semicircle is a hill."

"That's what I said," Jenny muttered.

Margaret ignored her. "Crescent Hill, perhaps." She pointed toward the next block. "This pattern of angled triangles shows a direction."

Alex squinted at the pattern. "It looks like geese, flying south."

Margaret nodded, pointing at the large triangle at the right. "Except in this case they are flying east."

Slowly, she critiqued each block, explaining what she thought it meant. Trees. A patch of flowers. A river. As Margaret started to examine the final three blocks, her watch chimed, and she glanced down at the time. "Your sister's expecting us in ten minutes."

Jenny shrugged. "She can wait a little longer."

"There's no telling what those children of yours have done to her house."

Jenny groaned, and when she met her friend's eye, Camden felt her frustration. "Can we finish this tomorrow?" Jenny asked.

Camden thought for a moment, wondering if she'd even be here tomorrow. "How about first thing in the morning?"

Margaret checked her watch again and patted Camden on the shoulder. "Maybe we could finish it tonight, after the kids are asleep."

"That's when I'm supposed to be sleeping," Jenny said.

"C'mon," Margaret prodded her toward the door. "We can't be late."

Camden walked the women to the door. When she returned to the room, Alex was still where she'd left him, studying the quilt. She came up alongside him and examined the final three blocks.

The first block on the row was stitched with four gray ovals. A tall, burgundy box was stitched in the next block along with a cross. And the last block held a large black circle.

A minute passed, and then two.

Alex tapped on the block with the gray ovals. "They look like stones . . . Stones by the river?"

"Stones?" Camden stepped closer, and her fingers brushed over the materials, resting on the cross in the second block. "I wonder . . ."

"What?"

"Maybe they're supposed to be tombstones."

Stephanie pulled up in front of the imposing mansion on the hill. The roof was sagging, and one of the gutters hung at the side of the house like a broken arm. It probably wouldn't be long before the house was gone, but for now the crooked shutters and broken glass added to the charm of Crescent Hill. The place screamed of heritage. History.

Ghost train moves in black of night. Hold your breath, child. Be still. Cross the river. Don't stop running. Til you reach the Crescent Hill.

She could only imagine what it must have felt like, running all the way from a state like South Carolina, trying to find this hill. No matter how tired, no matter how hungry, they must have felt some sort of elation to make it this far. To a place, as Howard said, that almost guaranteed passage to freedom.

Had William Ellison made it all the way to Crescent Hill? If so, where had he gone from here?

It wasn't like whoever lived in this home today—if someone still lived here—would have any connection with its past. But perhaps they could direct her to someone who'd heard stories about the place or even someone whose ancestors had once lived on the hill. Maybe there were some sort of records left, naming the slaves who'd once run through here, or even a map as to where the runaways had gone next. She could follow the path north until she found out what happened to William.

The sun was beginning to set behind her, but it wasn't too late for her to knock on the door. Climbing up the cracked steps, she rang the bell and the loud gong permeated the wooden door. No one inside could have missed hearing it. Either they didn't want to answer or no one was home.

Slowly, she walked back to the car. It was probably silly to come all this way to chase down an old family legend. But this was about more than stolen jewelry. It was about a family who'd been wronged. About a man who had fled with the admirable intent of helping his family find freedom.

Of course, what he had done after that may not have been as admirable. She wouldn't tell Howard Walters if she found out his ancestor sold the jewelry and spent the money on himself.

She started the car engine and began to cruise down the hill. Maybe a neighbor could tell her about Crescent Hill.

Edward slammed down the phone and swore. Twice.

"What's your problem?" Jake mumbled, his eyes on the computer screen.

"She found out."

Slowly Jake turned his head, his fingers still on the mouse, ready to defend his base. "Who found out about what?"

Edward looked over at the couch. Mariah was lying down, her eyes closed and both hands on her whale-of-a-belly.

"You mean Camden discovered the—"

"Shut up," Edward hissed, darting another look between him and Mariah. "You know what I mean."

It served the old man right to be nervous, especially after what he'd put Jake through the last week, making him crawl around like a deranged mole in that dark tunnel. The only fun he'd had was when he tucked Camden's purse under the edge of her bed. If only he could have seen her face when she found it.

"Has she been inside *it*?" he asked.

"How am I supposed to know?"

"You worry too much," Jake said, turning back to his game. One more round, and then he was taking Mariah out to a fancy dinner. They'd celebrate the windfall of the thousand bucks he'd earned when he sold the Bristow books this afternoon. Tomorrow, after he buttered Mariah up a bit, he would drive her to the clinic in Mansfield, and they would take care of her problem.

The doorbell rang, and Jake spun around. "Who is it?"

Edward was out of the den, partway across the floor of the living room when Jake caught up with him. After Edward looked out the peephole, he turned back. "I have no idea."

The bell rang again.

"You need me to answer it?"

"I'll handle her," Edward said. "You go out the back. See if you can find Camden."

"Find her?"

"Yes, Jake, go find her."

"What do you want me to do, go knock on her door?"

"I don't care what you do. Just find her and apologize or something, and then try and find out what she knows."

Jake huffed as he grabbed his jacket. He wouldn't apologize, but he could check and see if she'd changed her mind about selling the house. When he told her the truth about her family this morning, the shock on her face was priceless. He wanted to wait for her to come back to him, groveling to get some money out of the house before the city took it, but he would go now. She could think she was keeping the house because of some devotion to her family, but it always came down to money.

When he found her tonight, he'd sweeten the deal. Offer her more cash or something. Then he'd mention the tunnel, just to see what she knew.

He walked toward the kitchen to escape through the back door. Mariah followed him.

"Stay here," he ordered. Camden would want an introduction, and he didn't want to explain Mariah or her belly. He also didn't trust Mariah, not yet. She might try and run away from him again, into the forest. If she did, he'd catch her of course, but she might get hurt, and then the people at the clinic tomorrow might ask questions.

"Take Mariah with you," Edward called.

"But—"

"Take her with you," Edward barked again.

"C'mon." He motioned, and she followed him out the door.

The air was chilly as Camden and Alex walked down Crescent Hill. Camden pictured herself on a rug beside the grand fireplace that used to roar in the parlor, resting near her grandmother with a mug of hot chocolate and a blanket and a book.

Alex held back a tree branch, and she ducked under it. "Maybe we should wait until morning to come down here."

She stopped and faced him. "You don't want to wait."

In the remaining sunlight, she caught his grin. "Neither do you."

She turned away and stepped forward again, down the path. He was right; she didn't want to wait until the morning. Even if they didn't know for certain the meaning of the final blocks, the cemetery was a good guess. They would find out tonight if it meant anything.

The sky darkened as they walked down the path, and she switched on the flashlight in her left hand, washing over the path with light. How strange it was to have Alex Yates with her, walking toward the family cemetery. Strange and yet safe somehow. Like he was supposed to be part of this journey.

Was it less than a week ago that she'd been so livid at Alex? He'd been the enemy, out to steal her family's house away. Now, ironically, he was helping her save it. Or, at least, helping her understand it. Then they could talk about saving it from the city council.

They walked through the trees like the map directed. Beside the stream. Her light bobbed over the tall grass, and the beam captured two bright eyes, staring back at her. She gasped, and then laughed as a raccoon scampered off into the trees. Alex joined her laughter.

"Are you nervous?" he asked.

"I didn't think so."

"Don't let a raccoon spook you."

"I won't," she said, though she sounded more confident than she felt.

"How long until we get to the cemetery?"

She lifted her flashlight, and there it was, in front of them. The plot of seventeen graves was a grayish haze in the night. Bristow aunts, uncles, cousins, and grandparents she never knew. It had been a small family line, but a strong one.

The flowers on top of her grandmother's grave were wilted—she would replace them with a fresh bouquet in the morning. As Alex waited behind her, her fingers glided over the etching in the cold stone that marked her grandmother's life.

Perhaps her grandmother wanted to tell her the truth about her father's birth. Perhaps she'd even written about it in the missing letter.

Rosalie could have given her son up for adoption or found a place to abort him, yet she chose to birth her child—and keep him. And, apparently, she'd never gotten pregnant again. If she hadn't kept her son, there wouldn't have been anyone to carry on the Bristow name.

The leaves rustled behind her, and Camden swiveled around, illuminating the patch of trees. When nothing moved, she turned the light back toward Alex. "What was that?"

"Probably another raccoon." The concern on his face turned into a smile. "Or maybe a skunk."

She scanned the trees with her flashlight again, but all was still. "Do skunks bite?"

"You'd rather be bitten than sprayed."

She shivered. "I don't think so."

Alex glanced at all the stones. "Where do we go from here?"

She ran her fingers over her grandmother's tombstone one more time, and then directed her light on the brick structure at the side of the plot. The second to the last block on the quilt had been red. The block before the black circle.

She didn't know about the black, but perhaps the red signified the mausoleum.

CHAPTER THIRTY-SEVEN

Stephanie stepped off the porch. The lights were on in the house, but whoever was inside didn't answer the door—they probably thought she was a solicitor. She couldn't blame them for not answering. Maybe they had kids and were tucking them into bed for the night.

She checked the time on her phone. Her parents would be winding down for the day, probably watching the news while they rinsed off the dishes. Once she finished knocking on the doors in this neighborhood, she would give them a call. Her mom left a message a half hour ago, and she'd start to worry if Stephanie didn't check in soon.

She turned back toward her car and looked at the cross street. The house behind her was the closest one to Crescent Hill, but there were several houses nearby. Maybe she could knock on one or two more doors tonight and then start her search again in the morning.

The streetlamp buzzed in front of her, and then she heard the click of a lock. Light flooded the front yard, and she hopped back up on the porch, waiting until the door opened.

An elderly man answered, holding a cane in his hand.

"How can I help you?" the man asked, the words rolling smoothly off his tongue.

She introduced herself. "I'm looking for information about Crescent Hill."

The man studied her. "What kind of information?"

"Do you know who lives up there?"

"It belongs to a family by the name of Bristow."

"Bristow," she repeated. "Have they lived there for long?"

His laugh sounded more like a cackle. "A hundred and sixty years."

Her heart raced. Could it be possible that the ancestors of the people who ran the Underground station still lived there? After all these years? Maybe there was hope of finding out what happened to William and the jewels.

"My name's Edward." The man stuck out his hand. "Edward Paxton."

She shook his hand carefully, afraid she would crack the bones that protruded under his skin if she squeezed too hard.

He wrapped both hands around the head of his cane. "Would you like to come inside?"

She might be able to get more information from this gentleman if they sat for a bit, but she didn't have the same gut feeling she'd had when she visited Howard Walters. This man gave her the creeps. "No, thank you. I just wanted to ask a few questions."

"Are you a reporter?"

She laughed. "Oh no. I'm doing a research paper for college."

"Really?" His eyes lit up. "About what?"

"About one of history's many unsolved mysteries."

He stepped out onto the porch, leaning on his cane. "I'm a bit of a history buff myself."

She smiled at him, chiding herself for being afraid. He was a lonely man, looking for a little company. Like Howard Walters.

"What mystery are you trying to solve?"

She shrugged. "It's a family mystery, really."

"The best kind," he said with a nod. "Where are you from?"

"South Carolina."

"You've come a long way."

She nodded.

"There are all sorts of good stories about Crescent Hill," he said. "It was once a station on the Underground Railroad, you know."

Her heart raced. "Then it's the right place."

"What are you looking for?"

She swallowed. "I should probably talk to the Bristows about it first."

"The woman who lives there now doesn't know much about her family's history, but my family has been living in this same house for a hundred and sixty years as well. My ancestors helped the Bristows run their Underground Railroad station."

"Really?"

"Before they built the mansion, the Bristows ran the station in this house."

He'd left the door slightly ajar behind him, and she tried to sneak a peak inside, but she couldn't see anything over his shoulder except the edge of a fireplace. "Where did they hide the runaway slaves?"

He smiled at her. "I'd be glad to tell you, but we were talking about your family first."

She hesitated. It wasn't like the jewels were still around—what would it hurt to tell him? If his family did help the Bristows, maybe they passed along some stories about the runaways who'd stayed at their house.

"Back before the Civil War . . . a set of our family's jewels went missing."

His eyes grew wide. "Missing?"

"It seems that a runaway slave took the jewels before he came north. He was planning to use the money to free his wife and children."

"And now you want them back." His voice was as cool as the night air.

"Oh no," she laughed. "I'm sure the jewelry is long gone. I'd just like to find out what happened to the man who was carrying the jewels."

He stepped closer to her. "Why did you decide to look on Crescent Hill?"

"Rumor has it that William was headed here."

"Rumor?"

"There was a poem that talked about this place. A poem that William repeated often. It said not to stop until the runaways reached Crescent Hill."

The man didn't answer, looking instead at the streetlight and a couple walking by on the sidewalk.

She fidgeted with her hands. "You think I'm silly?"

"Oh, no," he said slowly. "I just don't think the woman living up on Crescent Hill is as interested in history as the rest of us."

"What's her name?"

He coughed. "Camden."

"You don't think she would help me?"

"I doubt it."

Her shoulders fell, but she kept her head up. "Well, I guess it doesn't hurt to try."

Edward pushed the door wide open with his cane, and she could see an armchair and black couch inside. "Do you want to see where my family used to hide slaves?"

"Where is it?"

He nudged the door even farther. "It's much better to show you than tell."

∞

Alex picked up the metal gate that blocked access to the small mausoleum and leaned it against the brick wall. A padlock dangled on one side, but a lock didn't do much good when the hinges had rusted through.

No windows had been cut into the brick, but it looked like there had been a door at one time on the other side of the gate. The doorway was wide open now.

Adrenaline rushed through him. Wasn't there some sort of penalty for opening a grave? And did that same penalty apply to mausoleums as well? It might be hard to convince a cop—or a court of law—that the chunky blocks of a quilt led them here. Even if they took Bryce Kelley to the house, showed him the quilt, he still might not believe them.

The only consolation he had was that they were on private property, and he was with the owner of that property. Perhaps it was okay to break into a mausoleum, after dark, with the woman who owned the cemetery.

Either way, he wasn't going to stop now. He and Camden were on the verge of discovering what the Bristows had kept secret for almost two centuries. A secret that now could help save the family home.

Louise may not have expressed enthusiasm for his idea to promote Crescent Hill as a destination, but he might be able to convince City Council to run with his idea. This was the kind of place they would cling to. It would bring in tourists. Promote new business. Increase their tax revenue. And they'd restore an Etherton icon in the process.

He stepped toward the dark room before him.

"Do you see anything?" Camden asked.

He glanced back. The beam from the flashlight in her hands illuminated the grave beside her. "It would help to have some light."

"Sorry." She handed it over warily, like she was giving up her only weapon.

"I'll take care of it." "I hope so."

He didn't know exactly what he expected to see when he shone the light into the mausoleum, but he thought there would be a number of crypts along the wall or across the floor. But only one cement slab rested there, and it was partially covered by a pile of decayed leaves. This entire building was erected to remember a single life.

He knelt down and brushed back the debris.

Herein lies the memory of our son.

Matthew Joseph Bristow

1845–1858

A boy who loved all of God's creation.

It was the boy he'd read about in the article. The missing child whose body was found on Crescent Hill.

He felt Camden slip to his side. The room was about ten feet by eight, and a beautiful tribute to this young life, but there was nothing else in here beside Matthew's grave.

Alex turned to Camden, disappointed. "Maybe the quilt leads someplace else."

She sighed. "Or maybe it isn't a map at all."

He'd been hoping for another doorway or even a ladder down to the tunnel. He looked at each bare wall. Nothing.

"Could it be in here?"

"There's nothing here," he said, kicking at the leaves in the corners of the room and then in the middle of the floor, hoping they might find something other than the crypt.

When he kicked again, his toe jammed into the cement block. He hopped back, clutching his foot, before he peered down at the floor. The slab that covered Matthew's grave had slipped an inch or two.

He leaned forward, examining the grave, and Camden fell to her knees, shoving away the leaves around the stone. When she pushed the slab, it scraped the floor.

"It's not that heavy."

"Do you think . . ."

She stood back up. "I don't know what to think."

"His coffin is probably under there."

"Or maybe just his bones."

"I'm sure they put his body in some sort of box," he said, although he didn't have a clue how they buried people in the mid 1800s. Plenty of places in the world didn't use coffins, although the Bristow family was certainly affluent enough to afford one. And they would want to honor their son.

Unless . . .

"We need to open the crypt."

Camden shivered. "Are you sure?"

Instead of answering, he handed her the flashlight and pushed the slab away from the opening.

Cool air erupted from the opening, chilling his fingers and arms. Camden aimed the light into the hole. "Is it the tunnel?"

"I have no idea."

Blackness met the beam of her flashlight.

"Can I borrow that again?" he asked, and Camden handed it over. Leaning even farther into the hole, he saw blackness trailing off to his left. The floor was only six or seven feet below. There was a brick wall to his right, and a ladder lying on the ground.

He whistled. "I think we've found our tunnel."

She shook her head, scooting backward. "But it's only a legend . . ."

"Not anymore," he said before he squeezed through the small opening, dropping onto the packed dirt floor.

"Don't move," Jake whispered to Mariah. She sat down on a tree stump, at the edge of the cemetery, as he crept closer to the gravestones. He hardly needed to say it—she'd be too tired to move anyway—but it was only fair to warn her.

They'd followed Alex Yates and Camden all the way down the hill to the cemetery. The two of them had gone into that tiny brick house fifteen minutes ago and never came back out. At first, he figured they were hooking up or something, but it was taking them an awful long time. You'd think they'd do their thing and get out before they woke up some dead people.

Then it occurred to him that maybe they'd left the building. Maybe there was a door on the back side, and they'd slipped away. He'd been careful all the way down the hill, staying quiet so they wouldn't know they were being followed. Halfway down, Mariah announced that her back was killing her. He told her to shut up, but Alex or Camden might have heard and snuck away from them.

Edward would kill him if he lost sight of Camden while she was searching for the tunnel. The woman was on to something, even though he didn't know what. Maybe she hadn't only found out about the tunnel. Maybe she'd discovered the location of the treasure as well.

The moon was halved tonight, giving him enough light to cruise through the graves without banging his shins, but still not enough to scare away the ghosts. For that reason, he was glad Mariah was with him. Ghosts seemed to stay away when there was more than one living person in sight . . . at least, he thought they did.

Slowly, he crept toward the building, ready to run and hide if Alex and Camden came back out. There were no voices though. No noise. The graveyard was as silent as it should be in the darkness, all ghosts asleep in their graves.

Finally he moved close enough to stand on the side of the building and listen, but he didn't hear any sounds. His heart pounding, he snuck to the front and peeked into the open doorway.

No one was there.

He swore. He'd kept his eye on the door the entire time—it was like the building had swallowed Alex and Camden.

He shivered at the thought, but Edward would have his head if he didn't go inside to check on them. As quietly as he could, he stepped into the dark building.

What kind of idiot didn't build a window or two into this building? Even with the stream of moonlight behind him, he could barely see anything. There was nothing in here except a slab of concrete and . . . he squinted into the darkness. A dark block on the floor.

An open grave.

His heart lurched as he stumbled backward. The grave had opened up and swallowed them whole.

Halfway back toward Mariah, his heart started to calm and another thought flashed into his mind. What if they hadn't been consumed? What if, somehow, they'd discovered the treasure below the ground? What if they were down there now, collecting what was meant for the Paxton family?

"Mariah . . ." he growled in the darkness.

"What?"

"Stay there," he said before he turned toward the riverfront.

Alex and Camden may find the treasure, but they wouldn't be able to do anything about it. He'd stop them before they climbed back up, and they would never know what happened.

In a week or two, he could return to the cemetery on his own—he wouldn't even have to mention it to Edward. He'd go down into the tunnel and collect enough treasure to set him and Mariah up for life. Then they could go far, far away from here. To West Palm Beach or San Diego or Maui. Or all three. He'd sell the jewelry online, just like Edward peddled most of his junk. No one—not even Edward—would have a clue about the jewelry or where he and Mariah had gone.

Along the bank of the river, he found a heavy stone and lifted it. Hauling it back to the brick building, he set it on the cement floor, lifted the slab that fit over the grave, and covered the black hole. Then he set the much heavier stone on top.

In the moonlight, he trekked around the tombstones again, collecting four more heavy rocks and piling them on the marker. No one would ever know what happened to Alex and Camden. They would simply disappear as well.

Walking back outside, he brushed off his hands on his good pants and moved back toward the edge of the cemetery, back to the place where he'd left Mariah waiting for him.

No one was there.

"Mariah," he shouted into the darkness, but no one answered his call.

CHAPTER THIRTY-EIGHT

Climbing up the wooden ladder behind Alex, Camden's arms trembled as she helped him push up on the slab overhead. When it didn't budge, her arms shook even harder. They were trapped below ground, in a long-forgotten tunnel, and no one knew where they were.

The tunnel wound up the hill about fifty yards or so, ending with a pile of dirt, stone, and bricks stacked to the ceiling. It may have caved in at one point, but it looked like someone had intentionally blocked it. It would probably take a bulldozer to get through the debris, and even then, the ceiling didn't look like it could handle standing on its own.

A few years ago, she'd taken pictures after a mining accident in West Virginia. The rescued miners were covered in grime and so dehydrated they weren't able to walk out on their own. One man was screaming as they brought him out of the tunnel. Delusional. But he was one of the lucky ones. Four hadn't made it out at all.

She looked down at the flashlight she'd set on the floor, the beam disappearing into the darkness. At least, for now, they had light.

"One more time," Alex said and they both pushed as hard as they could, but it felt like an anvil had been welded on top of the stone.

Had someone followed them down to the cemetery? And, if so, why did they want to trap them? Liza was the only one ticked at her for the moment, but she wouldn't resort to this, would she? It seemed too primal for Liza to be tracking them through the forest. But then again, she might do something desperate if she needed money.

Would Dan give Liza the house if Camden were out of the picture? The local police would investigate Liza first if they couldn't find Camden, but by then, it might be too late.

Camden stepped down a rung before hopping off the ladder, plucking the flashlight off the ground. Alex climbed down behind her and crossed his arms. "One of us should have stayed outside."

"You think?"

He pointed toward the ceiling. "Any clue who would have done this?"

"Only person I can think of is Liza." She paced beside the ladder and then reached into the pocket of her jacket for her phone. Alex had already tried to place a call, but neither of them had reception down here. Even so, she tried to call 9-1-1 again.

The call wouldn't go through.

She jammed the phone back into her pocket. "We've got to get out of here."

"Jenny and Margaret are supposed to come back tonight."

"They don't know we're down here."

"Maybe they'll figure out the rest of the map."

"Or they'll think we . . ."

Alex's eyebrows went up. "What?"

"Nothing."

Jenny would be thrilled at the thought of Alex and Camden on a date. It would be morning before Jenny even thought about worrying. Then, maybe, she and her mother could get into the house and decipher the rest of the map.

A chill ran through Camden. They'd be down here for at least twelve hours. Maybe she wasn't as strong as she thought she was.

She started climbing back up the ladder.

Alex reached for her arm. "Are you claustrophobic?"

"Only when I'm trapped under the ground."

"Let's pretend we're not trapped."

"That's a little hard to do." She pushed against the stone above her head again. She'd read that people had moved cars with a rush of adrenaline. Surely, she could move a cement slab.

He pointed the flashlight toward the other end of the tunnel. "We'll dig our way out of here."

"No, we won't."

He stepped toward her, and she could see his eyes in the light, pleading with her. "I need to try."

One more push on the slab, but it didn't budge. Her hands fell to her sides, and she began climbing back down again.

The Lord is my light and my salvation; whom shall I fear? The Lord is the strength of my life; of whom shall I be afraid? Grandma Rosalie's voice echoed in her head.

She looked at the dark tunnel and then sighed. "I'll help you dig."

Jake paced the floor of the living room. Back and forth. Back and forth.

Edward was in his armchair, puffing on his cigar like it was a lifeline, but Jake barely noticed the smoke. Everything seemed to be going right, and then in one moment, it all went south.

Alex and Camden were trapped—that was the one positive. He wouldn't tell Edward about Alex and Camden, but he had no choice but to tell him Mariah disappeared.

Edward was livid, but it was the old man's fault she was gone. Jake told him he hadn't wanted her to go along, and Edward insisted. Mariah didn't know what she wanted, and she was young. She needed his help to guide her, and now she was out again, alone, and he had no idea where she went.

His grandfather was ruining everything.

All he had to do was find Mariah and get her away from his grandfather and this podunk town. And then she would be fine. They would be fine.

Edward blasted another round of smoke into the air. "She was looking for the treasure."

Jake turned and walked toward the other end of the room. "Mariah doesn't know about the treasure."

"Not Mariah, you idiot. The girl at the door."

He stopped walking. "What?"

"Her name's Stephanie, and the jewels belonged to her family."

He gulped. "I didn't know they belonged to anyone."

"Of course, they used to belong to someone."

"But . . . how did she find them?"

"She had a letter from a relative." Edward drew on the cigar and blew out smoke. "The woman said they hid the treasure in the Bristow mansion."

Jake twisted his hands. Edward was lying about either the letter or the girl, but he wasn't sure which it was. If the jewels were in the house, then what were Camden and Alex doing down at the cemetery, in that hole? Maybe they were looking for something else.

Either way, Jake didn't have to worry about trying to convince Camden to show him the house. Nor did he have to worry about her bugging him while he was trying to search. Even without the treasure, he could haul out a load of valuable stuff tonight.

He could keep it in the tunnel—there was plenty of space. The cops would never know what happened. They might not even realize anything was missing, but if they did, they would never know where to look for it.

Edward leaned forward. "We've got to go in tonight, before that Stephanie girl tells Camden about the treasure."

"Camden is gone. I heard her tell Jenny she was going back to New York." He could lie just as well as Edward.

Edward snorted, like he didn't believe him, but Jake didn't care. Camden was out of the picture, and that's all that mattered. But the girl could still tell someone else.

Jake squeezed his fingers into a fist. "That girl knows about the treasure—why did you let her go?" *Who was being stupid now?*

"I invited her inside, but she declined."

"So you sweeten the deal."

"Maybe that's what you would do, Jakey, but I prefer to take things a little slower."

"That's why you haven't found your treasure."

Stephanie leaned back her car seat, exhausted from the long day of driving, and let the cool evening air wash over her skin through her open window. Reaching beside her, she swiped her phone off the passenger seat. She still needed to find a place to crash for the night, but if she waited much longer to call home, her parents would call Etherton law enforcement, and she didn't need the local police tracking her down.

In front of her was Edward Paxton's house, the light in the living room still on. Part of her was kicking herself for not accepting his offer to show her where his family had hid runaway slaves, but instinct nudged her away from him and his house. A bigger part of her was glad she walked away.

She'd gotten enough info from him anyway. After what he'd told her about the Bristows, she walked back up Crescent Hill and knocked one more time at the Bristows' door. No one answered her knock, but she waited a bit, hoping Camden would come home.

She was so close to answers, or at least a really valuable piece to the puzzle. If one of the Bristows kept a journal, like Miriam Ellison had, perhaps Camden would let her read it.

She thumbed in her parents' number, but before she called, she heard the slam of a car door behind her. In her side mirror from her reclined position, Stephanie saw a middle-aged woman with a gigantic purse hanging from her shoulder look both directions before crossing the street.

Stephanie edged up and watched the woman quickly beeline for Edward Paxton's porch.

Techno music blasted through the night, and Stephanie jumped in her seat, punching a button to silence her phone's ring. Startled, the woman outside turned and looked at her, a mix of frustration and fear on her face. Then the woman ran up the stairs and into Edward's house without knocking.

Stephanie looked down and saw her mom's cell number. This time she answered it.

"We were worried about you!"

"There's nothing for you to worry about," Stephanie replied. She glanced back at the Paxton house and saw the blinds crack as the woman peeked out at her.

CHAPTER THIRTY-NINE

Alex pried another piece of brick out of the wall and handed it to Camden. She tossed it into a much smaller pile at the side of the tunnel while he started tugging again. They'd been working for well over an hour, and he was covered in dirt and sweat. His lips were parched and his back ached, but he wasn't going to stop until he dug a hole through this wall of debris.

They were climbing uphill, and he hoped the other side of the tunnel would lead them to the house. They needed to be through the tunnel before the batteries in their flashlight ran out.

He never should have let Camden crawl down here with him. Not that she'd asked his permission, but he should have known better. In his excitement over finding the tunnel, he'd leaped through the opening and hadn't looked back, not even to protect her.

He should have waited until daylight and until they had let someone like Dan or Louise know where they went. Someone who would call for help if they didn't return.

It was his fault they were trapped down here, and he was going to get them out of this mess. Tonight.

When he handed back the next stone, a clod of dirt tumbled down onto his head. He coughed and brushed the dirt off his face.

"You need a break," Camden said behind him, her voice weary.

"I don't need a break."

With a click, the light in the tunnel disappeared. "Yes, you do."

He reached for her in the darkness, but couldn't find her. "Turn it back on, Camden."

"Just for ten minutes."

He sighed, stretching his neck. A break was probably a good idea though he didn't think he could sit for ten minutes. Not with the tunnel still blocked and no end in sight.

He stepped forward. "Where are you?"

The light flickered on, and he saw her at the side of the tunnel, resting against the wall. Her hair was covered in dirt too, her face smeared. And she looked beautiful.

Darkness surrounded him again, and he carefully made his way toward her, sliding down to the floor. Their shoulders touching, he felt her warmth, and it strengthened him.

He'd walked out on Angela when she needed him most, but he wasn't going to fail Camden. He would work all night if he had to. He was going to get her out of here.

His voice cracked when he spoke. "I'm sorry, Camden."

She nudged closer to him. "For what?"

"For getting us stuck down here."

Her fingers reached out to him, encircling his arm. "This isn't your fault."

"Yes, it is."

"No, it isn't," she said, squeezing his arm. "You didn't trap us down here."

"Still . . ."

She paused, and he could hear her suck in a deep breath. "This isn't about us, is it?"

Even though he couldn't see her, he turned toward her. "What are you talking about?"

"Alex . . ." She put her head on his shoulder, her hair soft against his cheek. "It wasn't your fault that your sister died."

He opened his mouth to protest, but the words didn't come. Of course it was his fault. He should have made Angela leave with him, should have come back to the house earlier. He should have skipped that awful meeting about paper towels.

"You didn't know what her boyfriend would do," Camden said.

"No," his voice hardened, "but I knew what he was capable of."

She lifted her head and softly kissed his cheek. "It's not your fault," she repeated.

He let her words wash over him as he enveloped her hand into his fingers. "Thank you."

The only light penetrating the tunnel was the dull glow of their cell phones as they sat beside each other in silence, the seconds slipping by.

She spoke first. "If this is Matthew's grave . . . where do you think they put him?"

He released her hand, forcing himself back to reality. If there was any hope for him and Camden . . . He knew what he wanted in the darkness, but he would wait and examine his heart when his mind was clear. "Maybe he's in one of the graves outside."

She shivered, and it was everything he could do to resist pulling her even closer. "My grandma used to tell me stories about Matthew."

"What kind of stories?"

"She said he was murdered by a man hunting slaves."

His mind wandered back to the articles he'd read at the library, all the speculation as to why Matthew Bristow had disappeared. "Did she know what happened?"

"She told me he was a hero, that he was trying to stop the hunter from shooting a slave."

"Did it work?"

"I don't know . . ."

"They must have built this tunnel after Matthew died."

"It seems impossible," she said. "People around here would have known about it."

"The only other house out here in the 1850s would have been the Paxton house, and according to Dotty, the Paxtons and Bristows were allies back then."

Silence surrounded them as she rubbed his arm. He took her hand again and squeezed it. "You doing okay?"

She paused. "Not really."

"We're going to get out of here," he said. "Do you mind if I pray again?"

"Please do."

He'd prayed in the minutes after they discovered they were trapped in here, and now he begged God for wisdom and protection and for help getting out of the tunnel.

"My grandmother used to pray all the time," she said when he finished.

"She loved God."

Camden clung to his hand. "When I was a girl I always wanted to be just like her."

"God loves you as much as He loved your grandmother."

"Then He doesn't know me very well."

He laughed. Not at her, but with her, and the general sentiments of the human condition. It was a miracle that a perfect and righteous God loved him or anyone else, with all of their flaws. And it was a love that knew no bounds.

She was silent for a moment. Her hand felt soft inside his. Small. "I've spent most of my life running from relationships."

"Running is never a good answer to your problems."

"Are you speaking from personal experience again?"

He rested against the rough wall and rubbed a cramp in his leg muscle with his other hand.

It had been two years since he opened the door and found Angela. Two years since his life began to spiral out of control. He'd been on a fast climb up the career track back then. A good job, new promotion, and a fiancée with whom he planned to spend his life.

Laura broke off their engagement about a month after Angela's death. He'd been too heartsick at the loss of his sister to comprehend losing his fiancée as well. He couldn't blame Laura for breaking up. He didn't understand the ugliness and anger and guilt that erupted inside him when Trent stole his sister's life. He couldn't expect her to understand either.

A year ago, he'd called Laura and asked forgiveness for spewing his anger all over her. She forgave him, but neither one of them suggested renewing their relationship. If their love couldn't stand up to the test of losing a loved one, he had no illusions about it standing strong for the rest of their lives. Forever would crumble the feelings between them.

"What happened?" Camden asked softly.

"After my sister and nephew died . . . I ran away."

She lifted her head from his shoulder. "Did you run far?"

He cleared his throat. "I took the job in Etherton, hoping a new surrounding and busy work would help me forget. When I still couldn't forget, I decided to go to Community Bible with Dan."

"So the church made you forget?"

"Not exactly, but I'm learning that this life isn't about me anyway nor is it about what I want out of it. Following Christ is about surrender and faith and about God working through me instead of me working for God."

"Rosalie knew what it was like to surrender her life." Camden took another deep breath. "And so did my grandfather."

"Dotty told me he was a good man."

"Apparently, he married my grandmother after she had a child, and he gave both her and her son a respected name, and a home."

"It's like he redeemed Rosalie and your father with his love," Alex said slowly. "And then Rosalie offered that same love to so many other women who needed someone to care for them."

"Just like Jesus does for us."

"Exactly," he said. "You've been redeemed into the family of God just like you and your father were redeemed into the Bristow family."

"That's what I want, Alex." Her voice broke. "To be part of a family."

He couldn't resist any longer. Stretching out his arms, he pulled her close to him.

"Hurry up!" Louise barked.

Hurry up? He was the one doing all the work. Carrying his grandfather partway through the tunnel on his back and pushing him through the rest of the way. The Honorable Mayor hadn't even offered to help.

He wanted to get this over with as much as the rest of them. They'd break open that locked room on the third floor, see if the jewels were somehow lurking in there, and if not, they were out of luck. He'd already cased every other room on the three floors.

Louise shined her flashlight back at him, burning Jake's eyes. "What is taking you two so long?"

"Why did you tell her about this?" he muttered in Edward's ear as he helped him across the broken brick path.

"Because I needed her."

"She's going to talk."

"Oh, no, she won't. She knows how to keep her mouth shut."

"She'd better keep it shut." He paused. "What's her cut?"

"Thirty percent," she called back. "Do you have a problem with that?"

"Yes, I do. I've been doing all the work."

She laughed. "You think you've been doing all the work."

"What exactly have you done?"

"The house was about to be condemned, Jake. Full access for you and Grandpa here except you went and put an offer on it yourself. Messed up the whole plan."

He shook his arm free from Edward's grasp. "No one told me there was another plan."

"It's not good for everyone to know all the pieces, Jakey. Keeps you out of trouble."

"You mean it keeps *you* out of trouble."

Louise laughed again, and he was glad he wasn't the only one onto Edward. The old man never worked his deals to benefit anyone but himself.

"Shut up," Edward shouted at Louise. "If you hadn't posted that condemnation notice . . ."

"You're the one who mucked this up, Edward. There wasn't supposed to be any information about the tunnel left."

"I'll deal with Dotty later."

Jake didn't know what Dotty had to do with it. "I thought this was a fifty-fifty split, Pops."

"You're getting thirty."

The headlamp digging into his forehead flickered on the path in front of him. "How much are you getting?"

"It doesn't matter."

He tried to do the math in his head, but somehow he didn't think he was coming out ahead.

CHAPTER FORTY

A loud noise interrupted Camden's sleep. Someone shouting her name.

"Camden," Alex said softly, and she snuggled in closer to his chest. She was meant to be here with him. She belonged.

"Camden!" Another voice shouted her name.

Slowly she opened her eyes in the darkness, and she remembered. They were still down in the tunnel. In the tunnel yet—

It wasn't a dream. Someone really was shouting her name.

Alex flicked on the light, and she cringed at the bright flash.

"Camden!" The shout echoed through the walls again.

She leapt to her feet and screamed back. "We're down here."

Alex rushed down the hill, and she followed until he stopped abruptly and put out his arm. "You need to wait."

"I'm not waiting."

He turned toward her, and the light cast shadows over the worry in his eyes. It felt strange, having someone concerned about her, but she could take care of herself. She'd done a pretty good job of it for the past twenty-eight years.

"We don't know who's up there."

She put her hands on her hips. "I don't need you to protect me."

"Please, Camden."

She dropped her hands to her side. Maybe she didn't need him to take care of her, but he needed to try. "Okay."

He stepped toward her, his eyes intent on hers. For a moment, she thought he was going to kiss her until someone shouted again. He turned and ran toward the opening.

Three minutes passed, and she prayed, starting from where he left off. Now, more than ever, they needed God to be with them. Needed Him to be faithful.

From the moment she'd left home, she'd never been dependent on anyone else, and now she was relying on so many. On her grandma's inheritance. On Alex. On God.

Now . . . she wanted God in her life, welcomed his presence in her heart. But without the house, how could she love his wounded children?

Don't be afraid to love. Or serve. Even when it hurts, I pray you will open your arms to the least of these.

Rosalie did what she thought was best, and she was faithful to what God asked of her—caring for her own child as well as the children of so many other women who needed her.

Camden closed her eyes, feeling the cool air on her face. How could she be faithful to God, like her grandma? What if God had a plan for her that she never expected? Would she be willing to serve him like Rosalie Bristow had?

Instead of asking why Mariah had stolen her purse, she had turned her away. What if Alex was right, and Mariah hadn't stolen the purse? She had sent an innocent girl back to a place where she would be hurt again and again.

It didn't matter so much that she found the tunnel. What mattered was that they find Mariah, and once she did, she would welcome her back. It might be temporary, but for the weeks or months that Crescent Hill was hers, she would do her best to make it a home for women and kids who'd been hurt, like Alex's sister and nephew.

Alex called to her. "It's safe, Camden."

She followed the trail of light all the way back to the opening and climbed up the ladder until she peered out into the mausoleum. In front of her was Mariah, sweat blotching her face and long strands of hair in her eyes.

Camden reached out and gave her a giant hug. "I'm so sorry," she said before she released Mariah's shoulders.

The girl's gaze was on her feet. "I didn't steal your purse."

"I believe you."

Mariah nodded, relief softening her eyes. "I didn't tell anyone about the house either."

Camden hugged her again. "How did you know we were here?"

"We followed you," she said. "He put the stones on the grave. When I was sure he was gone, I shoved them off the grave."

"Who put the stones—"

Mariah interrupted her. "Jake."

"Jake Paxton?" she whispered, looking over at Alex in the dull light. He didn't look surprised. "But why would he . . . ?"

"I don't know what he wants, but he's been looking for something in your house."

"He said he wanted to buy the house."

Mariah's laugh was bitter. "He doesn't have the money to buy a house."

Her stomach clenched. "Is he your boyfriend?"

"Used to be my boyfriend."

"You went back . . ."

Mariah's hands went to her stomach. "I didn't have anyplace else to go."

Alex nudged her arm. He was already on the phone with the police. "We need to move," he said to Camden, and then he spoke back into the phone. "We'll meet you at the top of Crescent Hill."

The storage room was wide open when they walked inside—Edward never would have believed it was locked except he had seen it with his own eyes. There was a cot on the floor, and the shelves were filled with boxes. The three of them picked through the shelves, checking inside filing boxes and hatboxes and ripping off the backs of framed family portraits, but there was no jewelry to be found.

The treasure was down at the graveyard. Jake was almost sure of it now. Alex and Camden and maybe even that Stephanie girl knew what they were doing, but as he watched his grandfather tear through another box, he realized that Edward Paxton didn't have a clue. He was chasing after a treasure the Bristows had hidden from people like him. They probably didn't even hide it in the house.

He took a step back toward the door. Why settle for thirty percent when he had a hundred percent waiting for him down the hill? He wouldn't have to wait until Alex and Camden starved to death. Edward had a couple of handguns he thought were well hidden in the house, but Jake knew their hiding place. He'd finish the job, find Mariah, and then scram before the cops knew what had happened. By morning, he'd be halfway to Florida, treasure in hand.

He took another step back and then turned toward the door.

"Where do you think you're going?" Edward demanded.

"I'm outta here," Jake responded over his shoulder.

"I don't think so."

At first he thought the clicking sound behind him was from a flashlight. He spun around, but there wasn't a light in Edward's hands. Instead, he held a gun. "You're going to help us find this treasure."

"It's not here, Pops."

The gun shook. "Stop calling me that."

He eyed the gun, weighing his options. "It's not here . . . but I know where it is."

Edward lowered the gun by an inch. "Don't mess with me."

"I found another entrance to the tunnel tonight. The jewels must be there."

"You didn't tell me?"

"I didn't want to rattle you."

"You mean, you didn't want to share." Edward lifted the gun again. "From now on, you are going to play fair."

Louise stepped up next to Edward. "Where is the entrance?"

"I'll take you to it."

"Right now," Edward said.

Louise grunted. "Don't be stupid."

Edward now had the gun pointed at her. "I'm the one in charge."

She put her hands in the air. "Then lead on."

The gun twisted toward Jake again. "Tell me where it is."

"I want fifty percent."

Edward laughed. "You'll be lucky to get twenty."

"You selfish, old . . ."

The gun blasted, and Jake fell to the floor, his hands covering his head. He wouldn't move until Edward stopped shooting.

But there wasn't another shot. Instead Jake heard Louise's voice as she nudged his side with her toe. "Get up."

Jake craned his neck, looking up. She was standing over him, gun-in-hand. He looked back and saw his grandfather, bowed over in pain but there was no blood. Louise probably kicked his shin or something. Hard.

Go Louise. Edward deserved every ounce of his pain.

He pushed himself off the floor and faced Louise with newfound respect. "Thanks!"

"I wasn't doing you a favor."

Then he heard footsteps pounding up the stairs at the end of the hallway. A bunch of them.

"Someone's coming," he said, lurching forward. He had to get to the entrance before they caught him.

Louise followed him toward the theater.

"Wait for me!" Edward yelled after them, but Jake laughed as he and Louise sprinted across the open floor.

Light flooded the lawn outside the Bristow mansion. Spotlights hung from poles, and fire trucks, ambulances, and police cars flashed a frenzy of red and blue. Camden sat on the tree stump where she'd collapsed. She shivered. It must be after midnight, but it seemed like half the town was gathered in front of her grandmother's house.

Jenny and Margaret brought several thermoses filled with soup and coffee up from Jenny's house. Camden didn't drink any of the coffee, but she slurped down almost an entire canister of hot chicken soup, wondering when her chills would wear off. She longed to feel warm again and dry, but she didn't complain. At least she and Alex were out of the tunnel.

Jenny piled another blanket on top of her. "Are you sure you don't want to go inside?"

Camden eyed the house. "Not until they find them."

Pastor Lambert and his wife swept Mariah away minutes after the police arrived so she wouldn't have to see Jake, but Camden wanted to see him again. She had a few things she'd like to say.

"We were so worried," Jenny said again as she poured another cup of soup.

Instead of taking the soup, Camden's eyes fluttered shut as the exhaustion overtook her body. She wanted to listen to Jenny and wait alongside the rest of the town for the cops to come out of the house, but she was so very tired.

She pulled one of the blankets close to her chest. It felt good to have so many people show up at her house, even if half of them were here out of curiosity at the spectacle atop Crescent Hill. The other half of the crowd was from Community Bible, and they all seemed to know both Alex and her grandma.

Alex guarded the front doors while the police were inside . . . and directed the curious away from the windows. Instead of wearing him down, their hours in the tunnel seemed to rejuvenate him.

He'd been so sweet to her while they were underground. So kind and protective. He hadn't stopped being protective when they got out, but he had sprung into business mode when they reached the top of the hill. With most of Etherton's police force inside, he took charge of the crowd. And that was just fine with her.

"They're coming out!" someone shouted.

Opening her eyes, she stood up. Above the crowd she could see Bryce Kelley, another officer, and the profile of the man named on her father's birth certificate. Edward Paxton had been inside her home.

"Where's Jake?" she heard Alex ask.

"We'll keep looking," Bryce said with a shake of his head. "Have you seen Camden?"

She handed Jenny the blankets and maneuvered through the crowd.

Edward glared at her, his head held high, but he didn't say a word. Bryce handed him off to another officer, and then pulled her and Alex to the side.

"It appears Jake and Edward got into your home without using a window or door."

"But there's no other entrance . . ."

She glanced over at Alex and saw his raised eyebrows. "Well, there's the legend," she said.

"What is it?" Bryce whispered so the throngs around them couldn't hear.

"There's supposed to be an entrance to the tunnel on the third floor."

"Any idea where?"

She shook her head.

"Can you help us look for it?"

Her eyes were blurry, her cold muscles aching, but she would help them search. She wanted to find Jake and find out what he and Edward were doing in her home.

If there was an entrance to the tunnel upstairs, it was a stroke of genius. First of all, no one would suspect a tunnel on the top floor, and second, the runaway slaves could always run upstairs when slave hunters stopped to search the house instead of having to get past them on the way down to the cellar.

Flanked by three other policemen, she and Alex knocked on the painted panels around the theater, but there was no secret door behind the pictures or on the stage or anyplace else in the room.

Bryce's radio buzzed, and he turned his back to them. Camden couldn't hear his words, but seconds later he was barking orders.

"Someone just ran out of the Paxton house," he shouted. "I want everyone outside and down the hill."

In seconds, the room cleared, leaving Camden and Alex alone.

She sat on the floor by the fireplace. "This is crazy."

"They'll get him."

She turned and looked at the fireplace. It was the same place she and her grandmother had stood arm in arm together for that snapshot, so many years ago. Back when they had filled the fireplace with twinkling lights instead of logs.

Leaning closer to the mantle, she squinted at the floor—something looked wrong with the grate. One end was higher than the other, by a half-inch or so.

Her fingers went to the base of the grate, and she felt a seam.

"Alex!" she shouted.

He rushed over to her and grabbed both sides of the grate. Then he tipped it over.

CHAPTER FORTY-ONE

Alex climbed carefully through the hatch, down the wooden staircase, and into the tunnel. The flashlight was starting to dim, but if it went out, at least Camden knew exactly where he was. The police were in the process of apprehending Jake on the other end of the tunnel, but he would find out where the passageway connected to the Paxton house. And when Bryce and the others came back to the house, Camden could send them down.

She volunteered to climb down with him, but her face paled when she said the words. He wouldn't have asked her to go into the tunnel with him. She'd been through way too much already tonight, and one of them needed to stay outside this time around anyway.

He missed her fingers wrapped around his arm, though . . . and her head on his shoulder.

Alex guessed he had gone fifty yards or so already. The dirt path was strewn with broken bricks, and he had to brace himself so he wouldn't fall. As he walked, he prayed again, but this time he didn't ask God for help. Instead he thanked him for rescuing them, and for protecting both Mariah and Camden from Jake.

God had protected them all.

A loud groan startled him, a few yards ahead, and he froze. Quietly, he turned off the flashlight.

"Help me," the voice moaned.

"Who's there?"

"I've been shot."

Alex turned the light back on and directed it toward the voice. Stepping forward, he could see Jake lying on the floor. Blood oozed from the man's chest and down his left arm.

Alex ripped off his jacket and knelt beside him, tying the material across Jake's chest. "The cops are looking for you."

"I bet they are." His laugh was hollow. "Did they catch Edward?"

"They did."

"Serves the old man right."

Alex shone his light beyond them, but didn't see anyone else in the tunnel. "Who did this to you?"

"She did it . . ." Jake started, but his eyes closed as he writhed in pain.

Alex shook him slightly. "Who is she?"

"She wanted the treasure for herself."

Alex stiffened. "Treasure?"

When Jake didn't respond, Alex felt for his pulse. It barely registered under his fingers. Part of him wanted to leave Jake here—he deserved to die after what he'd done to Mariah. Yet, as Shawn Lambert had once told him, they all deserved to die.

"I'm going to get help."

He stood to go, and Jake reached out and took his sleeve. "Tell Mariah I love her."

"I'm finding a medic," he said as he rushed away.

The tunnel ended at a much shorter staircase, and Alex rushed up through the door at the other end and into the Paxton house. The moment he exited the closet, someone shouted, "Put your hands up."

He stuck his hands in the air and looked into the face of a young officer with a badge that read "Reeve."

"Jake Paxton's in the tunnel," Alex said, stepping forward.

"Don't move."

"He's hurt."

"I said, *Don't move*."

"All right." Alex froze. "But a woman shot him, and she's still out there."

The officer grabbed his radio and called the sergeant. "I've got him. He's in the den."

Bryce's voice bellowed through the speaker. "We're coming."

A half dozen cops burst through the door, guns pointed. Bryce took one look at him and called off the dogs. "Let him go, Reeve."

"But . . ."

"You've got the wrong guy."

"That's what I was trying to tell him." Alex pointed back at the entrance. "Jake's down there, and he's been shot."

Bryce called for a paramedic, and then he signaled for Alex to follow him toward his patrol car.

"Jake said a woman shot him."

Bryce nodded, his hand on the car door. "We caught her running from the house."

Bryce opened the door, and there was his boss, her eyes focused on the opposite window.

"Louise?" he asked. What was she doing here?

When she didn't respond, he turned back to Bryce.

"Go home," Bryce said, slamming the door. "We'll sort this out in the morning."

Camden wrung her hands as Alex knocked on Dotty Sherman's apartment door. It was still early, but she hadn't been able to sleep much last night and neither had Alex. He met her at the Spragues' house before breakfast and told her he had someone special he wanted her to meet.

Dotty opened the door to them. "Well, who have we here?" she greeted them, then stretched out both arms to hug her.

The woman clung to her, and Camden didn't pull away.

"You are beautiful," Dotty said softly.

"Thank you."

"Alex better treat you right."

"Oh, no . . ." she started, lest Dotty think they were a couple, and then she caught Alex's eye. He was smiling at her.

Dotty invited them both into her apartment. "I hear there was a bit of excitement up on Crescent Hill last night."

Alex's smile vanished. "We wanted to talk to you before anyone else did."

"Don't look so sad, Alex. My neighbor already told me about Edward."

"He's probably going to prison."

"I hope they lock him up for the rest of his life."

"I found Jake in the tunnel. He was shot in the chest."

"Did he make it?"

When Alex shook his head, Dotty glanced down at her hands. "Not to excuse what he did, but he had a hard lot in life."

Camden's chest constricted. She didn't want to hear about Jake's hard life.

"His mother left when he was a baby, off to pursue her dreams in Hollywood, and Edward was the only one left to take care of him," the woman explained. "Jake was never the smartest kid on the block, but he could have made something out of himself if he'd been given a chance."

"Will Edward miss him?" Camden asked.

"Probably not."

Alex leaned forward. "He paid you to not talk about the tunnel, didn't he?"

She glanced out the window and then looked back at him. "He paid for me to stay here, but I'd like to think it wasn't bribery. I didn't know the tunnel was that important."

"And yet you told me about it."

"I've always been a proponent of the truth."

He reached for her hand. "What will you do now?"

"Aren't you sweet to worry about me," she said. "But you shouldn't. God will take care of me."

Her soft blue eyes turned toward Camden. "You look just like your grandfather."

"Edward Paxton is my grandfather."

"Maybe by birth, but God gifted you with Philip Bristow's smile."

Her eyes watered, but she blinked back the tears. "Thank you."

Dotty let go of Alex's hand and reached for Camden. "Edward wounded your grandmother's body and her spirit."

"Did he rape her?"

Dotty was silent for a moment. "Rosalie blamed herself."

Camden swiped her fingers under her eyelashes. She always thought her grandma's life had been perfect from the start, but her beauty rose up from the ashes. "How did she recover?"

"By God's grace . . ."

No wonder she had the heart and strength to help so many others.

"Not all the Paxtons were cruel," Dotty interjected. "But there were a few bad ones . . . going back for years. Did you find out why Jake was in your tunnel?"

"He said something about a treasure," Alex said.

"That side of my family has been searching for it for almost two hundred years."

Camden swallowed. "Your family?"

She nestled into her chair. "A long time ago my great-grandfather Charles and great-uncle Arthur worked alongside the Bristows to help slaves on the Underground Railroad until my uncle discovered something he couldn't resist. One of the runaways was carrying a collection of jewels north to buy his wife and children off a plantation in South Carolina."

Camden leaned toward her. "The slave told them this?"

"The man trusted them to keep his secret, but Arthur turned on him. He shot the runaway along with Matthew Bristow because the boy got in the way."

Alex rubbed his hands together. "The newspaper said the Bristows didn't know how Matthew died."

"They did, but they wanted to keep the cause of his death a secret. They buried him in an unmarked grave, blocked up the tunnel entrance to the Paxton home, and extended the tunnel out to the new mausoleum dedicated to their son."

"Did Arthur keep the jewels?" Camden asked.

"Oh no." Dotty whispered. "My great-grandfather hid the jewelry, but he wouldn't tell Arthur where it was. Joseph Bristow hoped to buy the runaway slave's wife and children through a friend in the South and then set them free, but the plantation owner refused to sell them.

"Joseph and Charles kept the jewels, hoping to purchase the man's family eventually, but the owner continued to refuse them. Then the Civil War began, and both men were killed in battle."

"What happened to the Bristows' wealth?" Alex asked.

"The original Camden Bristow spent most of it helping orphans and widows after the war."

"And yet they never told anyone where they kept the jewels . . ."

Dotty smiled. "I don't believe the Bristows told anyone, but Charles did."

"Who did he tell?" Camden asked.

"His wife, Emily."

Camden felt her pulse race. "And . . ."

"Emily told her son who told his daughter. My mother, of course, passed the story to me."

Camden clapped her hands together. "Have you seen these jewels?"

"Oh, no. Our family could never get to them."

"But you know where they are . . ."

"I have a pretty good idea."

Camden's heart raced as Alex drove her and Dotty toward Crescent Hill. This could be it, the answer she needed to save the Bristow home. If Dotty really knew where the jewels were, perhaps they could sell them to a collector and use some of the proceeds to restore Crescent Hill. She could welcome abused women into her home, just like her grandmother had done, and the city wouldn't be able to tear the place down.

Alex pulled into the driveway of the mansion, and Dotty laughed beside him, with the joy of a young girl bursting to share her secret.

"The jewels aren't here," she said.

Alex stopped the car. "Where are they?"

"A little farther down the hill."

CHAPTER FORTY-TWO

Stephanie waited until the clock on her dashboard clicked to nine, and then she went to the door of Edward Paxton's house and rang the bell. She'd tried Camden Bristow's house already this morning, but the woman still didn't answer the door. Perhaps Edward could recommend someone else for her to speak with about Crescent Hill.

No one answered the door at Edward's house either, and she sighed. She'd come so close to finding answers, yet if she couldn't locate someone in Etherton who knew the history of Crescent Hill, she may never find out what happened to William.

Reaching down, she fingered the doorknob before twisting it gently. The door edged open, and she stared at the crack.

"Hello!" she said, hoping someone would respond.

A silver passenger car pulled into the Paxton driveway, and Stephanie turned to watch a good-looking guy in his early thirties hop out along with a blond-haired woman. The man rounded the car and assisted an elderly woman out of the car and up the driveway.

Stephanie jogged down the steps to meet them.

"I'm here to see Edward Paxton," she started to explain. "Are you family?"

The blond woman eyed her warily. "Who are you?"

"My name's Stephanie. Stephanie Carter."

The woman introduced herself as Camden Bristow, and Stephanie almost hugged her.

"I've been wanting to meet you . . . " Stephanie started.

The story poured out of her about her family's history and Rachel and William and the missing jewels. When she finished, both women and the man stood silent for a few moments.

"How did you find out about this?" Camden asked.

"One of my ancestors kept a journal," she explained. "My aunt recently gave me the journal to read, and an ancestor of William's directed me to Crescent Hill."

Camden nodded and took the arm of the elderly woman beside her. "I believe Dotty has something to show us all."

Dotty led them through the open door. As she stood at the base of the main staircase, she explained they were the same steps the Bristow family and then the Paxton family used for almost two hundred years.

One, two, three . . .

Stephanie held her breath as Dotty slowly climbed the steps, counting each one. The woman stopped at the seventh step and smiled. "This is it."

The man with her leaned down and tried to pry off the top, but it didn't move. "I'll find a hammer," Camden volunteered, and minutes later she returned, hammer in hand.

With the claw of the hammer, he pried at the step until the wood finally broke loose. Dotty reached down and pulled out a canvas bag. Her hands shaking, Dotty slowly peeled back the canvas. And then she held out the bag.

Her pulse racing, Stephanie looked in awe at the transparent greens, whites, and blues of the jewels inside. She reached into the bag and pulled out a gold bracelet—the hallmark of a crowned lion was engraved on the other side.

Her voice quivered when she spoke again. "What happened to the slave who brought them?"

The elderly woman bowed her head. "My great-uncle killed him."

Dotty looked up at her, and Stephanie saw the tears in the woman's eyes, like she was responsible for William's death. It wasn't Dotty's fault what her ancestor did any more than it was Stephanie's fault for the terrible things her ancestors did to William . . . or even what her cousin did to Angela and Ethan.

Stephanie took the woman into her arms and hugged her. "Why haven't you told anyone about these?"

Dotty sat on the stairs. One of her hands clung to the bag of jewels and the other hand brushed over the worn wallpaper. "After my great-grandfather was killed, his brother, Arthur, inherited the house, and my great-grandmother refused to touch the jewelry in case they were somehow able to locate William's family. She firmly believed the jewels belonged to them, and my grandfather wouldn't touch them either in case William's family returned."

"And your mother?"

"She believed the story, but she was never invited to Edward's home to see for herself if it was true." She paused. "When she told me, I suppose I was afraid to find them—afraid that I would sell the jewels and use the money on myself instead of finding their real owner."

"I guess we should go talk to Bryce about this," the man said.

"I'm sorry," Stephanie said, turning toward him. "I didn't catch your name."

"Alex . . . Alex Yates."

She fell back against the wall. "Angela's brother?"

His face fell. "How did you know Angela?"

"Trent Ellison . . ." her voice broke. "My cousin . . ."

Silence settled over them before Alex reached out to her. Then the other two gathered around him, tears soaking their faces. The three of them encompassed her with hugs and they cried together.

Six weeks later

Camden shoved the tiller into the dirt and dragged it through the weeds. It would take months of work to restore the house and yard before she could sell the place, but at least the town wasn't going to tear it down quite yet. Not until they sorted out the whole mess of what happened on Crescent Hill.

Apparently there'd been a long history of kickbacks between the mayor and Edward Paxton—Louise helping Edward with his pet projects, Edward dumping money into each of her campaigns. Fifty thousand dollars was missing from the town's coffers, and Alex suspected Louise was responsible for the stolen money. Maybe Edward had a hand in the embezzling scheme as well—a greedy person always wants more money, no matter how much he or she already has.

Without the pandering and embezzlement of funds, Alex believed the town's new mayor would be able to do some productive things in Etherton like repair the streets and increase the police force—something that Louise had opposed for reasons that became clearer each day.

In the days after the arrests of Louise and Edward, Camden thought again about leaving Etherton to find work, but when Jenny learned she was out of money, she called a few friends and began lining up photo shoots of kids and pets. The small jobs would never provide enough income to keep Crescent Hill, but it was enough for food and to keep the lights on in the house.

Louise and Edward were being housed at the county jail, awaiting a trial that Alex thought would lead to prison time. And the heirloom jewels . . . the Ellison and Walters families garnered international attention with their find. They were in the midst of having the jewelry authenticated and probably sold, though Stephanie told her neither family knew yet how they would spend their newfound wealth.

A pang of envy raced through Camden. She wished she could have used at least a portion of the money that came from the sale of the jewels to save Crescent Hill. Instead she would enjoy the remaining time she had here . . . until she could find a buyer for the property. She hadn't told anyone, but she hoped it would be a long time before someone put an offer on the house.

Mariah was safe at a home in Columbus. Last she'd heard, the girl had chosen a couple to adopt her baby boy when he arrived, and she'd begun taking classes to become a nursing assistant for the elderly.

And just yesterday, Bryce brought Camden a letter he'd discovered in Jake's things. The letter from her grandma. She'd stayed up late, devouring every word.

Grandma Rosalie hadn't told her specifically about the safe house in her letter, but she did tell her to trust Bryce Kelley. She'd also apologized for keeping the secret of her birth grandfather for so long. She'd done it, she said, out of respect for Camden's father who hadn't wanted anyone to know this painful secret from his past.

So much had happened in the past six weeks, but God had traveled the journey with her. Even though she didn't know where she would go from here, she was learning to trust in His faithfulness for the future.

These days she even dreamed about staying in Etherton. Once she sold the property, she could rent a small place downtown and maybe she and Alex . . .

She thrust the tiller into the ground again. She had to stop thinking about Alex. Ever since Louise confessed to her crimes, Alex had been working around the clock, trying to patch things up at town hall. She sat with Alex at church, and they'd even gone out for dinner a few times. He seemed amiable, but distracted—like the hours they'd clung to each other in the darkness never really occurred. Both of them were still trying to sort things out, but in her heart . . . in her heart she hoped for more.

Jenny's minivan came flying up the driveway, and Camden set her tiller against a tree and stepped back, fanning the dust from the driveway out of her face. She was still fanning when both sides of the minivan opened and all the Sprague kids bounded out. They flew to Camden, almost knocking her over with hugs before they rushed out to the woods to play.

Jenny slammed her door and waved an envelope in front of Camden's face. "I've got an offer for the house."

Camden backed away from the envelope like it was coated in anthrax. "Really?"

"It's from someone who wants to restore it."

One of her eyebrows slid up. "Did you get that in writing?"

Jenny grinned. "I did."

"Because I don't believe it."

"He said he'll restore it, but there's one stipulation to the offer."

Camden cocked her head. "What's that?"

"That you'll live here with him."

Her mouth hung open. "What are you talking about?"

Jenny dug in her pocket and pulled out a small velvet box. Then she handed it to her.

"What in the—" she started.

"I said . . ." Jenny was shouting now. "There's one stipulation to the offer."

Her eyes were still on the black velvet box.

"Oh, drat." Jenny took the phone out of her pocket and started to dial. "Where is he?"

Then Camden saw him, jogging through the trees with all the Sprague kids in tow. Hailey broke in front of him and rushed into Camden's arms.

"Alex says he wants to marry you," Hailey announced.

Camden's heart skipped a beat. "Does he now?"

Alex smiled at her, and she smiled back.

"He told my mommy he wants to be with you forever and ever."

Alex was beside her now, taking her hand in his. The chaos around them seemed to melt away, her eyes lost in his steady gaze.

"Forever is a long time," she said.

Hailey hopped out of her arms, and Alex pulled her close to him, whispering in her ear. "Not nearly long enough."

Lifting her hand, he slipped on the ring, and she pulled it to her chest.

They could make new memories together on Crescent Hill. And this time around, she'd never have to leave.

EPILOGUE

One year later

Good morning, Mayor," Camden said as she jogged down the steps of the mansion to the first floor. Alex won the election by a landslide last fall, but she still liked to tease him about his new title.

Alex greeted his wife with a kiss and straightened his tie. "It's our big day."

Her face warmed with his kiss. "Are you ready?"

"As long as we do this together."

He took her hand and together they walked, through the entryway that sparkled with new paint and freshly scrubbed tile. Dotty Sherman joined them at the door, dressed in a lavender spring suit with tiny yellow flowers.

Dotty had been living with them since Camden and Alex married last August, harboring their secrets like she'd harbored the secret of the jewels for her entire life. Not that she needed the Yates family to provide for her—the Ellison and Walters families gave her a large sum of cash when they sold their jewelry to a duchess in Britain. Her desire, though, was to assist Camden and Alex in their work.

The three of them walked out the front door together to face the crowd gathered on the lawn. Fresh flowers bloomed in gardens around the base of the house—all of her grandmother's favorites were there to honor her life plus a few new varieties to commemorate her and Alex's life ahead as the Bristow-Yates family.

Camden waved to Debra Ellison and Howard Walters and Stephanie, of course, in the crowd of people. Louise Danner and Edward Paxton were both serving their sentences in a state prison—Edward would undoubtedly spend his few remaining years behind bars.

Between the money from Angela's life insurance policy and a generous donation from the Ellison and Walters families, her grandmother's dream—and now her dream—was coming true.

The first floor of their restored home was a community center for the town. There was space for art classes and drama classes and meeting rooms, and the parlor was set aside for the new after-school program run by Community Bible Church.

On the second floor was her photo studio, and a bedroom for Dotty and private rooms for her and Alex along with plenty of room to expand.

And the third floor was . . . well, the third floor was supposed to be for storage, but after the discovery of the tunnel, the town was abuzz with new stories about ghosts haunting the Bristow Mansion. Neither she nor Alex tried to squelch the rumors.

There was a woman staying in a renovated room on the third floor right now, along with her two children. Perhaps the ghost stories would keep people from wondering about the peculiar lights and shadows roaming up there during the night.

Alex took her hand and lifted it as she quietly thanked her Heavenly Father for creating beauty out of dark ashes. Then together she and her husband dedicated the Angela and Ethan Yates Community Center to God and to their hometown.

AUTHOR'S NOTE

I spent most of my childhood in a small Ohio town. On a treed hill near the downtown is a decrepit mansion shrouded in mystery, and it's rumored that the old house was once an Underground Railroad station. Another legend says a long tunnel under the mansion led to the family's underground mausoleum about a half mile away, but no one has ever found the entrance to this tunnel or proven that the house was a stop for runaway slaves.

Even so, the legends I heard as a child sparked my imagination, and *Refuge on Crescent Hill* began with the simple question of "What if?" What if the rumors were true and a tunnel really leads to the mausoleum? What if the tunnel once sheltered escaping slaves like so many tunnels along the Underground Railroad? And what if a house like this could be used in some way to help people today?

All of these questions inspired this story, and it was a joy for me to explore my hometown with fresh eyes and relive some of the wonder from my childhood.

A number of wonderful people collaborated with me on this story to help me get my facts straight. Any errors—and I'm sure there are plenty—are my fault.

Thank you to my parents Jim and Lyn Beroth for scouting out the information I needed about my favorite town in Ohio, Aunt Janet (Wacker) for uncovering a trove of history and legend about my favorite old mansion, Tom Nelson for supplying detailed information about city planning and growth, Patricia Pursley for helping me research my questions about the nineteenth century, Dobby Dobson and Gerry Nunn for being my contractors-on-call, Aunt Kathy (Bowers) for answering my questions about quilting, Detective Kit Branch for helping me understand online fraud and law enforcement, and Uncle Ham, Aunt Bev, and Katy (Hamilton) for allowing me to explore your home in wonder when I was a child.

Thank you Michael H. for permission to explore your beautiful property and Karen M. for your tour—I thoroughly enjoyed meeting you. Thank you Leslie Gould, Sandra Bishop, Kimberly Felton, Christa Sterken, and Kelly Chang for reading the many versions of this manuscript and for all your great ideas and encouragement.

My friends at SCC—Dorie, Mary, and Luke—thank you for letting me hunker down for days at your wonderful coffee shop to research and write.

Vennessa Ng—having you edit my work is like having eyes on the back of my head. You catch everything that I miss and help take my stories and characters to the next level. You're amazing!

Thank you to the entire staff of Kregel Publications including Dennis Hillman, Stephen Barclift, Janyre Tromp, Dawn Anderson, Miranda Gardner, and Cat Hoort for your excitement about this book. I'm honored to partner with you again.

Another big thank you to those faithful friends who read this manuscript before it was complete and thank you to those who encouraged and prayed for me as I wrote this story—Christina Nunn, Michele Heath, Carolyn Dobson, Tosha Williams, Beth Guisinger, Patti Lacy, Carol Garborg, Jodi Stilp, and Miralee Ferrell.

Thank you Karly and Kiki for dreaming up story ideas with me and for never letting me escape too far away from reality. You girls keep me grounded, and I'm grateful for it.

Thank you to my husband, Jon, for your love and support and for encouraging me to continue pursuing the dreams God has woven into my heart.

Isaiah 45:3 reads, "I will give you the treasures of darkness, riches stored in secret places, so that you may know that I am the LORD, the God of Israel, who summons you by name." I'm thankful beyond words to the Lord God for summoning each of his children by name and for giving us many treasures including the incredible gift of forgiveness through his Son.

Thank you for dreaming with me,
Melanie

P.S. If you'd like to see pictures of the mansion that inspired this story, please check out my Web site at www.melaniedobson.com. Also, I love hearing from my reader friends! My e-mail address is comments@melaniedobson.com.

Also Available from Melanie Dobson

Gold-medal winner in the 2008 *ForeWord* Magazine Book of the Year Awards

"This intense, well-crafted story will have you wondering long into the night." —Linda Hall, author of *Shadows in the Mirror*